ACKNOWLEDGEMENTS

I owe a part of this book to a tall, handsome man in Flagstaff who owned a horse named Fancy—oh, the memories of those long trails through the tall, fragrant Ponderosas, deep canyons, and a long-past companionship...

He aggravated the heck out of her...so why couldn't she stop thinking about him?

Hettie stopped in her tracks and waited for Jake to reach her. "Well, Sheriff La Force, what brings you out here so soon again?" She couldn't keep the ice from her voice as she greeted him. Knowing he suspected her made her feel off center and her anger rose.

He swung his long legs off his buckskin and looked at her. "Mind if I put my horse in your corral for the night?"

He intends to spend the night again? He stood before her, looking wiry, strong, and dead serious. Yet, the sight of him set her heart to racing like white-water rapids. It angered her even further.

Through clenched teeth, she replied, "Go right ahead. May as well plan to come in the house for supper then. I have another guest at the moment. You'll have someone besides me to talk to."

He could see that his arrival had set her on edge and he didn't mind it at all. It made things more exciting. He'd missed the sight of her to the point he'd drummed up an impossibly thin reason to ride all the way out here again. Now here she was, madder than a wet hen already.

"Sorry to ride in on you so soon, but I'll need to see that murder scene again. There's something I must have missed. If you'd consider taking me out there, I'd appreciate it."

He could easily find that site on his own since he wasn't exactly a greenhorn in the area, and knowing that made her even more suspicious. He'd drag her out there again looking for a way to involve her in Elmer's murder. She shuddered with disgust, thinking she'd have to see that place again.

That poor man had lain out in the open with those buzzards picking at him, fighting each other for bits of his body, and it made her feel sick inside.

Why doesn't the sheriff just leave me alone instead of trying to find evidence to incriminate me?

He makes her feel safe—when he isn't accusing her of murder...

Hettie Jamison lost her husband in 1892 and now, two years later, her ranch hand has been murdered and her cattle are being rustled. When the sheriff of Flagstaff, Arizona, Jake La Force, comes to investigate, Hettie's foreman hints at her guilt and Jake interrogates her. Hurt and angry, Hettie tries to deny the attraction between them and orders Jake off her property. But he won't stay away, using every excuse to come back and continue his assault on her heart.

He's determined to make her love him—but she's putting up one hell of a fight...

A tough, no-nonsense lawman, Jake is surprised to find himself falling deeply in love after just one look into Hettie's fiery, golden eyes. While trying to solve the murder and rustling on her ranch, he must deal with suspicion, jealousy, and horse theft—not to mention a troubled young girl who'll stop at nothing to have Jake for herself. Jake knows he must overcome nearly insurmountable odds to claim Hettie for his own...he also knows this feisty and fiercely independent widow just might be the death of him.

KUDOS for *Jake's Song*

In Jake's Song by Ramona Forrest, Hettie Jamison's life changes drastically when she finds her oldest ranch hand murdered out on a remote corner of her ranch. It's not bad enough that she loses a beloved old ranch hand, but now the sheriff suspects her in the murder and she has no idea why. I really enjoyed the story, even though historical westerns aren't my thing. But I liked the characters and the byplay between them. I also thought that Forrest wrote with an authenticity that either comes from countless hours of research, or from knowing a lot of really old cowboys. Forrest seems to have a good understanding on how life must have been for women in the old west, and especially for women who were widowed. It tickled me to hear the eighteen-year-old girl, who also wants Jake, refer to twenty-eight-year-old Hettie as "so old." It really gives you an idea of how hard life was on people back then if 28 was "old." – *Taylor Jones, reviewer*

Jake's Song by Ramona Forrest is the sequel, sort of, to Stranger on the Tonto. It has some of the same characters and, while it is its own separate story, it does continue at least one theme from the first book. (No I'm not telling which one—you have to read the book to find out.) Forrest again shows an uncanny understanding of life in the old west and she doesn't shy away from addressing such things as body odor, which I imagine was a major problem when people didn't have the ability to take regular baths. I thought her attention to details like, body odor, food storage, and meal preparation made the story a lot more in-depth and believable. As usual, Forrest's character development is first class...Her dialogue is also first rate. It is just different enough to let you know that you are in another time and place, but not so unusual that it takes away from the story. All in all, this is another excellent example of what a really good author can do with a little imagination. – *Regan Murphy, reviewer*

JAKE'S SONG

Ramona Forrest

A BLACK OPAL BOOKS PUBLICATION

GENRE: HISTORICAL ROMANCE/ROMANTIC SUSPENSE

This is a work of fiction. Names, places, characters and incidents are either the product of the author's imagination or are used fictitiously, and any resemblance to any actual persons, living or dead, businesses, organizations, events or locales is entirely coincidental. All trademarks, service marks, registered trademarks, and registered service marks are the property of their respective owners and are used herein for identification purposes only. The publisher does not have any control over or assume any responsibility for author or third-party websites or their contents.

DEDICATION

In memory of a rancher named Charlie Young, who took us on round-ups, taught us what impossible things a horse could do, and gave us a very real glimpse into the daily life of the Arizona rancher.

CHAPTER 1

Arizona 1894:

Hettie Jamison started her ride on Diablo this early spring morning to quiet a dreadful fear that had settled into her bones. Restless with fear, anxiety, and a hefty sense of guilt she began her search for one of her ranch hands. Elmer, an older man, and eager to prove he was up for it, went out to take on the hunt for rustled cattle.

Her shimmering black horse, mettlesome and testy this early in the day, kept her mind and hands occupied controlling him. But Hettie, always eager to be outdoors, could not enjoy her ride today.

In a state of turmoil, she'd left her ranch house to ride— anything to help relieve her tension. '*Doing is better than stewing,*' her long dead mother had often said. She remembered that, too, but worry kept her jaw gripped as tightly as the hands that ached inside her gloves.

Elmer, too old to be on a mission like this, or gone so long, was a proud man. He pulled his weight around the ranch, and rather than hurt his pride, she'd let him hunt for the missing steers. A lonely old man, he had no family, no one outside the ranch to care or worry about him. He'd been there forever, had come with the ranch when she and her husband bought it.

Elmer had settled into their everyday life, and with him gone, so was his kindly presence. He's always enjoyed milking the cow, making cheese, working in the vegetable garden, and taking care of the hen coop, mundane chores the other men despised.

The climate had warmed by this time. April in the northern part of Arizona Territory, 1894, was a fine month to be riding across the ranch. Hettie noted the new grass coming along, what there was of it. She smiled at her acceptance of their sparse cattle feed—it was nothing new to her.

Ranching in this part of the Arizona Territory required many acres to feed very few cattle. The ranch was hers, though a good part of it was through government leases that allowed ranchers in many western states enough acreage to feed a decent sized herd.

They'd had good snow cover this past winter, and the early spring melt had enriched and watered the poor, rocky soil. New growth sprang from the still dampened earth wherever it could, and the sight of the new grass helped renew her courage. Facing the problems she encountered daily as a lone female running a cattle ranch took about all the resourcefulness she had.

Though edgy with worry about her ranch hand, she appreciated the crisp, cool air, flowing past her taut features, and the smooth movements of her horse. The sweet air, and promise of coming warm weather, would have made the ride pleasant on any given day if not for fretting over Elmer Greenup.

Nearing the noon hour, she noticed the circling of buzzards over a rise to the west. She tensed in the saddle. That familiar and deadly sign sent her pulse racing. *Now what? A dead animal*? A sick foreboding spread throughout her body and into the pit of her stomach.

"Damnation, I hope it's nothing more!" she uttered in fear as she guided Diablo toward the ghastly, bald-headed birds that kept the landscape clean of dead and rotting carcasses.

Closer to the fluttering of the black-feathered birds, she heard their noisy bickering as they circled and fought over every available bit of decaying flesh. It was a normal thing in the wild, but it always made her skin crawl to see those birds in action.

Diablo flung up his head in alarm at the flapping of huge black wings. She turned him aside, dismounted, and tied him upwind. He wouldn't take to the smell of rotting flesh or go near the foul odor. Leaving him tied to a sturdy scrub oak, she walked the remaining distance to have a look. Her eyes narrowed, as she sought the cause of a gruesome buzzard's feast.

"Oh God, no! That's Elmer's shirt, I'd know it anywhere. He wears it all the time." Sickened and wanting to vomit, she took in the faded print, the partially shredded jacket, even his scuffed and nearly worn-out boots. But the bloated remains of his face, torn and partially missing, were not in any way recognizable. The buzzards had quickly gone for the softer facial parts, and their grisly work lay before her.

Hettie had allowed the old fellow to go alone on what had seemed a fool's errand, and now she bore the guilt of seeing the poor old soul lying dead beneath the blazing sun.

The sight of his torn body fed her guilt, and her nausea was rising at the sickening stench. She came closer and saw a rounded, partially shattered hole in the dead man's skull. The sight of it leaped out at her. "Oh no! My God, he must have run into those rustlers and they've shot him."

He had to be over seventy if he was a day. I'm sure of it and I let him go on a wild goose chase. "Poor Elmer, your life has ended so badly."

Looking about, she saw no wandering cattle nearby, only the awkward movements of the ghostly, red-headed birds. As scavengers, they kept the environment clean, but Hettie found it difficult to be thankful for that at the moment. They flapped and circled close by as they waited for another chance to tear at the old man's remains in their horrid, scavenger's way.

Some devil has shot poor Elmer and left him lying here to rot in the sun! She returned to her trembling horse. He nearly snapped his reins, wild-eyed and stamping his hooves at the vague scent of death on her. Hettie patted his gleaming neck. "Easy, Diablo, easy boy." Murmuring words to gentle him, she reached behind the saddle, untied her slicker, and returned to the remains.

She spread the slicker over the pitiable body lying across the rocks, face up and exposed to the unrelenting processes of nature. *I'll have to get the sheriff out here. Maybe he can get to the bottom of this.*

She secured the slicker with the largest rocks she could carry. Looking around the site, she spotted her husband's old 1866 Yellow-Boy Winchester Carbine, carelessly thrown on the rocky ground. *How on earth did Del's old rifle get out here?* Had it been left there by the murdering bastard who'd gunned Elmer down?

An uneasy feeling invaded her mind—someone had entered her house. But why? *Who would steal that old relic and used it on poor Elmer? It was so old, why even bother with it?* A treasure of her husband's, he'd only shot it on rare occasions. The brass plating had new scratches on it, and someone had left it to rust or rot in the sun along with Elmer.

She hadn't missed it from its place over the mantle. Maybe she'd been too preoccupied with the intense loneliness that continually haunted her days since the death of her husband, Del, and now, another death, another loss. Seeing Elmer lying there gave her a renewed feeling of hopelessness.

Fighting back the tears that threatened to flood her eyes, she longed for her husband, wishing for his warm, strong presence. She needed him. Her world had gone totally wrong the day her husband's horse had stepped into a prairie dog hole, throwing him headlong into the rocks. A stupid accident took the love of her life, and marital partner, leaving her to tend a failing ranch on her own. If it hadn't been for the recent mining leases, she'd have lost the place by now.

Upset that someone had entered her home, taken that rifle, used it, and thrown it away, like Elmer's life, she decided it'd be best to leave it where it was. *Best not touch anything, I suppose. Maybe that cold-eyed sheriff will know what to do.* She hoped the big rocks around the edges of the slicker would keep the huge black, birds away from Elmer until she brought help.

Heading home, she dismissed the missing cattle from her thoughts. Fretting with anger, and a touch of anxiety, she covered the rocky ridges and gullies, her grip on the reins making her knuckles ache.

She'd found her ranch hand, but the knowledge that her home had been invaded and the rifle stolen added a sense of unease to her deep remorse and guilt. Tears splashed down her cheeks and onto the wide, delicately tooled, horn of her Mexican saddle.

She went over things on her ride back through the scrub oak and clumps of twisted red-barked Manzanita. Patting the shimmering neck of her glossy black stallion, she pulled his head up when he attempted a quick nip at the new bits of green growth along the way.

ຕາຕາ

At the ranch house, Hettie found no one. Though tired and dispirited after what she'd seen, she couldn't rest. The matter was too urgent. Packing biscuits, jerky, and a couple of apples, she headed for Flagstaff, a long ride. It was already late in the day. Her heart was heavy and her head was bowed as she rode. She mourned the loss of the faithful old cow hand. Her hands clenched frequently, and bitter tears flowed over the loss of Elmer. No one deserved to die that way.

She rode the same horse. He'd been ridden all day, but she wanted him under her for this trip. She loved and trusted the horse and had named him Diablo because of his color and haughty spirit.

She'd never known the name his former owner may have used. The man was dead—her friend, Cherry Carmona, had said. She'd declined to give Hettie any details, only saying that she never wanted to lay eyes on the horse or his overly fancy tack, ever again. The tone of her voice, and the way her friend had shuddered when she'd said it, let Hettie know it was better not to ask.

"I can't bear the sight of that animal on my place," were her friend's parting words.

Hettie had given the splendid horse a new home along with his fancy tooled, silver-trimmed tack. It was indeed something to look at, and too fancy to use out in the brush this way, but Hettie had found the saddle very comfortable. Maybe her horse was overdressed when she used it, but she always did.

She glanced down to see how well his sides had healed from vicious spur marks left by the previous owner. Why such a horse ever needed spurs in the first place puzzled her. She'd come to love Diablo, and that he'd been ill-treated filled her with anger whenever she gave thought to it. Riding him, enjoying his smooth gait, she relaxed in the saddle. A stallion he might be, but she handled him well enough.

Well after dark, she reached the small, but growing, town of Flagstaff, Arizona. Located at a higher altitude, it was much colder and she felt the chill of the mountain air. The fumes and heavy metallic clanking of a passing freight train let her know for certain she'd just entered a big city. But compared to a metropolis like Phoenix, it would be considered a small town, little more than a village. She came here often for ranch supplies and the place was familiar to her.

She found the sheriff's office and, seeing a lamp burning within, dropped Diablo's reins over the hitching rail, stepped to the door, and pushed to open it. Finding it locked, she knocked and waited. She was very tired, and her patience had worn thin. Within a moment, she heard the shuffle of feet. The door was unlocked and opened.

A tall, thin-faced young man stood before her. "Yes, ma'am? Needin' somethin', are you?"

Hettie knew he'd been dozing by the befuddled look on his face, the tousled mess of his hair, and the way he rubbed his eyes.

"Yes, I need to see the sheriff if he's around."

"He won't be in until the mornin', ma'am." His questioning look bade her offer more information. Coming fully alert, he opened the door wider and indicated she should enter. "I'm Lin Sloane, deputy here if you're needin' somethin'."

"I'm here to report a death out at my ranch, but I guess morning will do. I've been riding all day and half the night." Exhausted and bedraggled, Hettie didn't care if she saw the sheriff right now. It wouldn't help Elmer, and no way could she ride back tonight. "I'll come back then."

"Wait just a bit, ma'am." The deputy motioned her to a seat. "Which ranch you talkin' about, and who might you be?"

the man asked, obviously seeking enough information to enlighten the sheriff when he came to the office in the morning.

Hettie gave her name and what details she had. When he was satisfied, she bid him goodnight. She headed to the town stables to board her horse. A sleepy boy came and took the stallion.

"Mighty fine horse there." He patted Diablo's neck. "I'll feed him and rub him down. Don't you worry none about him, ma'am."

Satisfied as to Diablo's care, Hettie walked back up Front Street to the Ayers Hotel, roused a sleepy-eyed clerk, and took a room. She quickly got the impression that being a lone woman out late like she was, raised a few eyebrows. But Hettie didn't care. She had a reason for being out late.

She requested the comfort of enough warm water to clean up before seeking her bed. Too tired for dinner, she decided the lunch she'd had would have to suffice. She mourned the loss of her hand for a while, until utter fatigue overcame her, and she sought her bed. Tomorrow was time enough to meet that icy-eyed sheriff.

CHAPTER 2

In the morning, feeling rested and dressed in her trail-worn clothes, Hettie entered the dining room. Though ravenous, she wished she'd thought to bring something better to wear. She found a seat at a small empty table and, when the waiter appeared, gave her order. Soon, she held a welcome cup of coffee in both hands, sipping it's hot, life-giving contents while it warmed her hands. She took the time to gaze about the room, looking at the other residents or townspeople having their breakfast, and realized she didn't know a single soul in the room. *I'll have to come to town more often.*

Her pulse rose instinctively when a shadow crossed before her and a long figure imposed itself on her vision. She looked up to see a tall, spare, man, somewhere in his late thirties, she guessed. His pale blue eyes held hers in a steady gaze. She knew instantly this no-nonsense gent had to be the icy-eyed, loner sheriff of Flagstaff she'd heard about.

"Pardon me, ma'am. You Hettie Jamison?" His voice, though soft and low, carried the unmistakable elements of command and power.

She took a long look at this man she'd only heard about. "Yes, I am, and by the looks of that star on your vest, I imagine you'd be the sheriff hereabouts."

She wasn't going to be unsettled by his look, but he'd made a decided impact on her senses and that bothered her plenty. Surveying his quiet strength, she knew she wouldn't want to be caught on the wrong side of the law with this stern looking law-dog around. Taking another look, she wondered if he ran enough ice in his veins to match those eyes.

"I'm Sheriff La Force. My deputy tells me you came in last night to say there was a death or a killin' out at your ranch. The Lazy J, is it?" He pulled out a chair and stopped, his look asking her if she'd allow him to have a seat.

"Yes, please do sit down." She wouldn't have to go to the office after all. "Had breakfast, Sheriff?"

"Well no, not yet. Mind if I have a bite along with you?" That quiet voice of his had a way of going right through her. Something in the timber of it sent waves of unease dancing up her spine.

"Certainly not. Please do." She shrugged casually, but her heart pounded uncontrollably, and she felt on edge like a silly school girl, instead of a mature, twenty-eight-year-old widow. Keeping her wayward feelings under firm control, she waited in silence while he ordered and then began his questioning.

He cleared his throat and directed his ice-blue gaze to her. "Now, tell me what you can of this death you're reporting."

He leaned back, settling his wide shoulders against the wooden slats of the chair. She'd already seen the way his narrow hips were belted with a double set of pistols in slick, well-worn leather holsters and how the belt that carried them was heavily loaded with bullets shoved into little leathern slots.

His searching eyes missed nothing, while his voice, soft and deep, asked for answers. Looking him over, she nibbled at her food, wondering if he'd had to shoot anyone lately. She knew the man could.

Hettie began slowly. She'd slept well and saw no reason to be in a hurry. Poor Elmer was already gone. "About three days ago, he rode out to find some missing cattle—we've been losing stock all along for more than three years. My other hands were out, and when Elmer never came back after two or three days, I rode out yesterday, looking for him. And...uh...came across his body." She shuddered, mentally picturing the squabbling buzzards, but felt unable to mention them. It made her ill to remember that ugly scene.

La Force must have noticed her reaction. "Pretty bad out there, was it?"

She nodded, and he continued his questioning. "Any idea who'd want to gun the man down? Any enemies you know of?"

His eyes took on the glow of a predatory bird on the hunt as he gleaned what information he could from her sketchy account. She felt her scalp prickle with excitement, watching the man at his job, and felt relieved to be on the right side of the law—at least his law.

"No, he had no enemies, far as I know. He was with us for a long time, the longest of any of my men." She shrugged. "I don't really know why anyone would want to kill a nice old hand like Elmer, unless it was rustlers."

"You don't mention a husband or father. Are you saying that *you* run that ranch, a lone woman?"

His eyes, narrowing as he took her in, set her on edge.

"My husband died in an accident over three years ago. I do the best I can." She didn't see the need to mention her recent mining interests to him. Besides, it angered her that he thought being a woman, she'd be helpless.

"Sorry for that, ma'am." Jake meant that, but his thoughts were racing wildly back to a time long ago in his own memories. Looking into those gold-shaded cougar looking eyes of hers did things to his mind and body he'd never wanted to feel again. Surprised at himself, he found himself wanting to see all of her and couldn't stop the insane thoughts and feelings that rioted wildly through his brain and body.

Trying to keep his head on straight, he nodded. "We'd best ride out there and take a look. I'll have a word with your other hands, too." He received his plate and took time to eat. Doing that helped him get his racing thoughts in check.

Hettie watched him devour a huge plate of ham, eggs, flapjacks, and several cups of coffee. The sight of a man eating had always been a joy to her. The picture of Jake La Force eating his breakfast forced painful memories of another time in her life. No dainty little bites here. Nor was he a sloppy eater. He merely ate like a man. Her husband, Del, had eaten that way, too. Her heart ached, hard enough to stagger her, seeing it again.

She enjoyed her own breakfast as well, though she hadn't really tasted much of it.

When they finished, the sheriff rose from his chair. "We can ride out soon's you're set. Come to the office when you're ready. I'll be ready to ride by then, myself." He shoved his hat on. "Nice havin' breakfast with you, Mrs. Jamison."

He tipped his hat to her, and she noted with surprise, the ice in his pale blues had thawed considerably. When he smiled, they crinkled at the corners. It gave him a solid, manly look and hinted at a sometime gentle nature hidden away beneath those glacial eyes.

She sat at her table watching the tall, lanky man walk out of the dining room. His long stride, the set and swing of his shoulders, along with the jaunty way he shoved his hat back on his head, attracted and held her attention. His hair, a bit shaggy, and a nondescript brown shade, suited him somehow. Even the musical ring of his spurs as he walked, pleased her. Hettie felt more than something warm swelling inside of her. It was downright heat and the flush of it rose, burning over her neck and face.

"He's a nice one, isn't he?"

A voice close beside her caught her attention and broke into her reverie. Hettie caught the scent of fine, pricy perfume and looked up to see a small, blonde girl standing at her side, a frown across her pretty features. Her fine little figure was nicely dressed in lace and ruffles.

"Hello, I'm Annabelle Nellis. My daddy owns this hotel."

Her uplifted chin and proprietary attitude regarding the sheriff couldn't possibly mean anything to Hettie, yet she found it interesting, if not a bit unsettling. The girl looked to be far too young for a man like the sheriff.

"Nice to meet you, Annabelle. I'm afraid I have to leave right now but perhaps I'll see you again when I return to Flagstaff."

She rose from her seat and laid money on the table for the waiter, but he refused it.

"No need, ma'am, the sheriff took care of your breakfast."

"Indeed!" Expressing surprise, she picked up her money. As she walked toward the main lobby, she felt the presence of Annabelle trotting along beside her. Hettie turned to her. "Was there something else, dear?"

"No nothing really. I wondered what the sheriff had to speak to you about. Idle curiosity, I suppose." She sniffed. "I see he paid for your breakfast, too."

Her peevish tone came as a surprise to Hettie, and she took that for jealousy on the girl's part.

Her eyebrows raised in wonder. "It wasn't anything of importance."

Shrugging at the girl's sudden interest in her affairs, Hettie left the little blonde standing in the lobby and walked down the boardwalk toward the stable.

Looks like that steely-eyed sheriff has made himself a nice little conquest. She chuckled to herself but found it unsettling somehow and wondered if the man was even aware of it.

She found her stallion munching his morning oats and asked the stable boy to saddle him.

The kid leaped to comply. "I seen this horse somewheres afore, can't recall right off, where though, maybe down Prescott way. I come up here from there." He finished brushing the satiny, ebony-hued hide and settled the saddle blanket in place. After he placed the saddle and tightened the cinch, he stood back, a smile on his face. "He's sure a looker, ain't he ma'am?" His appreciation was evident as he indicated the finely-tooled saddle and patted Diablo's glossy hide. "Real fancy riggin', too."

"Yes, everything about him is nice, isn't it? I don't know his history, not so far," she replied.

Diablo proved to be a handful this morning, tossing his head and shying suddenly at every leaf blowing across the street. Hettie rode to the sheriff's office and sat astride him with a good grip on his reins, waiting.

La Force seemed to have waited for her arrival and came out immediately. He took the reins of his own horse and swung his lanky frame aboard. His horse looked to be a good sixteen, if not seventeen, hands of solid, buttery-hided buckskin. She watched the sheriff's blue eyes taking in her mount.

"Nice outfit you've got there, ma'am. That horse is sure a beauty."

"Yes, he is. Thank you." She didn't feel the need to fill him in on the particulars of Diablo's past and wondered at her own reticence. She kept a tight rein on the stallion, but the horse eagerly awaited his chance for a good run. His pace, tight and bouncy, let Hettie feel the bunched power beneath the saddle.

La Force smiled at her. "That's a lot of horse for a woman."

"He is, but we get along."

The brisk mountain air had Diablo more than ready, and Hettie held him to tight, prancing steps, as they rode out of town.

The sheriff had a loose-limbed way of sitting his saddle and made a graceful picture as he rode. She noted the warmth and regard he had toward his own horse he called Bucky. They headed south of Flagstaff toward the Lazy J. A leathern pack tied onto his saddle along with a coiled rope, a sheathed long rifle and rain slicker, spoke of his readiness.

Storms came up quickly in this region, though no clouds threatened at present. In summer, clouds usually hit against the high mountains around Flagstaff in the early afternoons, bringing quick, heavy, summer showers. The sheriff tended to lag behind her as they rode and she wondered why he did so, but wouldn't think of asking.

Jake stayed behind the slim, athletic young woman on her black stallion. Most women couldn't manage a horse like that, but Hettie Jamison had no problems he could see. He never took his eyes off that tall, slender figure, sitting her saddle with the ease of long practice.

Once again, something about her jarred a load of painful memories to the forefront of his mind. He watched her easy sway in the ornate saddle and couldn't stop the warmth from spreading all the way through him.

Seeing a good stretch ahead, Hettie let Diablo out for a good run, taking some of the restlessness out of him, then she sat and waited for La Force to reach her. "Sorry, he needed to stretch a bit."

The sight of her clinging low in the saddle, the stallion's black mane and tail flying in the wind, were pictured in his mind and he found it hard to speak for a few moments. Her body had moved to the rhythm of her horse's gate, and her blonde-streaked, thick-braided hair made a sight he'd not seen in years. His tongue felt thick. His voice nearly broke as he managed a mumbled reply. "No problem, ma'am. A horse like that's got to have his head now and again."

Saying nothing more, Hettie rode beside the sheriff for the next few miles, finding it companionable and enjoyable. The man appeared to be a cool, quiet soul who dominated the scene whenever he was a part of it. He'd easily commanded her respect and, outside of his stern reputation, had done nothing in particular to earn it.

It neared the noon hour, and they still had a long way to go, when he pulled up. "There's a small stream just down there. We might stop for a bit, give the horses a drink, and have us a bite." He indicated a low area with trees and heavy brush to the right of the trail. Without awaiting a reply, he swung his lanky frame down and turned away to lead his horse along behind him, heading downward.

Hettie followed suit and shortly they entered a small glade of grass and trees. Scrub Oaks were clustered about with some Junipers, red-barked bushes of Manzanita, and healthy patches of lush spring grass. Hearing the music of a swiftly running stream, she led her horse to it. As he drank, she noticed La Force had his horse ground-hitched where he could drink and nip at the grass. He'd pulled off one of his packs, settled cross-legged on the ground, and opened it.

"I brought along a few things to eat, if you'd care to join me."

His narrowed, light-hued eyes held the invitation and, despite the unbalanced feeling his look gave her, she nodded her head. She was too hungry to worry about her emotions.

"I'd love to join you."

Her voice, soft as feathers, settled over him, bringing those long-forgotten sensations forging back. While he took out a small square of cloth and some cloth-wrapped sandwiches, he kept his eyes on his task and had a tough time hiding the trembling of his hands.

"The hotel put this up. It's only bread and roasted meat with a couple of apples. Sorry, no coffee, but the water's good in the creek, right there."

Hettie laughed. "I'll live."

She sat cross-legged opposite him. They ate heartily and enjoyed the heady feeling of companionship. Thirsty, she knelt down beside the creek and scooped water up in her hands to satisfy her thirst. She had a canteen, but the fusty contents were no match for the sweet water flowing close at hand. The creek was icy and shallow. Every pebble, clear as day, was outlined on the creek bed.

Jake watched Hettie kneeling at the water's edge, scooping water to drink from her hands. Her natural grace of movement, whether astride the horse or afoot, made a beguiling picture that caught at the heart of him. He tried to look away, but found his eyes on her, following every movement she made with a kind of tortured joy.

She washed her hands in the creek and he watched them turn cherry-red from the icy water. Then she caught up her grazing horse and waited for him to say when to begin the ride again.

His expression made her wonder at his thoughts. She'd caught a glimpse of something hidden in his eyes, either pain or sorrow. She'd seen that look one other time as well before he'd looked away. The man hid some deep, sad mystery. She didn't know why her heart ached for him, but she'd known her share of heartbreak, herself, and was familiar with the feeling.

He took hold of his buckskin and led him back up to the rutted trail and, slipping over a few stones, she followed.

He quickly mounted. "We'd best be on our way, ma'am."

"Thanks for the break, sheriff. That was nice. I rode all day yesterday, and this stop was very welcome." Because his look sometimes made her wonder, she asked him, knowing she maybe shouldn't, "Do I remind you of someone, or something?"

"Well, you might say that—in some ways, yes." His answer held enough reticence, that asking further would invade his privacy. She turned her horse toward the ranch and rode on ahead. Everyone had sorrows hidden away.

CHAPTER 3

In late afternoon, they entered the ranch yard. Hettie indicated a corral for Jake's horse and went about unsaddling her own. He'd need to spend the night as it was too late in the day to travel to the scene of Elmer's death. Hettie figured the bunkhouse would suffice.

Smoke coming from that rustic building indicated some of the riders were in off the range and, knowing she'd ridden in, they came out to satisfy their curiosity. She explained the sheriff's presence and introduced them.

"This is Handy Childs." Jake shook hands with the heavy-set man. "This is Miguel, been here three months or so."

Handy had readily held out his hand in welcome, but Miguel stood silent, nodding. He said nothing, though Hettie noticed his black eyes certainly kept track of things. Two more men, Windy Jones and Larry Potter, came out and met the sheriff.

Jake turned to her. "Ma'am, I'll just have a chat with these fellows for now. We can ride out to the scene in the morning, if you can find it again."

"I can find it." Hettie left them and went into the house. As she walked away, she felt the eyes of the sheriff following her and thought she might invite him for supper, not now—maybe later.

Jake went into the bunkhouse and sat down with the men. "Mrs. Jamison tells me she found one of your crew shot dead a ways from here. Rode into town to report it, yesterday. Any ideas you might have about it would be helpful. It's a shooting death and a crime has been committed."

"Aw, hell—it's got to be old Elmer then. The rest of us are right here. Shot, you say?" The dismay in Larry's blue eyes told Jake how he felt about the missing man. He had the non-descript look of a young, outdoors type, with his wind-burned features and streaked brown hair.

"He ain't been around the last few days, I seen that." Windy's weather beaten countenance and furrowed brow held a puzzled look. A spare man of early middle age, he wore fad-ed, frazzled clothing. His pants were stuffed into high-top boots, and a sweat-stained cloth hung loosely around his neck.

Handy Childs wore a frown over his ruddy, slightly ro-tund features. His stomach swelled out over his belt, and old sweat stains ran down beneath his arms. "Ain't seen old Elmer around the last three, four days, that's fer sure. She say it was him for certain, then?"

"That's the story so far," Jake replied, hoping to get a feel of the sentiments among these men. How they liked working for a lady boss—he wondered that, too. "Anything you boys might have to say I'd be glad to have a listen." He rose. "I'll be seein' to my horse."

After feeding a measure of oats to his buckskin, he head-ed to the ranch house and knocked. Hettie opened her door, a questioning look on her face.

"I thought to look around a bit before we ride out there tomorrow. Didn't you mention an old make of rifle you found at the scene?"

"Why, yes, I did." She led him into the large sitting room and pointed to the empty place it had hung. "He kept it right here and, as you can see, it's gone."

Jake looked about, relishing the chance to see the inside of this particular woman's home. It held a fireplace made of native stonework with empty hooks above it. Plastered walls held scattered pictures of early days, including herself and her husband in happier times. There were several chairs, a long couch, tables, and lamps—a right comfortable room for a man to come home to.

"Over a fireplace wouldn't be a good place to keep an older gun like that. Heat'll dry out the wood and might darken the brass plating, well...if it's got one." Not wanting to denigrate the skills of her recent husband, he tried not to be critical and wondered why he'd mentioned such a thing.

"My husband always kept it there. More like a keepsake, I guess. I wasn't sure if it worked anymore, being so old." She smiled then looked at him through slightly narrowed eyes. "Would you like to have supper with me?"

"Why, I sure would, and I thank you." He felt the heat rise on his neck and struggled not to show it as he headed for the door. "I'll come back later, then."

He walked over most of the ranch yard again, finding the place nicely put together with several out buildings, corrals, and stacks of hay. "Looks to be a right nice place," he murmured.

Out near the water tank, he encountered Handy Childs. His agitated behavior, as he scuffed his boots about in the soil, told Jake the man had something on his mind.

"I shouldn't be tellin' you this, but I think Mrs. Jamison had it in mind to fire Elmer. The old boy was gettin' on in years and couldn't do his work so good no more. Told me he was real worried about what he'd do or where he'd end up if she shagged him out of here. You won't be lettin' on to her I told you about this, will you?"

His tight-lipped expression mirrored the worried look on his face. Jake wondered why the man would deliberately incriminate his boss, female or not, and seem more than eager to do it. A thing like that usually meant there was a hell of a lot more going on under the surface than met the eyes.

Jake had the feeling there was an undertow of disagreement on this ranch between the men as well. It hadn't been brought out verbally, but he felt the undercurrent of it and needed time to get a handle on it. The Mexican hadn't said a word. Jake wondered how much English the man spoke or even understood. Something about Miguel gave him an unsettled feeling. He could usually read men, but this man was an enigma he hadn't been able to figure out.

After a time, he heard the soft clanging of the small dinner bell coming from where it hung on the wide porch. He found the water tank where his horse had watered, washed his face, and slicked his thick brown hair down as best he could. He hadn't brought fresh clothes. What he had on would have to do.

Refreshed and ready, he stepped up to the door and knocked. His heart beat a little faster, and the unsettled sensations, he'd had in the restaurant and on the trail, came back to haunt him. *Damn! What the hell's going on?*

Hettie opened the door and ushered him in. She'd washed and changed her clothes. Her waist looked tiny with the wide green sash she'd tied around it, to set off the sprigged calico dress she wore. She smiled up at him. "I had to put something together on short notice. I hope it'll suit you."

"I'm sure it will, Hettie." He used her given name for the first time and wondered if she'd notice. He took a seat while she bustled about putting dishes on the table for them. Her honey-streaked light brown hair was long, thick, and wavy, maybe from being in a braid all day. She'd pulled it away from her face and let it cascade down her back.

He saw a dish of mashed potatoes, beef in thick gravy, several kinds of vegetables, and a pile of fluffy biscuits. The sight of it made him swallow to keep his saliva from getting away from him.

"Say now, this supper looks mighty fine," was all he could manage as he reached for the pot of coffee.

She sat opposite him, helped herself to one dish after the other, and he did the same. "I haven't done much cooking since Del's been gone. Doesn't seem worth it somehow. It's a pleasure to feed a hungry man again."

She flushed at her admission. He thought she looked wonderful just now, with her face all rosy from the heat of the cook stove and the work of preparing a meal.

"Most days I take my meals at the hotel in town there, so this here's a real treat for me, too." He chatted easily with her, while his mind struggled with the impression he'd gotten from Handy Childs. He needed more information. "Tell me about this Elmer. Been here a long time, you said?"

"Oh, yes. He'd been here some time before we took over. He sort of came with the place when Del and I bought it about six years ago. He always did a good job for us, I must say."

"How old a man was he, would you say?"

"He was getting pretty gray. It bothered him some. The boys razzed him about it, so I've heard. He's always done his work as far as I know. But lately, I'd thought to find easier

work for him on account of his age." A tear escaped her eyes.
"I still can't believe that someone would take a shot at him.
We'll miss him around here. He took care of the milk cow. We
keep a few pigs for the meat, and he was good at curing hams,
bacon, and such. He even took care of the garden and the orchard. I don't know what I'll do with him gone. The other boys
hate that kind of work. Who'd ever think sending him out to
find that stock would lead to his death? I wish I'd never let
him go…I always will."

She raised her gold-shaded eyes to him, and he saw the
shimmer of tears along the thick dark lashes. With her honey-
brown hair swept back, her facial bones looked delicate and
finely molded. Her ears were nicely shaped, and so was everything else. Looking at her, he understood the many sorrows she
held hidden within herself. She felt a deep sadness at the fate
of her employee, and he caught from her conversation that
she'd completely loved her husband and mourned him still.

Being preoccupied in taking in the entirety of this en-
chanting woman had nearly made him forget his purpose until
he forced himself back on track. "I'll find out what happened
to your man, Hettie. Maybe tomorrow when we see the scene,
I'll find something to help me with the investigation."

He took his eyes off her and bent over his dinner. Her
cooking was excellent, better than anything he'd had in years,
short notice or not.

While he'd polished his plate with a remaining biscuit,
she rose to bring a thick crusty pie to the table, along with a
pitcher of cream. "This is from our apples of last fall if you'd
like a cut of it."

"I surely will have some of that, ma'am. You are one hell
of a cook!" He enjoyed the pie with a bit of cream poured over
it and nearly smacked his lips.

"This cream is from the last time Elmer milked our cow." She choked up as she said it, and Jake noticed again, her real sorrow over the death of her ranch hand. He wondered once more at Handy's incriminating words. Something wasn't right. Their stories didn't fit.

"Too bad it turned out this way," he said, wanting to comfort her. The pie finished, he rose and walked about the big room again, taking in the fine handiwork he'd seen, the books, old pictures, and a few old Indian artifacts they must have found together.

He noticed an old, well-used guitar, hanging on a peg. The sight of it gave him a deep pang. He suppressed it and sighed. "Well, I'd best get out to the bunk house and find a place to bed down. I sure do thank you for a right fine dinner, Hettie." He took her hand in his. "I'll say good night, then." He went out the door and into the night.

Hettie sighed. It was good to feed a man again. *He's a nice sort if you don't get on the wrong side of him. But I'll bet those eyes can drip icicles if he thinks you've broken the law.* She laughed at herself. *Those dirty dishes can wait,* she decided. She'd ridden hard for two days and needed some sleep.

⌒⌒⌒

Jake entered the bunkhouse and took a seat on a beat-up old chair sitting vacant. The men had been chatting, but grew quiet in his presence. "Say boys, don't stop anything on my account. I'm just passin' the night here. Which bunk will you let me have?" He saw several, knowing there'd be at least one to spare.

Windy pointed to an empty bunk. "You could take Elmer's there. Looks like he ain't needin' it no more. Might be some of Elmer's possibles on it. I'll clear it off." The stumpy-legged man hopped up and went to the bunk. He gathered some of the items laying there and made them into a nicely tied bundle. "Don't know what we'll do with this. Never heard if he had kin folk anywheres."

"Thanks, Windy." Jake sat on the narrow bed. It didn't bother him that it had belonged to a dead man. There were a hell of a lot worse things to worry about, and he'd ridden a long way that day.

Windy sat a while, holding the few personal things Elmer had kept in his bunk and the little cupboard beside it. It was something he appeared loath to look into. "Reckon I'll take these things up to the boss lady and let her deal with 'em." He picked up the personals of the dead man and headed out.

Half-asleep Hettie opened at his knock. "Yes, Windy?"

He handed the bundle to her. "These here are Elmer's possibles, ma'am. I don't know anything else to do but to give 'em to you to look through."

With reluctance she took possession of the small, ker-chief-wrapped parcel. "Thanks, Windy." Standing inside her home, holding the pathetically small remains of a good man's life in her hands, she murmured as she went to a cupboard and put the things away, "Doesn't come to much after all, does it?"

Hettie couldn't bear to look at what the old man had kept private—his personal treasure. She might do that later when there was time. Right now, she had to get some sleep.

She slept fitfully in her twisted sheets, fighting buzzards that grew bigger, noisier, and hungrier until escaping them, she found herself hiding from pale blue eyes that held her mind in a grip she couldn't escape.

CHAPTER 4

In the early morning, Jake knocked on Hettie's door. He'd eaten in the bunkhouse with the men, was ready to go, and had asked the men to ride along to bring the man's body back for burial.

Hettie opened the door. "Good morning, sheriff."

She was ready, too, and he filled his eyes with the sight of her walking out into the sunshine in a split riding skirt of a dark corded material over tooled boots that held small spurs. She wore a white blouse under a corded vest. Her thick, ropy hair, caught into a heavy braid, obviously bothered her until she flipped it down her back. The broad-brimmed hat she wore shaded her hair and face from the sun, pretty much, but it hadn't prevented the glow of tan across her fine features. A heated thrill shot through Jake just watching this young woman walk beside him. He turned quickly away lest she see the look on his face.

The party mounted up, and Hettie led the group out into the sage and scrub growth that covered the lower reaches of her ranch. The grass, though sparse, was fresh, green, and tender. Rocks were always plentiful. Jake believed she had a tough time making a living on the place.

He'd also noticed how easily she rode with the stallion's soft jog-trot that covered the distance so well. The men followed in silence, and Jake, nearly in a trance from watching the trim figure riding ahead, silently cursed himself for his thoughts. Hettie had an enticing amount of fullness in all the right places. He shook his head, trying to keep his thoughts away from her feminine assets.

What the hell's going on in your mind, you damned jackass? These feelings had been absent in his brain for so long, he barely remembered how mind-boggling the sight of a fine-looking woman could be to a man.

He was here to investigate a man's murder, not to look at a woman again for the first time in too many years. But that handsome figure and the thick waves of blonde-laced brown hair kept his eyes and mind way off track.

Along about noon, she turned to him. "I think you'll find him right about over that next ridge. But if you don't mind, I believe I'll just wait here." She pointed to a few black circling buzzards. "I hope those blasted birds haven't uncovered him." Jake saw the look of distaste over her face, as she slowed her horse's pace and stayed back from the site she didn't want to see again.

He nodded. "Wait here, if you like. We'll do what we must."

"Thanks, I will."

Hettie watched the men ride over the ridge and heard their horses snort and blow. As the men approached the site, several huge, black buzzards flew up from the ground. Hettie shuddered, knowing the grisly sight that lay before them.

Jake dismounted upwind and tied his mount to a handy scrub oak, hoping to keep the stench of rotting carrion from spooking the horse. He approached the dead man and flapped his arms at the birds. They scattered away, squawking, but circled about the area, waiting.

He pulled what remained of the slicker off the body. It wasn't difficult to see where the bullet had entered. The jagged hole in Elmer's skull made that easy enough. The ghostly, red headed birds had eagerly cleared away the skin. Flesh and bits of Elmer's hair lay scattered about on the rocks.

"Whoever did this got close enough to place the bullet right where he wanted it." He indicated the wound site to the men. Spotting the rifle lying on the rocks where it had been thrown, he muttered, "Must be the rifle she mentioned." The scratches on the metal of the old gun didn't look new to Jake. The rifle itself looked to be an older model. Yet he knew many were still in use. Maybe this one worked, too. He picked it up, sniffed the chamber, and nodded. It'd been fired.

Handy Bates came close to the body, muttering and kicking rocks about. "God damned! Poor bastard should'na ended up this way. It ain't right. It jest ain't right!" He moved away upwind, and the others followed.

They'd brought a roll of canvas to put the body in, and after Jake combed the site to his satisfaction, he told the men to roll Elmer in the tarp and pack him up for the return to the ranch. They completed the grisly task and tied the long parcel on the spare horse they'd brought along, but not without a fight. The packhorse let them know he wasn't partial to the stench of death. He snorted and twisted, trying to offload the canvas-wrapped bundle tied snugly across his saddle.

Jake came back to where Hettie sat her horse. "We're done here. Is there someplace you'd like him buried? The boys seemed to think he had no family." He added, his voice softening, "It'd be your say, ma'am."

"We have a small cemetery where Del's buried. I guess that'd suit Elmer all right. The boys can help with that and I'll get our minister. He's a rancher, too, but stands in for these things." She gestured toward the ridge. "They're bringing him?"

Jake nodded and again noted her deep sorrow regarding the old rider. It didn't set with what her man, Handy had told him. He wanted to question her further, but he decided to wait until they got back to the ranch. "Well, he won't be layin' out there anymore," was all he could say for now.

"Thanks, Sheriff." She indicated the rifle. "I see you're carrying Del's old rifle in the crook of your arm. Did the killer use that?" By the grimace on her face, he knew it hurt her to ask.

"Looks that way. Hard to be sure of much, the way things were around there." His taciturn answer gave her an idea of what he'd just seen. She didn't need him to draw a picture— she'd seen enough of that site herself. She shuddered and urged her horse to move out, turning Diablo toward the ranch.

On the way back her head drooped. She paid no attention to her surroundings or the wild beauty of the far-flung mountains that ringed her ranch. Everything went unnoticed or appreciated. Her heart ached in sorrow for the loss of that dear old man. The entire party rode in silence.

When they reached the ranch yard, they sat on their horses, watching the men bring in Elmer's body. Jake asked her about the Mexican. "What do you know about this Miguel? Who is he and where's he from?"

He'd noticed how the young Mexican rushed up to take care of Hettie's horse. *Is his interest in the horse, or are his eyes on Hettie?*

Hettie dismounted and handed Miguel the reins. As he led the horse away, she replied, "I don't know. He came out of nowhere, really. We needed another hand at the time. In winter, sometimes we have to feed extra hay out to keep the cattle going until the spring growth gets started."

"Just curious." Jake had noticed the quiet, all-seeing eyes of the slim, dark-skinned man. "Does he speak or understand enough English to get on with all the *gringos* here?"

"I guess he does, yet, I've rarely heard the man say a word about that or anything else. He seems to watch everything, especially my horse." She laughed about it, but he heard a note of worry in that, too.

"I'll be headin' back soon, but I need to ask you about something else. The man was getting' on in years. Had you planned on getting rid of Elmer any time soon, being he wasn't able to carry a full load anymore?" He'd tried to find a gentle way to ask the question, and instantly regretted the look on her face at his words.

"Why would you ask me that?" Her voice rose and she flushed in anger at the suspicion in his voice. She'd believed they were working together in this investigation until now. Suddenly, she felt like a suspect with his new line of questioning, and her temper flared. "No, as I mentioned before, I'd planned on having him do less strenuous work because of his age. Right now with Elmer gone, I don't see how I can get along without him, and I've never had a thought of letting him go. Never!"

"Just have to cover all the questions that came up."

Hettie fired at him. "Came up? What on earth put that idea in your head, or who?" She felt crushed and betrayed that anyone would accuse her, or even think such a thing. "Whoever said anything like that is plum loco! Was it one of my men who said that?"

"I can't say anything about that, Hettie."

He saw coldness and disbelief in her eyes, and the pain of it flashed clear through his body. He wanted this woman's good opinion above that of anyone he knew, and he'd just lost it. Her face, flushed with anger and tears, warned him she was ready to erupt.

"You've no business calling me Hettie, either!" She shook with rage. "I can't believe you're thinking I could be guilty of murdering that good man. The very idea! For all the help you've been, you can get yourself back on that buckskin horse you rode in on and damned well hightail it out of here. Now!"

"Well, I'll be goin' ma'am, but this case isn't over. Not yet, it isn't." With that he swung aboard his horse and rode out of her yard.

Jake grinned as he rode away. *That woman's got a hell of a temper.* He had to look at everything when a case came before him, but this one challenged him in ways he'd never expected. After many years of solitary living, he'd met a woman he looked at with interest—and way too much of it. "Dammit all to Hell, I thought all that business was dead and gone."

CHAPTER 5

L ater, after a long trip back to Flagstaff, Jake took supper at the hotel. Haunted with lingering memories of
the meal he'd enjoyed at Hettie's table, he ordered ab-
sent-mindedly from the well-fingered menu. With his habit of
eating at the hotel, he had it memorized.

He was surprised to see his order delivered by a smiling
young blonde girl. "I thought I'd just bring your supper myself, Sheriff."

She wanted to sit down, but Jake hesitated, being used to
eating alone or with some of his deputies or the townsmen. He
didn't want the intrusion of a rather forward young girl right
now and hoped the scowl on his face would discourage her.

"I'm Annabelle Nellis. My daddy owns this hotel. You've
been coming in to eat here for a long while and I just wanted to
make your acquaintance." She drew back a little, finding no
welcoming warmth in his icy-blue eyes.

He looked at her, wondering what she had in mind. "Very
nice to meet you, Miss Nellis. Can I help you in any way?"

She looked eighteen, not much more, and he didn't want
this child at his table, though he'd eagerly welcome Hettie if

she walked in. He wondered at the intrusion, but said nothing more.

"Uh, no, just passing the time around here…Um…want some company for dinner?"

Jake could see it took all the courage she had to ask that question in the face of his stony, tight-lipped expression. He tightened his jaw, and his body stiffened. He knew a spoiled child when he saw one, and he'd already figured that what Annabelle wanted, Annabelle got.

Without asking further permission, she plopped herself down across from him, determined to get acquainted. He felt an icy chill run through his insides, wondering what this young girl could possibly have in mind. He had no interest in her, and he sure as hell didn't want her company.

Seeing she had nothing in front of her and not wanting to seem rude, he offered, "Since you're sitting there, won't you have a bite of supper?"

"You buying, Mr. Sheriff La Force?"

The coy look she directed at him as she cocked her head made him decide to find another place to take his meals. He often frequented a small place called Ma James and decided he'd best eat over there. He didn't want any trouble in this town and could do without some silly girl hanging around him, certainly not a spoiled teenager.

"If you like," he replied, keeping conversation as short as possible.

His voice, terse and cool, didn't deter her in the least, and she plunged ahead. "Well, all right, then." She giggled and waved the waiter over to take her order. "Ben, dear, could you bring me the lamb shanks? And Ben, please make sure it has the minted sauce over it, and I'd like a small baked potato, opened with a small bit of cheese over it. Not too much now, and could you bring me a cup of that new tea Daddy just got in. It's imported from China, and I believe it's called Jasmine or something like that."

She let her voice drag over some of the words making sounds she believed were very upper class. "And, oh yes, don't forget the new tomatoes we just got in." She smiled in triumph at the waiter and turned her blonde head to see if Jake was impressed by her attention to each minuscule detail.

If he was, she couldn't see it, and it deflated her enthusiasm a bit, but only momentarily.

She kept on, and Jake suffered through a long, meaningless trial at dinner, hearing endless chatter about nothing of interest to him. He ate his food, remembering in detail the quiet dinner he'd enjoyed at Hettie's table.

Other diners took notice of the young girl at his table, and it made him increasingly uncomfortable. He barely kept up a decent conversation with Miss Annabelle. She paid no heed to his reluctance, non-attention, and clenched, tightened jaw, as she rattled on with her nonsensical blather.

Across from him, the blonde curls continued to shake and tremble with her animated chatter, and the full red lips spouted endless items intended to impress. A long ride over a hot desert with a dry canteen looked a hell of a lot better than Annabelle Nellis as far as Jake was concerned.

The dinner finally ended and with a sigh of relief, he rose and took his leave, after leaving a generous tip for the waiter. He tipped his hat to Annabelle and said, "Goodnight, miss."

Walking out into the fresh air, he wondered, *What the hell brought that on*? He shook his head, muttering to himself, as he stalked across Front Street.

That brassy little female had moved in on him without invitation and he hadn't enjoyed one moment of it. *What in hell has that silly girl got in her head*? Whatever it was, it reminded him of a pesky blowfly, but one he couldn't swat.

Constantly puzzling over the murder of Elmer Greenup, he found it impossible to think Hettie could have had a hand in it. Yet what Handy Childs said clung to his mind. "Why would the man say something like that?"

The undercurrent among the men remained a mystery, but it was there, and he'd felt it. With Childs's accusation pointing toward Hettie, he'd seen it in action.

He had a hanging to keep an eye on in a couple of days and headed to the office for a few moments. Lin Sloane met him at the door.

"Say, I saw you havin' chuck with the little blonde. Takin' an interest in the ladies, are you?"

Lin couldn't seem to hold back his sly chuckle and Jake gave thought to pasting a hefty blow to Lin's grinning chops.

"Sure as hell wasn't my idea," he growled in answer. "Anything happen here while I was gone?"

"Nothin' much. Vonokovich beat his wife again last night, but she wouldn't say a word against the man. Couldn't arrest him." He sighed. "How'd it go out there?"

Jake filled him in on what he knew. "I can't figure it right now, but something smells like an overripe outhouse at that ranch, and it sure isn't the owner. It'll take some time to get it sorted out." He kept his hat on and headed for the door. "I'll be sayin' goodnight now. See you in the mornin'."

Jake was in a rotten mood. He'd made an enemy of Hettie. He remembered the anguished look on her face, and it tore him up in ways he couldn't understand. The whole case bothered the hell out of him. He couldn't stop thinking about it. When he saw a rock lying in his path, he gave it a good kick.

જાજાજ

Hettie heard no more from the sheriff. Madder than a yellow jacket when she thought of it, she cursed the man and his buckskin horse. "He'd better not show his face around here after what he's accused me of."

She missed Elmer, his weathered face, his smile with a few missing teeth, and all the small wearying tasks he did for her around the home place. She hated all those small chores as much as the men did, but they had to be tended to. Gone was the old man's smiling face and his fussy way of working in the garden or tending the chickens or pigs. It had been like they were his and he enjoyed the care of them. Hettie liked the products and produce, but not the additional work.

She picked wild flowers, blue spiky lupine and wild roses whenever she found them, to put on the freshly turned earth of his grave and her husband's, too. She longed desperately to talk to her friend, Cherry, but she'd married and moved to Prescott. That loss left Hettie feeling more alone than ever.

When she heard the clatter of hooves coming into the ranch yard, she hoped it was her friend and hurried to the door. Looking out, she felt her spirits slump. The little blonde girl from the Ayers Hotel came driving up in a spanking new, red buggy, outfitted with gleaming brass and a fringed shade to cover the driver. Her small bay mare, dressed in the finest leather harness and trimmed with silver studs, looked tired and sweaty.

As the girl got out, Hettie recalled their previous meeting at the hotel in Flagstaff. *Annabelle is her name, I think she said. What on earth could have prompted this visit?*

She went out to greet the young woman. "Hello there. I'm surprised to see you way out here, so far from home." Hettie stepped to the side of the small carriage and helped the girl down. "What a lovely rig you're driving!"

The girl paid no attention to the complement about her carriage as she gushed, "My goodness, you really live way out in the wilderness, don't you? I didn't think it was this far."

"Won't you come in and stay awhile? It's getting warmer every day and you must be dry as desert dust after your long drive." While Hettie waited for an answer, she unhitched the buggy horse and led her to water. "Want me to put her in the corral for a while?"

"Oh, why, yes. That'd be wonderful, now wouldn't it?" Annabelle didn't offer to help, merely stood waiting while Hettie took care of the animal. After watering the horse, she let her into a small corral and tossed in some hay. Then, together, she and Annabelle walked to the ranch house and went in.

Hettie found the girl a drink of sarsaparilla water. She didn't really care for it herself, but kept it around to offer a rare visitor. Coffee was much preferable to Hettie's way of thinking.

"My, you have this fixed up quite nicely, don't you? I always wondered how folks managed, way out like this. Must be terribly lonesome." She looked around, seeing a picture of Hettie and her husband together. "Is this you and your husband? Where is he?"

"He died about three years ago—an accident with his horse."

"Oh, and you're all alone here, then?"

From the fretful tossing of Annabelle's head, Hettie guessed it wasn't what she wanted to hear. The girl looked sharply at Hettie. "Any plans toward marriage again?" she asked and waited for an answer.

"I haven't given any thoughts to it. My husband would be hard to replace. We were very happy together."

The girl gave a sigh of relief, and Hettie wondered about it. She'd met Annabelle right after her breakfast with Jake La

Force and, by the girl's actions and words, had the feeling Annabelle Nellis had her eye on the sheriff. *Could it be she is worried I might be in her way?* She uttered a chuckle at the thought.

"What's so funny?" Annabelle asked, her eyes narrowing.

Hettie easily saw she was intrigued by an older, yet handsome enough, woman. One who could be a real adversary if she set her sights on that cold-eyed sheriff, or any other man. The girl couldn't hide the jealously rising within her.

Hettie found it amusing to think that this girl had her eager young eyes on the sheriff and ached for his attention. She instantly felt sorry for the girl's misplaced ideas. The silly little fool didn't seem to know that La Force hadn't taken up with any woman, for as long as he'd been in the area. Even Hettie had heard that about the man.

She wondered if Annabelle seeing her as an adversary had niggled at her until she had to drive this far to find out. It rang a bell in Hettie's mind and she hid a smile. *That fool girl has come out here to find out if I have designs on the man.*

Annabelle caught the sly smile. "Why are you smiling like that?" She wore a frown across her flushed, heated cheeks.

"Nothing, really, just a passing thought I had. Would you like a slice of pie? It's from yesterday, but it's still good." Hettie didn't want this girl to know her thoughts, so she changed the subject. However, she couldn't help feeling a bit of elation at the ridiculous idea that Annabelle saw her as competition.

Still burning inwardly at La Force's suggestion that she had something to do with Elmer's death, she laughed silently at the thought. *If that fool girl wants that steely-eyed sheriff, he is hers for the taking, and God's pity on them both.*

It was nearly dark outside when Annabelle decided to leave. Alarmed, she looked at Hettie. "Oh dear, I've stayed way too long! My mother will be worried sick and think I've had an accident or something awful, like that."

"Why don't you spend the night? They must realize you couldn't drive all the way out here and get back before dark. They do know where you are, don't they?"

"Of course, they do. But, could I stay the night?" She appeared flustered at being caught out this way. Yet Hettie saw the calculating look beneath her anxious exterior, understanding this girl and her underlying machinations.

Spending the night out away from home wouldn't do her any good—unless it brought the sheriff out hunting for her. *She'd be capable of a little trick like that. And wouldn't it serve that suspicious lout just what he deserved?*

"I'll fix up the second bedroom for you," Hettie offered. "We'd best go out and make sure your horse is properly cared for before we turn in." Looking outside, Hettie saw the men were in the bunkhouse. The lamp had been lit and their horses were in the corral. "Looks like the men are here. I'd like to know if they've found out any more about Elmer's death, so I need to speak with them."

"Well, all right."

Annabelle hung back, hesitant about going out in the dark, Hettie noticed, but she didn't give her the option of staying inside.

"Let's go see what the boys have been up to." She pulled on a jacket against the bracing evening air, handed one to Annabelle, and opened the door. They walked first to the corral. Someone had tossed hay to Annabelle's horse and removed her tack. Diablo had been cared for as well. They went on to the bunkhouse and knocked.

Handy opened to admit them. The lamplight threw an orange-tinted pattern across the steps and on the two women who stood there.

Hettie went in, nearly dragging the reluctant girl by the hand. "Boys this is Annabelle Nellis, come to pay a visit."

Annabelle immediately brightened at the sight of the sun-browned men, a whole room full of them. At the girl's increased excitement and fluttering eyes, Hettie wondered if she had some sort of need for male approval.

Annabelle greeted the men in turn. "Nice to meet you. I got caught out here and have to stay the night." She rambled nervously until her eyes fell on Miguel. She spent more time looking at his dark, slender form than was proper, and when he kissed her hand, and murmured in soft Spanish, "*Ah por dios, la muy hermosa senorita,*" she nearly went into spasms of delight.

Neither woman knew for sure what he'd said, but his black eyes had said plenty. Hettie, seeing it was time to leave, pulled the shining-eyed girl along with her.

"I'll check with you men, tomorrow," Hettie said, as they left.

She hadn't had time to question her men, but Miguel's overt interest in the blonde girl gave her an uneasy feeling, one she understood and didn't trust. Annabelle appeared ready to flirt with any male even close to her own age, and though Jake was older, that included him as well.

They checked on the horses again and entered the house for the night. Annabelle enjoyed a cup of hot chocolate, and Hettie found her a nightgown to sleep in before they settled for bed. Hettie lay awake thinking of poor Elmer and how that cold-eyed sheriff had accused her. She also enjoyed the company of another woman, even knowing Annabelle's nefarious purpose. In fact, she found the whole thing pathetically humorous.

❧❧

After a healthy breakfast of ham and sourdough biscuits, but before she drove away in the morning, Annabelle exclaimed, "Hettie, I almost forgot to mention it, but there's a big community dance next week. Why not come into town and go with me? You could spend the night at my home. We have a lovely big house and I'm sure my mother would approve."

She pleaded for Hettie to come with her voice—but her glittering eyes said something else. Hettie saw no sincerity in them.

Miguel was on hand to hitch her horse to her fancy little rig, getting next to Annabelle as often as possible. The girl enjoyed his attentions and responded with giggles and frequently tossed blonde curls. Finally, with a cheery wave to Hettie and Miguel, she clicked to her little bay mare and drove away.

Disgusted with the girl's overt flirting, Hettie turned away from the sight of her departing buggy to enter her house.

"Well, well, since I need supplies, I just might make it into town for this dance."

She figured the hands would all be raring to go as well. No one missed a chance to attend a dance when they got the opportunity, and some people came from as far away as Prescott.

After careful thought, she decided to go. She hadn't gone to a dance since losing her husband and this would be her first.

She couldn't help wondering if Jake La Force attended those dances. Being so sober and serious like he was, she doubted he'd give himself over to a frivolous thing like dancing. *If he does, he can go whistle if he thinks I'd waste my time dancing with him!*

She couldn't imagine it. Yet, she found herself thinking about wearing a wonderful new dress and shoes, her hair in a fancy, upswept hairdo, and being held in his long, strong arms.

Whirling around a dance floor with that man holding her, invaded her thoughts continually, and she censored herself firmly as she dug though her closet for something suitable. "I must be insane!"

CHAPTER 6

Hettie heard no more from the sheriff and wondered if, finding no further evidence regarding Elmer's death, he might have put the case aside. Any further investigation seemed to be forgotten. Del's old rifle hung in its usual spot over the fireplace, and she missed seeing the old man going about his daily chores.

She wondered if her presence at the dance would stir the sheriff into trying harder to find her complicit in Elmer's death. "Maybe he's forgotten the whole thing," she said to herself, but she knew better.

Worrying about that cold-eyed sheriff won't stop me from going into Flagstaff. We need supplies, again, and if I choose to attend that dance, I will. Her temper flared when she thought about him accusing her of any crime, especially murder.

She spent time worrying over what to wear and finally settled on a dress she'd not worn in years. It was form fitting on top, with a square neckline—a dark cream shade with tiny violet flowers delicately embroidered throughout the skirt, with a matching row outlining the neckline. Small purple buttons ran in a row down the front and below the waistline, set into a V above the flowing skirt. It had the effect of making her waist look as trim as any sixteen-year-old's. The color complemented her tanned skin and thick ropey hair. She hadn't decided on how she'd fix that yet. "Something up high, I imagine," she said and laughed at her image in the mirror.

"I wasn't sure I'd want to go to this dance, yet I've gotten more excited over it than anytime I can remember. I must be lonesome. Or going plumb crazy." She whirled before the mirror—what there was of it. She wasn't completely sure how she looked, and Elmer wasn't around to ask. He'd been the one man with whom she'd easily discussed anything, even how she looked.

The boys, except for Miguel, headed to Flagstaff. Hettie had packed her things into the wagon they used to bring supplies and drove along with them. The dance wouldn't start until the evening and she'd have time enough for a good bath and smoothing out her clothes. She decided to take a room at the hotel rather than accept Annabelle's offer. Spending more time with that silly blonde was too much to consider. She uttered a hollow laugh at the thought.

She planned to watch the goings on at the dance and figured if she had a few turns around the floor, it would make the entire night one to remember. She wondered how La Force would react to seeing her again. Part of her felt more than eager to lay her eyes on that lonely soul. He was a man who kept his past very carefully hidden. It made her wonder what lay behind the few glimpses of deep sorrow she'd seen in those pale blue eyes. Memories of a life gone before? What sorrows did Jake La Force carry deep inside that chilly exterior?

It was coming on summertime these days, and the hot sun bore down on her bonneted head as she drove the team and wagon. It was tiring, so she asked Windy if he'd drive awhile.

"Why, shore will, ma'am." He tied his horse behind the wagon and hopped up onto the seat beside her. "Getting hot, ain't it?" he observed.

He emitted the sweaty odor of a hard-working man, pungent, but nothing she hadn't noticed before. It went along with the deep voice and hard muscles of a healthy, working, male body.

She nodded in agreement. "Sure is, Windy."

With him driving, she relaxed as they moved over the rutted road better suited to horseback. But they needed what the wagon could haul.

They reached the hotel around three in the afternoon. Hettie always enjoyed the cooler air of the heights around Flagstaff, particularly during the summer and spring months. The many times she'd been in town during the winter months, she'd found it blustery and cold.

She carried her bag into the cool interior of the Ayers Hotel and took a room. She saw nothing of Annabelle and felt relief because of it. Glancing into the dining room, she saw the sheriff sitting at a table.

Jake had come in for a late bite to eat, chancing he'd miss out on the pleasures of Miss Annabelle's annoying attentions. His heart rate quickened at the sight of Hettie. That tall, slender form at the front desk, with her wild mane thrust under her weathered hat, had the power to turn him inside out.

"If she's plannin' on goin' to that dance, I believe I'll be attendin' that fandango myself." A smile played about his mouth. "She hates the sight of me, but I figure on claiming at least one dance with that hot-headed lady."

Hettie ordered hot water and a light meal delivered to her room. She ate a few bites then took a nice bath. It gave her the quiet time she needed to quell her thoughts regarding the man she tried her best to dislike. Yet Sheriff La Force continued to occupy a large place in her thoughts. Wanting to hate him, she failed. He was constantly on her mind.

She sat at the desk and pulled out a sheet of paper. "It's time I dropped a line to Cherry. There are things I must know—maybe she'll tell me now. It's been a long time since they'd had that trouble on their ranch. Diablo came to me after that, with no explanation. A horse like that has a history, and I need to know what it is."

She set out the inkpot and got busy. It struck her as unusual that Miguel had such a proprietary attitude toward that black stallion, unless the man had an eye for exceptional horseflesh. If there was a connection of some kind, she needed to know.

The letter finished, she dressed carefully. Not wanting to venture in alone for some reason, she'd asked Windy to come and escort her to the dance.

When he knocked on her door, she opened it to see him spruced up in his Sunday best. He was about forty or more, she guessed, thin built, with long, sandy sideburns on his weathered face. He wore a red shirt tucked into black pants, and his best boots had been shined to a nice glow. He appeared more than proud to take his boss to the dance.

"Here I am, ma'am, all ready and rarin' to go." A wide smile lit up his rather homely features as he held out an arm. "You look right smart tonight, Mrs. Jamison."

"Thanks, Windy." She tucked her hand through his arm. "You look pretty darned fine yourself. I hope escorting me won't keep you from one of your lady friends."

"Aw, no, ma'am. Don't really have one, but I might meet a few at the dance tonight."

He flushed, but his words held a hopeful sound. She wondered if he'd ever been married. You never knew about men. They kept their secrets.

She walked with Windy down the staircase and paused to hand her letter to the man at the desk. "Would you see this goes out in the next mail?"

The man took the envelope and gave her an admiring glance. "Sure will, ma'am."

It made her feel good to see affirmation in the eyes of another male. She moved with confidence as they left the hotel and walked the short distance to the community meeting rooms/dance hall. With the increasing sounds of fiddle music, piano, and drums pounding away, it seemed the very walls swayed and pulsated with the beat of the music.

Her excitement mounted as they entered. She'd kept herself isolated for nearly three years. She had no one to blame as it had been her own doing. Most young women wanted to attend as many dances as possible, but she'd neglected social things far too long. After losing her husband, she'd found it difficult to go to dances or meetings alone.

Trying to hold her ranch together kept her busy enough. But, lately, keeping solvent hadn't been a problem after selling her mineral rights to the government. She totally enjoyed the freedom from her burden of debt, and with her financial problems eased, she felt ready to step out a bit.

At a time like this, Hettie missed her husband terribly. She found it hard to be a lone woman at any gathering. It didn't seem right or even natural, but she held her head high and would do her best tonight as well.

She wasn't sure she could bear the sight of that sheriff again and hoped he'd not be attending this dance. She held a good bit of anger inside, even while realizing he was only doing his job. Would that lonely creature show his face at this dance? "You fool, why do you even care?" she murmured, censuring herself.

Her heart rate quickened as they entered the dance hall. She bade Windy to leave her as she settled into a chair. "I'll be fine on my own. You have a good time now, you hear?"

"Well, I shore will, ma'am, but I might have to ask you for a dance 'afore the night's over." Windy moved away toward a group of young women laughing and chatting together.

Hettie sat next to Alma, the wife of mercantile owner, Bib Williams. The woman grinned. "Goodness, it's been an age since I've seen you, Hettie." Alma laid a warm hand on her arm. "My dear, how have you been?"

"Just fine, Alma, and I'll ask the same about you. I—"

She stopped speaking. A figure crossed in front of them as the music began again. A handsome man in his forties stood before her. He held out a clean, smooth hand. "Might you favor me with a dance, ma'am?"

"Why certainly, sir." Delighted at the offer, Hettie rose and, with a shrug to Alma, she let the man lead her out on the floor. He proved to be a solid, mid-height gentleman, wearing dress clothes. By the softness of his hands, she decided he definitely was not a ranch person. He wore a nice cologne, was clean shaven, and she hoped he'd be a good dancer.

"I'm Martin Banks, ma'am, just passing through town. I haven't seen you around here before, but I must say you're the finest looking lady I've seen in a long, long time." His arm tightened around her back and he swept her along in a fine waltz. His cologne smelled masculine and wonderful.

Most men of her acquaintance never wore anything that nice. They used mostly soap, Bay Rum, and some kind of hair dressing to slick down their sun-dried locks. This man looked directly into her eyes, and at nothing else, as they moved along. His gaze soon became uncomfortable. It had the power to make her feel hunted, and he held her a bit too tight for comfort.

As they danced, she caught glimpses of people she knew and, in spite of her adverse feelings about him, looked to see if La Force was there. Then she decided she'd best pay attention to her partner. "You're a very good dancer, sir. I haven't been to a dance for so long, I thought I'd forgotten how."

"No worries there, my dear. You're doing just fine." His arm tightened around her further, to the point she felt increasingly uncomfortable.

Affronted by his bold actions, it set her afire with indignation. He'd gone too far with his grip on her person, and her temper flared.

She uttered a low growl through tightened lips. "You'd best loosen your grip on me, mister, or I won't be responsible for what I do next. But I can guarantee you won't like it."

Looking at him with ice in her eyes, she felt relief as his grip loosened.

He smiled at her. "My God, you're really something, aren't you?"

He laughed and she caught a glimpse of gleaming teeth that vaguely reminded her of a ravening wolf. Yes, he might be rather handsome, but now, she saw him as predatory, and that feeling caused ice to fill her veins. Though he'd proven to be a fine, skilled dancer, she eagerly waited for the dance to end.

When it did, he returned her to her seat. "Thank you, miss…"

Hettie didn't give him her name. She didn't want him to know it. He stood there for a moment, towering over her, before leaving in search of another conquest.

He'll be back. She knew enough about men to know a man like that wouldn't be put off so easily.

She sat next to Mrs. Williams again. "Alma, that man was too much! I had to threaten him about the grip he had on me."

She smothered a laugh, remembering how quickly he'd complied and loosened his hold on her.

"We see him quite often. He sells goods all over this part of the country and he hit town yesterday. Don't know that much about him, though. Nice looking gent, isn't he?" Her eyes held a twinkle, and Hettie decided that Alma, knowing she'd been widowed, felt she should be looking for a new husband.

"Maybe so, Alma, but he's not too trustworthy, is my guess." Watching out of the corner of her eye, she saw him choose another woman for the next dance just tuning up. "Best watch out for that one, Betsy, my dear," she murmured.

At that juncture, Annabelle made her entrance, dressed in a shimmering frock that must have cost her daddy half the hotel. It outlined her fine little figure. Her blonde curls, swept high to increase her diminutive stature, added to the picture she presented. An enticing bit of femininity, she quickly had a willing partner before she even found a seat. Hettie wondered if she'd notice her sitting there and question why she hadn't taken up her offer of hospitality.

A shadow moved across her and Hettie looked up to see Jake standing there. She gave him a mocking smile. "Am I under arrest?"

"Not yet. I'd like to have a dance with you before I put the handcuffs on."

He grinned at her and reached out his hand. Hettie wanted to refuse him, but his pale blue eyes looked darker just now and had a glow she'd never seen in any man's eyes before. He looked so fine and well dressed in his western-cut suit that she rose to her feet automatically and let him lead her onto the floor.

"I believe this is a waltz," he murmured as he circled her waist with his arm and swept her along in a very well-done waltz. "Been a long time since I've done this. Hope I don't walk all over your little feet."

"You're doing just fine, Sheriff La Force, just fine." She had to smile. She felt so good right now, her anger at him had a hard time staying focused. Elated after seeing that certain gleam in his eyes, one she hadn't seen in a man's eyes for far too long, she knew full well this man saw her far more as a woman than a suspect. Not that it would change anything with him. He was a law man before he was anything else. She already knew that much about him.

"You could call me Jake, Hettie. It wouldn't kill you, would it?"

"So you could accuse me of murder again and use my first name to do it? I should say not, and I'm not Hettie to you!" The sudden elation at sparring with this man made her heart sing, and she felt it racing wildly.

Ignoring her hasty comment, he breathed softly in her ear, "My God, woman, you look like a queen in that outfit you're wearing. I thought you were a looker before but, tonight, you take my breath away!" His arm tightened around her just a bit more.

Fighting off the wave of heat his words sent through her, she warned, "Don't you dare hold me so tight. I've been through that already tonight, but he let loose after I gave him a good piece of my mind." She held back a giggle as she watched Jake's face tighten with anger.

"Who was it?" he demanded, holding her back to search her eyes.

Well, what next? He's being protective of me? Enjoying herself, being in his arms and sparring with him, made this evening a total joy. Then, out of the corner of her eye, she saw Annabelle edging their way. The little blonde was on Jake's trail and Hettie waited, wondering what he'd do about it.

He looked about the room. "Was it that traveling sales-man over there, getting too close to Betsy Martin?"

The dance had ended and he hadn't seen Annabelle approaching as they stood in the middle of the dance floor as Jake continued trying to find out who'd bothered her. The concern on his face was difficult for her to believe. "Was it that salesman over there?" he repeated.

"It was my business, and I took care of it." After a clipped, terse answer, she turned to greet the approaching girl. "Oh hello, Annabelle, my dear, what a lovely dress you're wearing."

The overly bright sound of Hettie's voice went unnoticed by the young girl. She stood looking Jake La Force up and down with a possessive gleam shining in her eyes. Hettie actually began to feel sorry for the man. Without a doubt, this young girl had plans for him.

"Oh, thank you." Annabelle said, remembering Hettie's comment on her dress but keeping her eyes on Jake. "It cost my daddy dearly but he always wants me to have the very best." She drew in a quick breath, thrusting her small breasts outward. "And here *you* are, Sheriff La Force. I wondered if you'd be here tonight. I really hoped to have a dance or two with you." She gushed her excitement as Hettie stood silently by, being completely ignored.

With absolute delight, Hettie watched the frozen look spreading over Jake's face and said ever so sweetly, "Thanks for the dance, Sheriff La Force. It was a pleasure. You were very good out there."

Hettie left him standing there with the eager young Annabelle, who definitely had the sheriff in her sights. Part of her wanted to strangle the girl, but the rest of her enjoyed the sheriff's utter discomfort.

"Serves that suspicious lout right," she sniffed in disdain as she returned to the chair next to Alma.

The music started again, and Jake took Annabelle in his arms for a dance. The stony expression on his face warmed her heart. He'd been trapped, and she'd had a hand in it. Yet, she ached inside, wishing it was her body he held as he whirled the little blonde around the dance floor.

Remembering her turn about the dance floor, she decided Jake's grip hadn't been too tight. The way he'd held her in his arms suited her just fine.

CHAPTER 7

Hettie's thoughts were interrupted by the salesman, Banks. "Care to dance again, ma'am?" Rather than make a scene, Hettie complied. He kept his distance as far as holding her too close, but his words were something else. "I'd like to spend a lot more time with you, lady." His dark blue eyes fixed her with a gaze that could melt the forged steel the mining people had blathered on about when explaining their need for Molybdenum and its uses.

She felt her temper rising again. "I don't care to spend *any* time with you, Mister Banks, and I don't want what you hint at."

"Just what am I hinting at, then? You know what I mean, and don't lie to me. A woman your age has been around a bit. I'm no fool, lady."

"No, you're not a fool. You're a filthy bastard! You're lucky I don't want to make a scene, or you'd be lying on this floor, holding onto you precious whatevers!" She tried to pull away, but he tightened his grip on her.

"Such language for a fine, fine, lady!"

His voice had turned angry, even menacing. Hettie's desperation grew as she sought a way to leave the man without creating a scene. A wave of relief and utter gratitude swept over her when she heard Jake's voice.

He'd stepped up and tapped Banks on the shoulder. "Mind if I cut in?"

His cool drawl and forceful mien made the salesman loosen his grip. Hettie turned and poured herself into the safe haven of Jake's arms with a sense of relief so great, she almost burst into tears.

Jake tightened his welcoming arms around her. She laid her head against his broad chest and closed her eyes as he swept her across the dance floor. She'd come into a warm, safe embrace and, without thought, pressed even closer into his long, lanky frame, heaving a troubled sigh.

"Oh God! Thank you, Jake."

She had no trouble saying his name, now, but she fought the threatening tears, not wanting him to see how upset she was. He seemed to know. He held her close and swung her across the floor with his arms wrapped tightly around her. While it felt so very good—and safe—she couldn't help the insidious deviltry she felt in asking, "Where's Annabelle?"

"I have no idea, Hettie."

His eyes squinted as he smiled down on her with an *I'll-get-even-with-you-later* look in his pale blue eyes. As they moved across the floor, she realized again how skillful he was. Was it the natural grace of the horseback rider? she wondered. Hettie saw Annabelle watching and couldn't help giving her a wide smile as they passed by.

"What was your new conquest saying to you just now to make you look so het up?" Jake had a sly grin spreading across his face. "I was beginning to worry about that poor man."

"He's no conquest of mine. Alma Williams says he's a traveling salesman. Probably chases women in every town he goes to." Out of the corner of her eye, she spotted Annabelle's eyes shooting daggers in her direction. She laughed and looked into Jake's gaze. "It seems you have a little conquest of your own to worry about."

"Not my idea." He kept his taciturn mien but pulled her a bit closer, and she didn't resist. She felt secure in his arms, despite his suspicions of her. He had a good odor about him, all man with a dash of Bay Rum. It made her remember Del. He'd had that, too, and the closeness she'd known with him came back to haunt her.

It struck her again how lonely her life had become as she relaxed against Jake's hard body and stayed close while they moved around the floor.

Surprised, he put his head down close to hers. That kind of closeness, so very intimate, sent a searing heat cascading all the way through her. She pressed her face against his broad chest and held him tighter as they danced.

When the dance ended, he released her and led her to her chair. She could barely walk, and his face was slightly pale as he walked away. While she composed herself and her wayward thoughts, Annabelle came and sat beside her.

"I see Sheriff Jake has asked you to dance several times." Her tone, low and sulky, came heavily laced with envy and anger.

"I suppose he has. Did you enjoy your turn with him?"

Hettie kept her own voice all sweetness and light. She'd heard the angst in the girl's voice but felt no pity for Annabelle. The sheriff was too old for her and had shown no interest that way, whatsoever.

"He was like a block of ice when we danced. He's good at it though, isn't he?" Annabelle shook her blonde curls. "I think he likes me." She turned questioning eyes toward Hettie. "What do you think about it?"

Amazed at the girl's obtuse thinking, she answered, "I hadn't noticed." Scanning the room for her men, Hettie hoped they were enjoying the dance and wondered if any of them had found a lady to share the night.

Annabelle chatted on about Jake. "I think my daddy being a hotel owner kind of puts him off. Maybe it'd be him stepping out of his class or something if he courted me." She sniffed. "It wouldn't bother me if I married a sheriff—well, one like Jake." She giggled and shifted in her chair.

Hettie drew back in disbelief at the girl's stilted thinking. For all his rough exterior, Jake La Force was a better man than most, including Annabelle's father, or anyone else in this town. Surprised that she wanted to defend the man, she kept those opinions to herself.

Annabelle pattered on. "I hope he isn't interested in any-one else around here. I'd not take it lightly, and my daddy al-ways knows what to do if I need help." Her thinly veiled threat meant nothing to Hettie since she had no interest in Jake. She did feel certain Annabelle had her work cut out for her if she was going to corral a man like him.

She couldn't stop a smile from spreading over her face but she held back the hearty laughter that wanted to burst forth. She'd have to wait until she got to her hotel room for that.

"I hope you don't think it's funny!" Annabelle exclaimed. Spotting Jake across the room, she got up to head in his direc-tion. Before she left, she asked, "Hettie, why didn't you come stay with me?" Her frown indicated her disappointment. "You aren't interested in Jake, are you?"

"Certainly not, my dear, but I have business to attend to, supplies to order, and I thought a room in the hotel would be better. It's difficult to spend my time talking about clothes and things with so much I must get done." She hoped the girl was sensible enough to realize being a ranch owner carried many responsibilities.

Annabelle left her and headed toward Jake, but suddenly, the man was nowhere to be seen. Hettie shook her head at Annabelle's machinations and managed a small amount of pity for the deluded young girl.

Surprised to see Miguel standing along the sides, she wondered, *Does he look for Annabelle after the encouragement she's given him?* She saw no other Mexicans at this dance, then she realized these dance steps might be unknown to him and he could not ask Annabelle to dance.

Hettie danced with each of her ranch hands and noticed Windy had found himself a nice widow woman about his age, a bit weathered and faded, much like him. He'd danced with the woman several times. Hettie noticed how close he held her, with his head down, whispering words in her ear.

When she got set to leave, she found Jake at her side. "I'll see you get back to the hotel without running into that salesman again." He took her elbow and walked with her out into the air.

"You don't need to walk me, Jake. Believe me, I can handle that man if he gets in my way again." He'd been good on the dance floor, sweeping her about the room in his arms like he had, but she faced the reality that she couldn't trust him, nor could she trust the way he made her feel. She held her arm stiff, feeling uncomfortable. *Is he planning to question me again?*

He chuckled. "Aw, loosen up, Hettie. You're still carrying on because I asked you a couple of routine questions. Aren't you carrying your grudge a little too far?"

It made her temper flare. "I can't believe you'd ever suspect me of killing a nice old man like Elmer. Of course, it upset me."

She tried to pull her arm away, but he wouldn't let go. He caught hold of her hand and kept her close.

"What are you doing?" she demanded. "Right now I'm beginning to think you're worse than that traveling salesman! I may have to make a few threats on you, too."

He fought back a roaring laugh, knowing it'd only make her madder and she'd hate him more than she did already. As much as he liked seeing her flare up, he held his humor and walked alongside her, keeping his body close against hers, saying nothing more. Being with her and touching her gave him a deep, aching pleasure. She made him feel alive, and he was rapidly getting used to the wonderful way that felt.

"What are you planning, now?" she queried, her jaw tight.

She believed he wanted to question her further and awaited the chance. She couldn't imagine what about, but it made her feel tense. And she didn't like it.

"I'm not planning anything, but you seem to have a corral full of ideas. Is there anything more I can do for you?" He pulled her arm closer yet as they reached the entry of the hotel.

"You don't need to do anything for me. We're here and you can let go of my arm." She struggled a bit, but not overly much. In spite of her anger at him, he felt way too good walking next to her.

He finally released her. "Good night, Hettie."

In truth, Hettie felt a sense of loss when he turned and walked away. She couldn't believe she felt that way, yet, something in his voice, his touch, made everything seem right. Or was it a sense of completeness he brought to her? He'd gone, and the feeling of closeness had left her. Loneliness set in again.

As she headed up the stairs to her room, Annabelle appeared at her side and took hold of her arm. "I saw Jake walking you back here. You sure you aren't chasing after that man?" She looked at Hettie with narrowed eyes and sounded sulky. "He's spoken for as far as I'm concerned."

The petulant look on her small face prompted Hettie to push her a little. She laughed. "Oh, really! Does Jake know he belongs to you?" She thought she'd best add, "I'm not after any man in this world. I've already had the best there is. I hope you'll be as lucky." She resented the girl's intrusion and, suddenly feeling very tired, she wanted to get to her room and fall into bed. "I'll say good night then, Annabelle."

She disengaged her arm and walked on down the hall to find her room.

The girl said nothing further, but her tight, grim expression as she stood in the hallway, let Hettie know she had an enemy of sorts. She entered her room and locked the door.

"The nerve of that silly girl!"

She washed and slipped into her bed. Her feet ached a little, and she smelled of smoke, but thinking back over the evening, she decided it'd been a good night out. She relived some of the dances, but a soft ache of pleasure came over her, remembering how safe she'd felt in Jake's arms as they'd swirled about the dance floor.

❦❧

During the night, a shadowy figure approached the room where Hettie slept. The man leaned against her door, listening for sounds inside.

When he grasped the knob and tried the door, Jake stepped out of the shadows and growled in his lowest voice, "You try goin' in that door, mister, and you're a dead man."

The salesman jerked and turned to stare at Jake.

"I thought this was my room." Banks blanched pale in the dim, lantern-lit hallway. He'd been caught and he knew it.

"I'll just say one more thing. If you ever set foot in this town again, I'd best not catch sight of you." Jake nearly laughed as he watched pale shades of fear cross the man's face.

Martin Banks slunk back to his room, but Jake watched Hettie's door the remainder of the night. He'd quietly dispatched Martin Banks, not wanting a loud, brawling ruckus to awaken the woman sleeping within. Not really sure why he sat watching over Hettie, he just knew that doing so gave him a deep sense of joy. She brought out his protective instincts. He chuckled softly, thinking of her. *She'd be mad as hell if she knew I was sittin' out here.*

CHAPTER 8

Hettie's wagon sat in front of the mercantile, stacked high with supplies. The team stood hitched and ready. She'd ordered a packed lunch from the hotel for the drive home. The others had left earlier, but Windy had stayed to ride his horse along with her. "I could spell you with the drivin' if you'd like, ma'am," he offered.

"Thanks, Windy. I'll let you know." She took the reins in hand and, before slapping the reins across the horses' rumps, asked him, "Meet any nice women last night, Windy?"

She smiled a knowing smile at him from her seat on the wagon and saw the sweat break out on his forehead.

"Shore did, ma'am."

He flushed rosily at her question, but the smile on his homely features said enough to satisfy Hettie's curiosity. He had the look of a man who'd spent some private time with a woman. She knew that look all too well herself and grinned with fond remembrance.

She flapped the reins across the horses' backs and set the wagon in motion. The wheels ground and crunched on the gravel of Front Street as she left the town behind, as well as the cool, crisp air of Flagstaff.

Deflated this morning, the fun and excitement of the dance over, she again faced the rigors of ranch life on her own. At times like this, she missed Del the most. He ought to be sitting beside her on the wagon seat, but the lonely spot in her heart reminded her that he was gone from her life.

She'd missed seeing the grasping, chatty, Annabelle this morning but, without overtly doing it, looked around every corner to catch a glimpse of the tall, spare form of that icy-eyed sheriff.

Unless Jake had more investigating to do, she didn't expect to see much more of him and that realization gave her a great sense of loss. Heading downward toward the canyons and mountains of her ranch, she felt more alone than ever and couldn't understand the why of it. She ought to be over the loss of her husband by now. Windy kept up a steady stream of cheery chatter going about the dance, but it was in no way what she needed.

Later in the day they arrived at the Lazy J, and Hettie felt her pulse quicken at the sight of an upscale Concord carriage sitting in her ranch yard. She saw no one about and, after climbing down from the loaded wagon, gave Windy his orders and headed toward the house, her curiosity heightened.

A tall, well-dressed man rose from one of the rustic wooden chairs, placed haphazardly along the wide, roofed porch. He stepped down with long strides to meet her.

"Mrs. Jamison, I believe." He held out a hand. "I'm Alexander Hodges of the Centralia Mining Company, the folks who hold the mineral rights to the Molybdenum mine on your ranch."

She took the proffered hand. "Nice to meet you, sir." She hesitated. "I did meet one of your people about a year ago, but no one since then." Puzzled at his being here, her face felt icy, and her heart rate increased. Had something gone wrong with her leases? She'd come to rely on the extra funds. They'd kept her and the ranch from going under. The look on her face must have expressed her fear that her finances were about to evaporate.

Seeing her distress, he sought to placate her worries. "I came to update you on our most recent plans for the resources at that site and one other one. The government values what we've uncovered here very highly." Hettie relaxed inwardly as he hastened to add, "We don't need it at the moment, but in case of war or unusual public need, we would of course want to begin mining in rather quick order." He smiled at her, observing her sigh of relief. "I'm sorry if my coming here set you worrying about our intentions, ma'am."

"Yes, it did a little. I don't understand much about this mineral you mention, but I'm glad it's of value." She sighed quietly then smiled at the man. "It certainly has been for me."

Remembering her role as a hospitable ranch owner, she asked, "Won't you come in and have something? Have you waited long?" She gestured for him to follow her as she started up the steps.

"No, not too long. I arrived here a couple of hours ago. My horse has been taken care of, and one of your hands offered water." He uttered a small laugh. "I had a drink as well as my horse."

She led the way inside her home and bade him sit in one of the larger chairs in the open sitting room. The fireplace commanded a large portion of the rock-lined wall he faced, and there were bookshelves on either side. Del's old rifle hung in the hooks over the long flagstone mantle where La Force had left it.

Looking at it and seeing the old scratches on its stock brought the memories of Elmer's killing back to her, and how La Force suspected her of the murder. Remembering that day made her temper rise to the point she nearly forgot her guest.

"Nice home you have here," Hodges said, sitting back, relaxed.

She got herself in hand and brought him a drink of sarsaparilla water, having nothing else to offer at the moment.

"I'll make coffee if you'd care for a cup. I could use a cup myself after that long wagon ride." She felt travel worn and worried that she looked it.

Looking out the window, she saw her men unloading the supplies she'd brought. They knew where everything belonged and that gave her the space and time to entertain this man. She pushed her heavy braid back and sighed.

"Why, yes, I'd certainly enjoy that," he replied.

Hettie noticed his look as he took in the sight of her and understood his thoughts, as well. She was worth the look—a slender woman with thick masses of honey-brown hair—and like any man, his interests weren't all in mining. She'd seen Del take a look at a pretty girl when he could and was fully aware that few men can overlook the sight of a finely put together female. It made her smile to be appreciated in spite of her travel-worn appearance.

As they shared cups of coffee, he explained, as well as possible in layman's terms, the uses the government had for the materials in her mine. "It enhances the power of steel exponentially. In construction, arms, and most industries, that is a real bonus where stability, accuracy, and strength are required. The mineral was discovered over one hundred years ago," he explained further. "But we are only now, after experimentation, finding ways to put it to good use. It's a national asset, should we ever need to use it, and the government keeps their eye on its whereabouts."

"I think I understand. Actually, those very qualities are valuable in just about every capacity, human as well as making steel." Smiling at him, she felt she understood things more clearly and was comfortable around the man. He wasn't a bit like the fancy-dude salesman she'd met at the dance. She didn't compare him to La Force, either, believing they were not at all the same sort.

He walked about the room and, looking outside, saw beginning dusk gathering over the mountains. "I wonder if I might spend the night here on your ranch since it's much too late to start back to Flagstaff. And before I leave here, I'd like to inspect the mine site, too. I can catch my train for the East from there whenever I'm ready to leave."

"Certainly you may stay the night. We have a good sized bunk house and one bed is vacant at the moment." She saw no reason to fill the man in on Elmer's death. "The boys will make you comfortable, enough." She paused. "Perhaps you'd join me for dinner. It will be a while before it's ready, but I'll call you when it is. I usually ring a bell."

"Why, I'd be delighted, ma'am," he replied as she led him outside and toward the bunkhouse. The corrals had enough animals present that she figured most of the men were there. Larry Potter was feeding calves in a far pen, and Windy tossed hay to her horses. She'd asked Handy to do the milking and pick up the eggs, daily chores he absolutely despised. They reached the bunkhouse where Handy was busily making their supper meal.

About to introduce the two, she soon realized they'd already met earlier. She wondered why Handy had been in from the ranges that early, instead of out with the stock. She'd speak to him about it later.

With Hodges at the bunkhouse, she headed toward the house. Nearing the porch, she heard the sound of a horse's hooves and saw the sheriff riding up on his big buckskin. A chill passed through her. *What is that man after now? Coming to arrest me?*

She stopped in her tracks and waited for Jake to reach her. "Well, Sheriff La Force, what brings you out here so soon again?" She couldn't keep the ice from her voice as she greeted him. Knowing he suspected her made her feel off center and her anger rose.

He swung his long legs off his buckskin and looked at her. "Mind if I put my horse in your corral for the night?"

He intends to spend the night again? He stood before her, looking wiry, strong, and dead serious. Yet, the sight of him set her heart to racing like white-water rapids. It angered her even further.

Through clenched teeth, she replied, "Go right ahead. May as well plan to come in the house for supper then. I have another guest at the moment. You'll have someone besides me to talk to."

He could see that his arrival had set her on edge and he didn't mind it at all. It made things more exciting. He'd missed the sight of her to the point he'd drummed up an impossibly thin reason to ride all the way out here again. Now here she was, madder than a wet hen already.

"Sorry to ride in on you so soon, but I'll need to see that murder scene again. There's something I must have missed. If you'll consider taking me out there, I'd appreciate it."

He could easily find that site on his own since he wasn't exactly a greenhorn in the area, and knowing that made her even more suspicious. He'd drag her out there again, looking for a way to involve her in Elmer's murder. She shuddered with disgust, realizing that she'd have to see that place again.

That poor man had lain out in the open with those buzzards picking at him, fighting each other for bits of his body, and it made her feel sick inside.

Why doesn't the sheriff just leave me alone instead of trying to find evidence to incriminate me?

Disheartened by this turn of events, she muttered, her voice so low he barely caught her words, "I'll ring the dinner bell when supper's on. It won't be much, since I just got back here myself and didn't have all day to cook, no matter who's eating." She turned away toward the house, her shoulders slumped and her pace slow.

"I'll be along then," Jake called to her, his voice soft as silk while he led his horse to the watering trough.

She turned to watch his lanky form walking away with his arm over the big buckskin's neck and couldn't take her eyes off the man. Aggravated to no end, she didn't know what to do about it.

Hettie fumed and fussed about fixing a hasty meal. "That mining man likely has fancy Eastern tastes in food. I suppose he won't think much of anything I can fix." She peeled potatoes and had water heating. She opened a Kerr Mason jar of pie apples, made a quick pie and when the oven had heated enough, shoved it in. The meat would have to be dried jerky since nothing fresh was around for the day and she wasn't about to kill a chicken for either one of those men. She whipped up a batch of biscuits and made a salad from a few greens that weren't too wilted.

She took time enough to wash up and change her clothes while she prepared dinner. It took a while to put the meal together with what she had on hand, but she did the best she could. She thought it was good enough to suit just about anyone. If not, it was just too bad, wasn't it? For the pie she found fresh cream from the cow and chuckled. "Handy hates milking that cow so much."

In the bunkhouse, Jake came face to face with Alexander Hodges. They stood toe to toe and introduced themselves. Jake felt a sudden wave of discomfort sweep over him as he looked at this fine specimen of manhood. He noted the refined, studied look of the well-educated man and had no idea what he was doing out here at Hettie's ranch. "Pleased to meet you," he said as he shook the man's hand. "New out here, are you?"

"I'm here from the Centralia Mining Company to consult with Mrs. Jamison on some of her claims. While I'm here I plan to have a good look at the sites." For some reason, he couldn't imagine, he didn't hesitate to let Jake know he held a position of some importance. "I'm one of their planning engineers."

They sat and talked while they waited for dinner. The feeling they were adversaries crept into the conversation, and the sparing had just begun when Hettie rang the dinner bell. Darkness had settled over the landscape as they walked to the house, side by side. "I'm spending the night in the bunkhouse, there," Hodges informed him.

Jake knew the bed he'd hoped for was taken. It'd be a haystack or pile of straw somewhere, and that didn't set too well with him. He figured Hettie would never stand for him spending the night under her roof, but he'd happily accept if she did. He grinned to himself, thinking about spending the night in the same house with that tawny-eyed woman.

Feeling unsettled about the woman, he wondered how long this fancy dude was staying. And furthermore, he'd never heard of any mining interests Hettie had. Now he wondered if she'd struck gold or something. She was a closed mouth one. He knew that, too.

Hettie ushered the two very fine men to her table. *Wouldn't Annabelle bust her silly little garters if she saw me right now?* "Have a seat, gentlemen, I'll put the food on right away." While the two men took their seats, she bustled about, placing hefty bowls and pots on the table while dressed in a dark green dress with a creamy-shaded sash tied around the waist. The color green enhanced her looks and the thin, silky sash outlined her small waist and trailed down the back of her full skirts. She looked good, knew it, and held her head high as she busied herself with dinner.

Setting the hot coffee pot on a small trivet at the far end of the table, she added a big dish of mashed potatoes, thick gravy with simmered jerky in it, a bowl of cut corn from the garden, the few greens she'd set up with vinegar and sour cream, and a huge plate of fluffy biscuits along with a pot of honey.

"Help yourselves now, there's plenty here," she chirped sweetly as she passed the dishes around and helped herself when they came back to her. She got up to pour the coffee, but Jake moved to get hold of the pot before her.

"I'll do that, Hettie." Using her given name let Hodges know they were on intimate terms and that suited him in some perverse way. He poured the coffee, spilling a small amount of the scalding liquid on Hodge's hand. "Excuse me, how clumsy," he murmured as Hodges jerked his burned hand away and blew his breath over it.

Jake lingered too long near Hettie as he poured her cup of the dark, heady brew. Hettie felt the tension between the two men and, though surprised, was elated by it. Since she couldn't change things, she settled down to enjoy the sparring males, right along with the biscuits and gravy.

It made her heart swell with pride at the small ways Jake invented to put the finely cultivated gentleman in his place, relying on the fact he wasn't familiar with this territory. He did it every chance he found and didn't hesitate to invent new ways to show up the greenhorn. But Hodges was a man who exuded confidence. Jake had met his match, whether he knew it or not.

Finally, she served them warm apple pie with a bit of thick cream poured over it. "I can be ready anytime you say in the morning, Jake, if you must see that terrible place again." Frowning, she added, "I should have thought you'd have gone over it well enough the last time."

Hodges perked up with interest. "What sort of site are you speaking of?"

Hettie caught the feeling the man was alert to anything happening between Jake and herself, and her eyes squinted with mirth. She'd never been the bone of contention between two such men in her life and found it a delight. Hodges had expressed an interest in seeing more of the country, and having a sheriff lead the way on an unexpected search, only added to his interest.

Jake answered. "One of Hettie's hands was found murdered a couple of weeks ago. Wasn't a place we wanted to spend a lot of time at right then, and we cut it rather short, so, I need to take another look." He figured the star on his leather vest spoke for him.

"I'd like to ride along if I may." Hodges cleared his throat. "This is my first trip to the West and I find this country rather marvelous. I'd like to see as much of it as I can while I'm out here." He looked Jake straight in the eye and raised his eyebrows when he said marvelous.

Jake, being no fool, knew Hodges appreciated a fine, handsome woman when he ran into one and understood Jake's interest in her, plain as day.

"Why certainly, you may," Hettie replied. "We have plenty of horses and tack. You'll find it very rough country out that way, but our horses can handle it." She thought a minute then added, "You mentioned catching a train. Do you have the time to spend on a ridiculous, wild goose chase like this?" She gave Jake a narrow-eyed, tight-lipped look, letting him know what she thought of his latest visit to her ranch

Hodges grinned at Jake. "I have no particular time constraint." He let that bit of information soak in to edge Jake's jealousy a little farther.

With the dinner over, the men took their leave. Where they slept was up to them. Hodges had the bunk, which left Jake to do the best he could.

CHAPTER 9

After a good breakfast in the bunkhouse, the men got their horses saddled. Hettie came out of the house, dressed for riding, entered the corral, and caught her gleaming stallion. Seeing the surprised look on Hodges face, she said, "He's really quite gentle."

She waved Miguel away from Diablo and told him to get Patches ready for Hodges. Jake took care of his own mount.

After they set out, she let the edgy stallion out for a brisk run before they hit the rockier part of the trail. Both men watched her racing over the trail ahead on that fine black horse, her thick braid flying behind. Hodges exclaimed, "Man, oh man, that woman's quite a wonder, isn't she?"

"Great on the dance floor, too. Had a good time up in Flagstaff, couple nights ago," Jake replied, grinning. He wasn't letting the man get any ideas about Hettie as he feasted his eyes on her willowy figure clinging low to the running black. He knew Hodges did the same.

Hettie waited for them to catch up and, when they reached her, she turned to lead the way, her slim figure outlined against the deep shades of the early morning lavender that colored the far mountains.

Worried about what Jake might be doing, she couldn't believe he hadn't covered the area well enough previously. She couldn't imagine he'd find anything incriminating enough to send her to the hangman's noose. She'd had no part in Elmer's death, but Jake had her worried to the point that it made her blood boil. She stayed ahead of the two men, not wanting to look at either of them.

Near the noon hour, she drew to a halt. "It's right over that rise. I'll just stay here. I never want to see that place again." She rode to a small mesquite tree, tied Diablo, and found herself a rock to sit on. Her heart rate had increased along with her worry that Jake would find something. *How could he, when I had no hand in Elmer's death?* Right now, she hated the sight of Jake La Force with his lanky frame and crazy ideas.

Soon, Hodges came back over the rise. "I don't know what that man's searching for out there. I see nothing there but rocks and brush." He chose a narrow rock near a large greasewood bush and sat in the little bit of shade it offered. "Kind of warm, isn't it?" he asked and wiped his brow with a finely made lawn handkerchief.

Hettie laughed. "At this altitude it can be very warm during the day and freeze your bones at night. It's the dryness, I suppose." She hesitated then asked, "May I ask a personal question?" At his nodding assent, she continued. "Do you have a family back where you come from? Illinois, is it?"

"Yes, I sure have—wife and four sons—and I can't wait to get back to them. I go on these trips all too often." He narrowed his eyes. "Why do you ask?"

"No reason. Nosy of me, I suppose. I didn't have a child before my husband was killed. Sometimes I wonder if I ever will. I think you're a very lucky man, Mr. Hodges." She liked him. He was a decent sort.

"From what I see, you won't be widowed much longer." He grinned at her look of surprise then nodded at Diablo. "Will you tell me about that saddle on your horse? I've never seen one like it—rather ornate, to say the least."

"I believe it's the way they make them in Mexico. I don't know anything much about the horse or his saddle. He was a gift." Dismissing his interest in her horse's rigging, she changed to a more important topic. "Mr. Hodges, if you think that sheriff is interested in me, you might remember, he's out there right now trying to find enough evidence to hang me."

"I hear the anger in your voice and see tears beginning," he said, seeking to placate her. "But I have to say, Mrs. Jamison, if he's looking for anything out there, it'll be for some way to solve this murder and find the real killer. Why would you think he's after you?"

"He *does* suspect me, and if I know that man at all, his job comes first. Something's going on around here, or someone has pointed a finger at me." She twisted her hands and wiped her brow. "Why me? And who would do that to me, for heaven's sake?"

"Of course, I wouldn't have any idea about that, but I'm certain it'll all come out in time. These things usually get resolved. My brother's a lawyer and I hear a lot of things from him."

She looked at Hodges with a frown on her face. "Wish he was out here. I may need him."

He looked her in the eye. "What I see in you is a trusting, open countenance and gentle nature. La Force would have to be a damned fool to think you guilty of murder." He smiled at her. "Try not to worry yourself about this. I believe you can trust him to be on your side. That man thinks the world of you, Hettie."

He seemed comfortable using her given name, she noticed. "You think so?" She grinned at him and, with a conspiratorial idea in her head, asked, "Mr. Hodges, do you think you could forget to mention your wife and family for the rest of your stay?"

"You naughty girl. You want to make that poor man suffer, and he is, you know." Hodges laughed aloud. "I'm a married man and understand you ladies to a certain extent."

When Jake came over the hill, leading his big buckskin, and caught the two of them sharing a laugh, he felt his world spinning down into a bottomless pit. As angry as hell was hot, he pictured Hodges swinging from the tallest tree, with a rope snugly tied about his fancy neck. But he managed to force a grin across his face as he approached them.

Hettie had seen the deep frown come over Jake's face *and* how he'd tried to hide it. It made her feel good, especially after hearing Hodges take on about her situation with Jake. She smiled her sweetest at him. "Find anything over there, Jake?" She couldn't keep the lilt from her voice and watched it make him wince.

"Not what I was lookin' for. I'll have to keep on."

He looked her in the eye and saw her face pale with his words. He hated to make her afraid, but he noticed she wasn't above scraping his wounds a little, either. She'd flirted and laughed with this Eastern dude right in his face, and it burned him to the core. He had no real claim on her affections, but that fact completely escaped him.

"It seems to me there isn't anything to find or you'd have found it."

"Well, you'd be right surprised, missy, now wouldn't you?" His pale blues bore into hers with a touch of anger.

Could he be jealous of Hodges? Hettie wondered.

Her tawny eyes twinkled with mischief. "We're heading back, then?"

Her voice rang sweet as honey in Jake's ears. It further irritated him, but he held it in check.

He fought his rising temper along with those other feelings he'd lost touch with for so long. But he shrugged. "Nothing more to be found at this site, I reckon." He walked over to his buckskin, shoved his knee into the big horse's belly, and heard him grunt as he tightened the cinch before he swung into the saddle. He headed toward the ranch. Hettie and the mining engineer followed.

Jake, his usual taciturn self, said nothing on the ride back, while Hettie chatted intimately with Hodges, pointing out the names of trees, shrubs, mountain ranges, and cattle breeds if they saw any along the way. So animated and informative to the engineer, her actions aggravated Jake to the point that his mind settled into a slow burn. He stayed ahead of them, lest they see the look on his face.

She'd chanced into his life unexpectedly and something about her shook him to the core. It hadn't taken long for him to see, in her, a woman who could completely fill that empty hole in his life. He'd unwillingly come to hope she might see, in him, a man she could trust and maybe fall in love with. *Now, along comes this damned Eastern son of a bitch!*

Jake spent the last miles of the ride devising ways to do the man in or make a complete fool of him in her eyes.

It neared sunset when they entered the ranch yard. Miguel came out and took Diablo. "I weel take heem," he said, laying an arm over Diablo's neck as he led him away.

With renewed interest, Hettie heard him crooning to the horse in Spanish. Since Jake had questioned her about Miguel, it had entered her mind that there did seem to be some sort of emotional connection between the Mexican and the horse. It added to the puzzle about Miguel and made her wonder why he'd come to this particular ranch when he did.

But she had another meal to make, tired as she was. They'd be hungry after a day out in the wilds. Her words were short and she frowned as she headed for the ranch house. "I'll make supper—it'll be awhile." She left them standing near the water trough and walked away.

Both men watched her retreating figure with pleasure. If Hettie was unaware she had an intriguingly feminine walk, it wasn't lost on either man. Hodges broke their silence. "What were you looking for out there, exactly?"

Jake wondered what was on the man's mind. "I never found any empty shells layin' around and I expected to see some. Thought I'd best take another look. It's easy enough to miss small things," he replied. "I'm thorough when I investigate. Lots of things don't add up at first and this case is no different."

"Just wondered. I wouldn't know much about that sort of thing."

Jake had to ask. "Hettie has mining interests on her ranch, here, is that right?"

"She hasn't told you?" Hodges sounded surprised.

Jake shook his head slightly in the negative. "Don't see the woman that much. In fact until this case came up, I'd never heard of her."

"She tells me you suspect her of killing the man found out here. You couldn't possibly, not a woman like that!"

"Just somethin' I heard and had to ask her about. She didn't take to my questionin', and I thought she wanted to shoot me for askin'." He laughed and shrugged.

Hodges seemed a good sort, and Jake found it difficult to dislike the man in spite of feeling like he wanted to see him hanging by his fine neck from a tall tree somewhere.

Hodges laughed in reply. "She's got a temper, I suspect. Handsome woman, that's for damned sure. It'll be a lucky man who *is* able to interest her." He paused in his comments then decided. "She knows I have a wife and family back in Illinois and asked me not to mention it to you. My telling you gives you a friendly heads up in that department, but you ought to know she's really burned that you suspected her of murder."

"So, that's it." Jake laughed and Hodges saw the relief on his face. "If I pour the coffee tonight, I'll forget to spill some on you." After a moment, he said, "If you're heading to Flagstaff in the morning, I'll ride along with you. It's too damned late to start tonight. I'll have to spend another night in that God damned hay loft."

They both had a good laugh, but Hodges didn't offer the bunk, either. Instead, he said, "I won't be heading back to Flagstaff for a few more days. I need to inspect a couple sites before then." He noticed his words didn't seem to ruffle Jake's feathers that he'd be staying on a while.

Jake took the time to seek out Handy Bates before supper. "Anything else you can tell me about Mrs. Jamison and any of the other crew members?"

A slick sheen of sweat shone across the man's face. It was getting toward dark, and maybe the man was tired. Jake took note of it, however. This man looked to be of interest in several ways. Maybe he had his own ax to grind.

"Well, just what I said before. She was fixin' to fire the old coot. Couldn't get his work done anymore." He stood his ground, belly protruding. "I heard her say it more than once."

"Well, that's it then, just wanted to be sure." Jake wasn't satisfied with what Handy said. The man could have a grudge against Hettie for some reason. "I wonder if she'd let on to me if there *was* trouble among the men around here," he said, once he was out of the man's hearing.

At times he observed Miguel listening intently. Did the man understand enough English to make out what was said? He'd also noticed how tenderly the Mexican cared for the black stallion. That was a curiosity in itself, as if he knew the horse from somewhere in his past. But then the man might just have a love of fine horseflesh. Frowning, Jake realized he had more questions now than when he'd ridden out here.

When the supper bell sounded, he and Hodges walked together into the house. Hettie couldn't help but notice they were on good terms after all the earlier sparring, and it unsettled her. She had nothing much to say as she set out a platter of steaks, potatoes, some cut corn from yesterday's picking, and a few thin-sliced cucumbers in sour cream. Handy had done some cutting from the beef they'd hung in the storage room. He'd have to dry or salt the rest very soon. Fresh meat was welcome when they had it. The men in the bunkhouse would be having steaks, too.

"How's that country where you come from?" Jake said to Hodges, his voice brimming with congeniality and friendly curiosity.

Hodges went on at length, speaking of farming communities, local granges where decisions were made, what the homes looked like, and how big the cities had grown. Jake poured the coffee without spilling a single drop, and Hettie hid her puzzlement behind a serene exterior. The animosity and vying for her attention between the two men had disappeared. Her eyes narrowed as she suspected what had passed between them. Did they even notice how nicely she had dressed for this meal? Her white dress with a dark green apron clung to her figure, but it was wasted on those two.

She was the finest hostess imaginable and completed the meal with thick slices of yesterday's apple pie. She offered cream with it, and they helped themselves as they continued talking with each other in their newly found jovial mood. Inside, she wondered how Jake knew he had no real competition from Hodges. Deflated, she directed a look at Hodges. He colored only slightly but she knew he'd betrayed her. *You men stick together, don't you?*

Before departing to the outside the two men spent time in the great room. Hodges was interested in the old gun and while they discussed it, Jake took up the guitar, tuned it, and strummed a few bars of some nameless tune. He was a man who could do with a little *investigating* himself. What hidden secrets lurked in that particular lonely man's heart?

CHAPTER 10

The next morning Hettie saw Jake on his way, again noting the general camaraderie between the men as they parted. If they had ever been rivals, they were no longer. When Hodges asked her to take him out to the site of her mine, she said she would. But as far as she was concerned, he had some explaining to do.

Hettie, though ready to ride, decided to have a look at the bundle that had been Elmer's. She hadn't wanted to open that small pack, so close to his death, feeling she'd be invading his personal privacy. But she retrieved it now from the cupboard where she'd placed it. The scent of it reminded her of the poor lost soul, so like him—slightly soiled, stained from use, and nicely tied in an extra-large bandana.

She undid the bundle, finding two worn shirts, dingy underclothes, a shaving mug and brush, and a few coins and bills. Beneath those things lay several old, worn letters with the writing long since faded. She also found a small box. It rattled as she opened it. Gasping in surprise, she saw several small bits of shimmering yellow metal, interlaced with a darker material, laying inside. "Could this be gold?"

Spreading the contents out on the bed, she saw several nuggets, fine grains, and small, irregular bits that gleamed a dull, rich yellow in the morning light. Wishing she'd looked sooner, she felt her heart rate quicken. *Is this why Elmer was killed?*

Having already trespassed on the old man's privacy, she opened the letters and felt a deep sadness to learn of the man's lost happiness. She read an old letter from someone who had loved him once, the date, more than thirty years ago. Hettie supposed the woman to be long gone, the same as Elmer.

She heard a soft patter as her tears dropped onto the yellowed paper. Turning her attention to the contents of the tin, she wondered what to do. Where did it come from? Was it really gold?

She shoved everything back where she'd kept it and went out to ride with Hodges, the very man who could identify those samples. She couldn't bring herself to mention the gold nuggets, if that's what they were, but thought she ought to let the sheriff know about them.

She rode a different horse this morning and caught a nice bay gelding for Hodges. She decided he sat his saddle well enough to handle the rough terrain as they headed toward the mountains south of the ranch. She wanted to ask him about Jake but waited for a good opportunity.

About noon, they reached the mine site. It was nothing much to see as far as Hettie was concerned—markers and a few fading paper signs nailed to wooden stakes, delineating the area, claiming the mining rights.

To Hodges that site became a thing of wonder and excitement. Hettie sat on a rock and huffed in her impatience. *Men*! *Important things like relationships melt away at the site of a pile of dirt and rocks.*

After he'd done his poking around, collecting a few rock samples, he joined her on a nearby rock. "I guess that's all I need for now, just had to get a look at the site. Don't see something like this every day."

His excitement eluded her. She held back a strong urge to giggle at him, but she was hungry and frustrated. She'd put together a decent lunch of cold steak sandwiches along with several apples. She gestured at her pack. "Won't you have a bite of lunch?"

"Surely, I would if we find a place with some shade." He had the gleam of discovery and excitement shining in his eyes, after poking about in that broken pile of rocks.

She was glad for the money the mine brought her and relieved it would continue, but she'd waited hours to question him about something far more important to her right now—that nosey sheriff, Jake.

She didn't mention the gold, needing to think more on that. But she should have asked him to put her mind at ease. Being a mining engineer, he would know about those yellow grains and pebbles. She rode on ahead of him until they came into a nice grove of Piñon Pines. She dismounted and tied her horse, a smallish pinto called Patches. She often rode him to spell the stallion.

"How's this?" she asked as he rode up.

"Looks wonderful to me." He swung off his horse and tied him to a small tree. "This country is amazing, you know. It looks completely desolate in every direction, yet here we are, finding shade in a nice grove of trees."

"I suppose it is. I've always lived in the West. Before I married, I lived in New Mexico. It's different from here in some ways. They surely get more rain over there than we do." She frowned. The new grasses of spring had already begun shriveling beneath the unrelenting sun. But she knew it would retain' its food value for cattle feed for a long time.

"Say, this is a good lunch! I didn't know how hungry I was." He sat back and looked at her. "What's on your mind? I see something's bothering you."

"I know you told La force about your family and all, but I wonder why you did that." She smiled. "You men stick together, don't you?"

"I wanted him to know he had a clear track with you if he was worried about me in any way. He's a very good man, Mrs. Jamison—Hettie, and I think he has great deal of interest in you." He laughed and colored a bit. "I will say, if I wasn't happily married, however, he'd have a *whole* lot to worry about."

"That's nice of you to say. I've been lonely since I lost my husband." She fought back a tear. "It was very good between Del and me. I never thought to find anyone else, ever. About Jake, I don't know. How can I trust someone who keeps looking for something to incriminate me?"

"I wouldn't worry about that. He's on your side, Hettie. Don't go turning your back on him. He's a good man, the way I see it."

"Well, it may be as you say, but from his questioning, I know he suspects me of killing our ranch hand, Elmer Greenup. And he's been out here looking for some piece of evidence to hang me with." She felt her anger building.

"I find that hard to believe. I know what I saw, too."

"You don't know that man's reputation. He never quits, so they say, and nothing stands in his way." She smiled sadly. "The next time you come out here, if you do, I'll probably be behind bars or standing up high on the platform waiting for the trap door to spring."

"That's not possible."

He threw his head back and let out a deep hearty laugh. He was indeed a fine looking man and his wife was likely just as nice.

"If you come out again, why not bring your family? Wouldn't it be a great adventure for them?" She laughed herself. "My place might be standing vacant by then."

"I'll never believe that, but I might consider the invitation for my family."

He finished his lunch and took up the reins of his horse. Hettie followed suit. The conversation had set her back, and she couldn't imagine why she felt that way. Asking about the gold slipped her mind completely.

Jake had said he'd be back in a week or so to continue his investigation and though she always enjoyed looking at him, she didn't look forward to another of his visits. Not when he sought to put her behind bars.

He'd dog her trail until he found some way to send her to that nasty Yuma Prison or the hangman's noose. She didn't know which would be worse. She'd heard the horror stories of the cave-like cells with snakes, scorpions, and humidity off the Colorado River. Each added their own form of misery to the place men called a hell on earth. Endless days of torture awaited if she went there.

Fear prompted her to harden her heart against Jake. And deep inside, she'd began to hate his relentless methods.

༺༻

Hodges spent one more night and, after Miguel hitched up his team, he left in his fancy Concord the next morning. His parting words rang like a bell in her mind. "If Jake is looking for anything, it's not to send you to prison, but to clear your name and find the real killer. Take my word for it. I know men, and he's as fine as they come."

She looked Hodges in the eye, her chin lifted. "I wish I could believe you, but how can I when I've seen the way he hunts constantly to find something against me?"

Shaking his head, Hodges smiled and drove away.

CHAPTER 11

A week later, Hettie saw Annabelle's fancy rig pull into the yard behind her small, sleek, bay mare. Things had been so quiet around the ranch Hettie almost believed this silly girl's visit would be a welcome diversion—for whatever reasons the devious young woman had in mind.

Hettie stepped out to welcome her, deciding to be a friend. "Well, what a nice surprise," she said, reaching out to help the nicely dressed little blonde step out of her rig. "You've driven all the way alone?"

"Why, of course I did," Annabelle said as her shiny boots hit the dust of the ranch yard. "No one would dare to bother me. My daddy would never let anything happen to me." She reached back to retrieve her overnight things and by the size of the bag, Hettie knew she planned a fairly long stay.

Miguel appeared almost instantly. He came to take care of Annabelle's horse but took a long look at the girl, with his liquid, dark eyes smoldering hot enough to melt the clinging moss off rocks.

Hettie decided she would make sure the handsome Mexican was sent to the far corners of her ranch after this. Why was he at the ranch today, anyway? she wondered. She'd speak to Handy about it.

Simpering and batting her eyes at him when he looked her way, Annabelle watched the darkly handsome young man un-hitch the horse. When they'd met before, she'd more than at-tracted Miguel's attention. Now the little nitwit egged him on, seeking another conquest to boost her ego. *The girl's a damned fool if she thinks she can flirt with that man*! Hettie worried Annabelle was playing with fire, several times over.

"Come inside. I'll fix something to refresh you after that long drive," Hettie said, eager to hurry the girl away from those black, exciting eyes.

She realized Annabelle believed she was every man's de-sire and, consequently, she did her best to conquer every male she met. The way the girl threw herself at Miguel made Hettie shiver with apprehension. Enticing a man like that could lead to trouble.

Dragging her feet with every step, Annabelle followed Hettie into the ranch house. Miguel stood holding the horse's reins, watching her walk away in a purposefully exaggerated and undulating fashion. Hettie wondered if she'd practiced that walk in front of her mirror.

Once inside, Annabelle slumped down into one of the big chairs in the large room and heaved a small sigh. "My, it's nice and cool in here. That sun is getting warmer every day." Her creamy, peach-toned face was flushed with heat from her long drive. Her carriage had a hood and she'd kept herself covered while she'd driven through the sun-soaked landscape, but summer's heat approached. Hettie's ranch sat at a lower alti-tude than that of Flagstaff and the sun burned even hotter dur-ing daylight hours.

"It's still springtime, but yes, summer's just around the corner." Hettie left her settled in the chair and rustled up a drink. Already tired of Annabelle's vacuous small talk, she knew it had only begun. The little ninny was too empty headed for true companionship as far as Hettie was concerned. And now she worried the silly girl was headed for trouble if she kept on with Miguel Maldonado.

Though Miguel looked young, he was certainly no longer a boy, and Hettie feared he'd take Annabelle's flirting more seriously than the girl ever intended.

Annabelle gasped, then, giggled. "Oh, my goodness, I nearly forgot! I asked the postmaster if I could bring your mail out. He fixed it in this sealed package—for privacy, I suppose." She sniffed. She reached into her overnight pack, pulled out a good sized package, and handed it to Hettie. "My, it seems like such a lot. I never get anything much." She started to chatter on, but Hettie interrupted her, anxious to see if Cherry had written back.

"Excuse me, dear, would you mind terribly if I look through this mail you so kindly brought me?" she asked, tempering her request with praise.

Slightly miffed, Annabelle replied, "Why yes, please do. I'll just sip this nice cool drink and look around." She rose and went to look out the window, not at the mountains soaring high in all their purple glory, or the outbreak of the wild spring flowers over the rolling hills, but toward the ranch yard, no doubt searching for the sight of the handsome Mexican.

Hettie opened the pack of mail and sorted through it until she came upon the letter she sought. She tore it open and read:

My dearest friend, Hettie,

So glad to hear from you again. We are doing well here in Prescott and are planning a trip to San Francisco soon. It's all so exciting,

*but I do miss you very much. You asked about
the black horse. It brings back dreadful memories but time has a way of smoothing things
out, doesn't it? And you certainly have the
right to know everything about him.*

*That horse belonged to a hired killer
named Matìn Maldonado. He tried to kill my
husband and do terrible things to me. He was
killed and buried where it happened. I
couldn't bear the sight of that animal or his
fancy rig after that. I thought if you didn't
know about these things, you would enjoy the
horse for what he is, a fine, magnificent animal. I don't know why you have asked about
this, but have honored your request.*

*I hope all is well with you there. I miss
you very much.*

Sincerely, Cherry Carmona

Hettie's scalp prickled and icy chills ran through her body
when she compared the last names of Matìn, the murderer, and
her hired hand, Miguel, both men named Maldonado. Against
her will, she questioned whether that vicious killer was actually dead. Was it possible he lived and had sent this man, perhaps a relative of his, to exact some hideous revenge?

Was this the reason the man's eyes lingered over that
black horse? Had she hired a man with evil on his mind—
vengeance? The horse? Surely, that name was common
enough.

She fought for control over her wayward thoughts, trying
to reason away her unfounded fear. If she said the man was

dead, Cherry ought to know what she was saying if it happened at her place.

Frightened and on edge, she wished longingly for the sight of Jake. He'd know what to do, what action she ought to take. She decided she'd best keep a closer eye on young Maldonado, too, should he be thinking of stealing Diablo.

Taking her gaze from the window, Annabelle noticed her distress. Her eyes had widened with alarm. "What's the matter with you, Hettie? Have you had terrible news? Your face is white as snow."

"No, not bad news really, just rather unexpected and if that sheriff were here right now I'd have something to tell him that he'd find very interesting."

She'd deliberately mentioned the sheriff, hoping to hear what Annabelle would say about the man and to divert her from further questioning.

"Oh, that man! He hasn't had a meal in our hotel for days now. Someone must have said something to him. I don't understand what he's afraid of." She shook her blonde curls in frustration. "If he only knew how much I liked him, he'd come around more. I've tried not to be too forward. He wouldn't care for that, I'm sure."

Hettie smiled in amazement at Annabelle's inane remarks. The silly girl had no idea what Jake really thought of her.

Then Annabelle remembered the letter. "It was that letter you wanted? What did it say that's got you so alarmed?" She directed her blue eyes on her hostess, her brow wrinkled, her curiosity high.

"Nothing of importance, really," Hettie said as she shoved everything back into the pouch. Those other things could wait, she decided. She had to deflect the girl's interest. "What would you like to do for now? We have the next couple of hours before supper?"

Hettie kept her shaking hands clenched together. She couldn't relate the letter's contents to a chattering ninny like Annabelle, but found herself wishing Jake would ride into her yard. She'd welcome the sight of him, even if he did believe her capable of murder.

"Why not let's go for a short horseback ride?" Annabelle suggested.

Hettie knew instantly the girl hoped Miguel would saddle her horse, and she could continue her flirting. Hettie didn't want to further the relationship between Annabelle and the young Mexican, but the girl was her guest and there were a few hours of daylight left. She decided to go along with Annabelle's idea. "Why yes, I think that would be fun. Let's do."

They dressed for riding with Annabelle trying on several of Hettie's riding togs to find a fit. She decided on a split riding skirt that was rather long, but better than wearing a dress certainly. She tried on a pair of boots and found them too large. They stuffed socks in the toes. Hettie laughed. "Good thing you won't have to walk in them, but they'll do for riding."

"Oh, it's so exciting. You know, I never do much riding, but I do know how it's done."

She was very emphatic about her skills, but Hettie adopted a "wait and see" attitude. So far the girl hadn't shown much interest in outdoor activity.

When they were dressed and ready, they went to the corral. Hettie indicated the small pinto. "Take Patches there. He's nice to ride. I ride him quite a bit to spell Diablo."

Miguel rushed out to assist the ladies in getting set to ride. He wasn't much help to Hettie, but he paid every attention to

Annabelle and, when Patches was ready for her, he stood close to the girl and helped her mount the horse.

When he adjusted her stirrup leathers, Hettie was very sure his hand was on her leg more than needed. She didn't hear any words of protest from Annabelle. If the fool girl allowed him that sort of familiarity, she was asking for trouble. Not a good idea!

Patches flung his head up, restless once the girl had mounted. He wanted a good run, which he always had when Hettie rode him. Annabelle held the reins well enough to suit Hettie. Perhaps she did know how to ride.

"Oh, my heavens, he acts so restless! Are you sure he's safe to ride?"

"Just hold him in until we get going. He wants to run, but he doesn't need to. Remember, *you* are the boss of the horse when you're riding, not him."

Hettie mounted Diablo and they started out. Annabelle kept looking back at Miguel. Hettie shook her head in disgust, seeing her wave a small gloved hand at him as they rode away.

"You'd best be careful of that man, Annabelle. He's from another culture. He may think you want him, if you know what I mean." She hoped she'd gotten through to the girl but had her doubts, seeing the knowing look that came over her pretty face.

"Oh, I know how to handle men. I can't help it if they like me so much." Shaking her blonde curls, she uttered a careless laugh. "But I must say, that Miguel sure is a handsome one, isn't he? And, oh my, I can't believe the way those black eyes go right through me!"

They had come to a long, flat stretch of trail. Annabelle giggled and twisted around in the saddle for a last look at Miguel before she let Patches out for a run.

She stuck to the saddle and Hettie thought she handled the horse well enough.

"At least that's one worry I don't have with this man-crazy girl." She let Diablo go and caught up with her. "How do you like him?"

"Who, Patches, or do you mean that handsome Miguel?" Annabelle let out a pealing laugh at her own humor. Her curls bounced and floated in the soft breezes. She made a lovely picture, for all her nonsense.

Hettie laughed along with her. "Well, I did mean the horse." It was cooling and turning into dusk. The colors coming into play were a marvel of mauves, pinks, and several shades of purple when they stopped for a long view of the far mountains at sunset. "Isn't it beautiful out here as the sun sets?" she asked the girl, hoping she'd gotten her mind off the handsome young man back at the ranch.

"What? Oh, why yes it certainly is real pretty. I was never much for looking at scenery, but there are lots of real nice colors when the sun starts going down."

Hettie thought the girl did her best to enjoy the soaring peaks and valleys colored with the hues of a western sunset, but the majesty and massive scope of the higher ranchlands of Arizona held little interest to a young lady who had her mind set on a lanky sheriff or a dark-eyed man from Mexico.

"Hettie, what do those men do at night before they go to bed?" Obviously, her concern lay in another direction entirely.

"I don't really know for sure. They play some card games, I know, but what they talk about, I'm not sure I'd want to know that, anyway. Cowboys are terrible cussers if they're alone." Hettie laughed as she said it.

"What about I go out there and play cards with them?"

"Not while you are my guest. It wouldn't be right, Annabelle," Hettie said, her voice firm. She could never allow something like that, especially with a man like Miguel among the men. "We'd best get back. It's turning dark now and it'll get colder as the sun sets."

"You are no fun at all sometimes, Hettie." Annabelle's red lips pouted and her shoulders slumped as she rode on ahead. "I don't see what harm there'd be in a few hands of cards."

Hettie turned Diablo's head and started back, following Annabelle. That the girl was more than eager to return as well was in her body's attitude as she leaned forward and hurried her mount along at a walk or into a gallop if they hit a good stretch of trail. *So much for looking at the scenery. It's obviously much better at the bunk house.*

When they returned, Miguel was immediately at Annabelle's side, helping her dismount. As he unsaddled and put her horse away, Hettie knew full well the man-crazy girl was headed for trouble, sooner if not later. She seemed mad for Miguel's attentions and the quicker the silly creature was on her way home, the sooner Hettie would heave a sigh of relief.

"Let's get some supper," she said, nearly dragging the girl inside the house. "Have a seat and I'll see what I can rustle up."

Annabelle plopped herself down in one of the chairs in her large sitting room, and Hettie saw the sulky, petulant look come over her features.

Working quickly, she fired up the massive iron cook stove and fixed a plate of hot beef and gravy over biscuits from the left over roasted beef. It was still good, but wouldn't last much longer. She'd learned to use things as fast as possible to avoid waste and spoilage. Most ranch folks did the same.

She wanted to sit down and go over the rest of her mail, but having an empty-headed visitor negated those chances. Lighting the biggest lamp she had, she placed it on the table along with a fresh pot of coffee and called Annabelle to come eat.

"I'm not so hungry," she said as she picked at her food and drank the coffee. "We've gotten in some really nice tea at our hotel. If you come in town one day, Hettie, we'll have a cup and I'll give you some to take home. We could sit in Daddy's restaurant." She kept looking out the window toward the bunk house, a wistful look on her face.

Hettie had to speak her mind. "Annabelle, if you have any kind of interest in that young Mexican man, please, I want to warn you, he's no one to fool with. We don't know much about him. He's only been here about four months." Hettie wondered if the girl heard a word she'd just said. "Just a warning. I hope you don't mind my saying what I think."

"He wouldn't dare do anything to hurt me. My daddy wouldn't allow it." Annabelle giggled. "But he is wonderful handsome, don't you think?"

Hettie flared. "That man never heard of your father, and your daddy isn't out here to watch over you, is he?"

"I can't help it if you're jealous that men find me so attractive. I didn't see them swarming around you at the dance, either." Her little pink nose was in the air and her cheeks flushed with anger as she sat at the table, stiff as a board, arms crossed over her chest.

Hettie was angry, too. "I won't have you come out here and make a lot of trouble for me, and there will be, if that man takes advantage of you."

"I can take care of myself. And I already have a mother!" Her disdainful look and nose-in-the-air attitude let Hettie know she was in for trouble with Annabelle Nellis.

Mad as a hornet at the girl's inference at her advanced age, Hettie sternly advised, "Well, my dear you go right on ahead, then, but not on my ranch. I won't have it!" She felt the heat rise in her face. "Go ahead. Make a damned fool of your-self if you want to, but I'll not be responsible for what happens."

Annabelle must have realized her host was trying to be helpful and Hettie's veiled warning finally took hold. She turned to face her new friend.

"I'm sorry for what I said. I forget my self sometimes." She held out her hand and Hettie took it. "But, he is absolutely the best looking man I've ever seen outside of Sheriff Jake." She couldn't suppress a simpering giggle.

"Let's walk out in the orchard before going to bed," Hettie suggested.

"Oh, all right, I guess we can." Annabelle had apparently decided to try to forget about enticing the handsome dark-eyed man and be a good house guest.

They walked about under the trees. With the oncoming warm weather, the apple trees were blooming and a fragrant scent filled the air. It was very pleasant and tempers cooled as they walked together. Hettie didn't trust the girl as far as she could throw her, but she was a visitor and deserved Hettie's full attention and hospitality.

Still, a strain had developed between them and they passed a tense, rather boring evening.

CHAPTER 12

In the morning, Annabelle announced, "I think I ought to drive back early today. My mother needs me since we've planned on choosing the fabrics for my summer wardrobe." She appeared unusually restless and edgy, and Hettie had the sick feeling the fool girl had arranged to meet the young Mexican on her way into Flagstaff. *Is she really that foolish?*

Annabelle was ready to leave, and Hettie, hoping to head off disaster, decided to intervene if the fool girl *had* planned to meet Miguel out on the trail. She casually made her own announcement. "I believe I'll ride right along beside you on your way into Flagstaff. Won't that be fun? I need a few things in town, myself." She wanted Jake to know the contents of the letter she'd received and decided this would be a good time to inform him.

The frustration on the girl's face was plain enough that Hettie was sure she'd thwarted her plans. Miguel would be far more trouble than little Annabelle could handle, and Hettie was determined that nothing should happen on her watch. *When did they hatch this plan? In the middle of the night?*

She caught Diablo while Miguel hitched Annabelle's horse to her rig. The disgusting flirtation on the silly fool's part made Hettie bite her tongue and hold her temper. While Miguel got Annabelle's horse ready, Hettie saddled her own horse with his fancy Mexican trappings.

Suspecting who Miguel was, she decided his attentions to Annabelle were far more dangerous than she'd first believed. She planned to fire the man when she returned home, remove him from the ranch, and avoid the trouble he was destined to cause.

There was nothing Annabelle Nellis wouldn't do if she took it into her dizzy, blonde head, and Hettie felt she was right to see her home in safety.

When Annabelle was settled in her rig, they started off. In her rush to be off, Hettie had not packed a lunch or even remembered to take water. Those things would have to wait until they arrived. However, she did remember to pack her pistol and had the belt and cartridges strapped around her slim hips.

Hettie easily saw that she'd ruined Annabelle's plans. The girl was exceedingly angry, as displayed by her tight lips and the hard-bitten expression on her pretty face. Hettie couldn't have cared less.

Glad to see the last of the conniving little ninny, she was never sure why the girl had come to visit in the first place, unless it was her desire to make sure Hettie wasn't involved with the sheriff. She scoffed. *Not a chance in hell would Jake take up with that little baggage. He isn't* that *crazy.*

They never stopped to rest and, by early afternoon, they'd reached Flagstaff and parted company with barely a word spoken between them. Hettie hoped the girl wouldn't come to the ranch again, if it was Miguel she had in mind. If she met him somewhere else—Hettie shivered, thinking of the trouble ahead for Annabelle if that happened.

She tied her horse in front of the sheriff's office and went inside. The deputy, Lin told her the sheriff was out somewhere. "Might I help you with anythin'?"

"No, I received some information and needed to speak to him." The letter she'd received from her friend Cherry filled her with worry. If it had any bearing on what had happened to old Elmer, she couldn't figure how, but the idea of a blood-thirsty devil having a connection to her horse made her extremely uneasy. "I'll be at the hotel and see him later. Thanks Lin."

She took a room at the Ayers Hotel, hoping she wouldn't run into Annabelle any time soon. She washed the best she could and decided to go out and shop for fresh clothing, since she hadn't thought to bring any. She walked along the boardwalk until she hit the largest mercantile, the one owned by Bib Williams and his wife Alma.

Walking among the racks of things ready to wear, looking for something to catch her eye, she overheard Annabelle's speaking to her mother and decided they must be shopping for those fabrics she'd gone on about—for her new spring wardrobe.

"Mommy, you wouldn't believe how rude she was to me. Imagine her thinking I'd be interested in that old Mexican she's got working out there. She's after that sheriff, I know it! She's got his mind poisoned against me. She has, Mommy, I know she has!" The petulant whine in Annabelle's voice rang in Hettie's ears.

"Hush, child. Someone will hear you! You know perfectly well, that sheriff hasn't as much as looked at a woman in all the time he's been in this town. Some say he has a tragic past or something dreadful like that. Besides, he's too old for a young girl like you. Why don't you step out with that Robbie

Lacombe? He's such a nice boy, and he's always asking after you. What's so difficult about that?"

"Oh, Mommy, he's such a baby! Have you ever taken a good look at him? He's sort of flabby. And have you ever noticed the way his stomach sticks out?" She giggled. "Can I help it if men make eyes at me all the time? They just can't seem to help it."

She changed the subject abruptly and they babbled on about dresses and fabrics until finally the two of them left the store and crossed the street. Hettie stayed out of sight. She'd seen enough of Annabelle for a while and, after hearing that exchange, felt sorry for her parents.

"That poor mother. There's trouble ahead with that girl. She doesn't see it, but I sure do." Hettie tended to mutter things aloud as she busied herself picking out under garments and a new dress to wear, should she go somewhere to have dinner. She wasn't sure about eating at the hotel for fear of running into Annabelle.

She also found some slim-fitting slippers to go with the new dress she'd chosen and, as she stepped to the counter to pay for her things, she felt a hand at her elbow. "Hettie, I'm surprised to see *you* in town. Special occasion?"

She looked up to see Jake standing right next to her. The scent of him, his clothing, his tall, lanky frame, set her heart pounding madly in her chest. His presence bothered her, made her angry, and...*Why does the man have to stand so close?*

Upset, she stood her ground. "Hello, Sheriff. Glad I've run into you. I wanted to speak to you about something that has me more than a little concerned."

"Someone breakin' the law out there, again?"

He had a mischievous twinkle in his light blue eyes as he spoke, but his voice was low and soft, almost crooning, and the very sound of it sent those familiar thrills racing through her body. *Stop it, you darned fool!*

"No, but when we can talk, I'll tell you about it." She paid for her things and headed out of the store. Jake moved right along beside her and kept her nerves in an uproar.

"It can wait a bit," she said, thinking he'd move away. But he didn't leave her side, so she asked him, "Was there something you wanted from me?"

He flushed at her remark, thinking, *My God, if she only knew what I wanted from her!* "Nothing at the moment, but if you're in town for the night, would you consider having dinner with me?"

"Where?" she asked. "The hotel?"

Annabelle might see them there, enjoying a quiet dinner together. The girl was capable of making a nasty scene, but Hettie thought she'd enjoy exactly that after the visit she'd had to endure from Annabelle's trip to the ranch.

"Certainly. Why not? Chuck's real good. Stayin' at the hotel, are you?"

He seemed to be in an unusually light-hearted mood. She didn't know him well, but he wasn't acting like the stern lawman she'd come to expect. It had her puzzled. She remembered what Hodges had said and wondered. *Could it be he's attracted to me that way?* If he was, she'd welcome it. He had made a deep impression on her in too many ways. She always longed for the sight of him, in spite of his continually trying to find incriminating evidence against her.

She went to her room and called for a tub of water, hoping a real bath would wash away the crazy feelings surging through her body after running into Jake. Soon enough, she'd face having dinner with that forbidding man.

She washed and took a short nap before dressing for dinner. She hadn't had a new dress for a long time and enjoyed the feeling of softness and smell of the fresh new fabric. She'd bought a long, slim-cut dress of pale green muslin with small, embroidered green leaves, scattered about the skirt.

Spring was in full bloom and it suited the time of year. She fixed her thick, ropy hair in a knot high on her head. A few tendrils had escaped and the wispy strands curled down the sides of her face. She looked in her mirror and was pleased with what she saw. She'd been alone for a long time and having dinner with a man once again was exciting, in spite of his relentless suspicions against her.

A soft knock sounded on her door. She opened it to find Jake standing there. He took in the sight of her and softly gasped. "My God, woman, you're so damned beautiful!"

Without warning, he stepped close, swept his arms around her, and bent her backward for a long, deep, and gentle kiss. He released her and steadied her on her feet with his arms close around her.

"Sorry, Hettie, I've wanted to do that for a terrible long time."

His kiss so affected her, she could barely stand. It had been a long time since she had been kissed, and his lips had been soft, yet firm, against hers. The warmth that swept through her body sent her into a swirl of emotions long denied and she barely knew how to respond. In a heated glow, she nearly cooed. "Well, really! I guess...when you aren't out searching around for some reason to hang me."

She couldn't help saying it, and they laughed together.

He couldn't let go of her, not yet. It had been so long, and he'd never expected to feel this way again. He held her close for another deep, searching kiss then held her ever tighter.

"Oh, my God, woman, I don't want to stop. I don't know if I can."

Her warm body felt like heaven against him as he nuzzled her hair. Finding her neck, he kissed her there, too.

"Well, you'd better if we're to have anything to eat."

She realized she ached for more of his kisses herself. He'd set her on fire, and the burning deep inside her body made her want it all from him, everything he was capable of giving. His tender, searching kisses had set off a terrible storm of need. An incredibly strong desire burned all the way through her and cried out for completion.

"We've got to go to dinner," she cried out, completely weak and unable to move.

She knew full well Jake didn't care if he ate anything. Things had happened so fast, she had to fight for stability. He wanted her and there was no mistaking it. Helpless to fight it, she returned his burning passion fully.

She tried to remember that she hardly knew the man and pulled away, trying to stop what was happening—to steel herself into the behavior of a decent woman, instead of some overheated, tavern wench.

Jake smiled softly, seeing her flushed, heated features, so filled with need and want. He finally got his feelings under control enough to hold out his arm to escort her to the dining room, but he wasn't finished with this evening, not by a long shot. He'd hold off if she wanted that. Maybe over dinner, they could face what had just happened and try coming to grips with it.

His heart leaped in his chest just looking at this lovely woman in her soft green dress. He placed his other hand over hers where she'd put it through his arm, and they moved slowly down the wide staircase. Jake kept his body as close to hers as he could manage—without being run out of town.

On the way to the dining room, Hettie walked in a trance. In total disbelief at this sudden turn of events, she couldn't begin to imagine what he must be thinking. Yet she knew what was on his mind because the same ideas burned on hers, and every bit as hotly. *What's happened? Where has all this come from?*

In a whirl of confusion and emotion, she sat across from the taciturn man who'd just made her head spin with the kind of maddening desire she'd tried for years to forget ever existed. She'd never forgotten how it was between a man and a woman. She'd sorely missed that when her husband died. And now, this quiet, reserved man had brought it all back in a mad, heated rush with more intensity than anything she'd ever known. She looked in his eyes, feeling hopeless. "Jake, I don't know what to say or do."

"Well, Hettie dear, you might take a look at the menu right now," he offered quietly. His voice had deepened and softened with the heated emotions that roared through his mind, but he knew his eyes were alight with his desire for her. "Later, we can discuss a few other possibilities."

He looked so deeply into her eyes that she thought she just might die right there at the table. *What is this man doing to me?* She felt her world spinning out of control. She wanted to stop him. Yet, she didn't want him to stop anything he might want to do with her, not ever.

"You might like a sip of this."

He offered her a glass of the pale wine he'd ordered. Her head, muddled to the point she hadn't even heard him order it, cleared a bit, and she reached out to take the glass like someone in a trance.

"Thank you," she said, her voice barely above a whisper. She put the glass to her lips and drank, not caring or tasting what it was. She couldn't take her eyes off him. He'd done something to her that made her feel lost. She kept trying to straighten herself out. "I can't go on this way. What's wrong with me, anyway?" she murmured low.

"What's that, Hettie, dear?" His voice came from too far away.

"Did you put something in this drink?" she asked and felt silly for thinking such a thing. "I don't know what's happening to me."

"Shame on you for thinkin' I'd do a thing like that." He chuckled softly. "You know, my dear, whatever's happened to you has happened to me as well. We need a very quiet and private place to try and sort this out." He reached across the table and took her hand in his. "Don't you think that's a good idea?"

❧❧❧

Annabelle, hoping to see Jake, hurried in the side entrance to the dining room. Suddenly, she stopped. In shock and surprise, she saw Hettie and Jake in close conversation. Seeing how they leaned toward each other and looked into each other's eyes, she froze inside. When Jake's hand reached out to enclose Hettie's, a new and poisonous hatred for them both filled her with resolve.

She'd show them! He had no right to be looking at an old woman like that when here she stood, in the same room, so young, so beautiful. She stamped her foot in anger, her mind racing a mile a minute. *I don't understand it! He's never looked at me the way he's looking at her. Why her? She's so old!*

Bitterly angry, her young heart breaking, she turned and left the hotel dining area the way she'd come. Running blindly out the hotel's side entrance into the night, her arms flailing out, she ran toward the street. Reaching Front Street, not knowing or caring where she went, she fled, sobbing, down the darkened sidewalk. Scalding tears flowed down her cheeks.

Behind her and only steps away, Miguel moved rapidly and silently. He'd watched her most of the day and all afternoon, when he could catch sight of her. Seeing her immediate distress and how upset she was, he saw his chance. She needed him and, elated, he hurried to catch her, neither knowing or caring about the cause of her distress. He knew women enough to realize the little blonde *chica* needed someone strong and manly to comfort, pet, and soothe her wounded spirit. And he was just the man to help her.

"*Mi amore,* so sad. I help you. You come with me."

When Annabelle heard his soft voice behind her, she stopped running and turned to look into the dark, familiar face of the young Mexican from Hettie's ranch.

"Oh, it's you, Miguel!" She was breathless. "I didn't expect to see *you* in town."

He stood so close, it made her nervous and she babbled wildly as she looked into his eyes. They seemed luminous, dark, and mysterious as they burned into hers. Something else burned in them, too, and sent a shot of alarm through her. She ignored it and stared at his face, so fine, so handsome. His eyes were so dark.

But, now, she finally saw something new and dangerous burning in them. His look held a message she didn't understand, but the edge of fear took hold inside her body as she remembered Hettie's warning: *That man is no one to mess with.*

"You so sad, *mi amore,* so beautiful, I don't believe it. *Por favor*, I help you. I weel take care of you, if you like." He took her arm. "You like come weeth me?" He tugged gently, urging, crooning softly in Spanish, words she did not understand. "Come, *mi senorita, mi amore,* come with me. I take care of you."

"Where, Miguel?" She hesitated. It hit her full force how little she really knew him. His strengthening grip held her fast, and her heart beat frantically as she struggled against his hold. She quickly realized he *was* a man and not some young boy to flirt with. He smiled at her. "It's no far, just 'roun' here, *pobrecita.*"

He led her, struggling and trembling, to a darkened doorway. It opened under his touch and he pulled her struggling young body inside. He closed the door with a kick of his foot. Glancing frantically around, Annabelle saw no way to escape. He took her into his arms, crushed her to his chest, and his seeking mouth pressed a soft kiss to her lips. He went deeper until he met her resisting teeth, locked tight against his assault.

From that moment on, he became wildly aroused and rudely shoved his tongue into her mouth. She felt his teeth grinding against her lips as he reached inside her dress to fondle and cruelly squeeze her young breasts. She gasped in pain as his callused, work-hardened hands fondled and crushed her tender flesh.

"Oh, no, oh please, my goodness—stop, stop it! You're hurting me, Miguel!" She stamped her foot in anger. She'd had enough of his unwanted advances and wanted to go home.

"You want me, *senorita*! I know thees. Here, take leetle dreenk, *mi pobrecita.* I come here to find you.*"* He pressed a flask against her lips and forced her to take a good swallow of the fiery tequila it held. "Is good, no?"

"Oh, God, that's awful!" She choked and coughed from the burning liquid. "That's the worst stuff ever. I want to leave now!" Frightened, she pleaded with him. "Please, I have to go home now, Miguel! My father is looking for me." She cried anew in terror when the man tore open the front of her dress, and his hard, seeking hands and mouth explored her tender breasts, nipping and sucking painfully.

"Oh please, don't! Please don't do this!"

He did not hear her refusals, only what he wanted to hear. His passion had risen to extreme heights. This woman wanted him, he knew it. Had she not spent much time flirting, making eyes at him so filled with sexual innuendoes, telling him how much she wanted him?

He threw her onto the hard wooden floor and ripped off her under things. As she shivered in shock and, without further attempts to soothe her or croon sweet words to soften her fears, he tore into her soft, female flesh and took his pleasure, hard and forcefully. Driven mad with desire, he heard no screams as he covered her soft mouth with hard, brutal kisses.

Driven mad by her small curvaceous body, her wonderful softness, and those shimmering blonde curls, he took her again and again. Her cries and moans mirrored his own wild passion, and her desperate screams seemed to echo his joy.

CHAPTER 13

Hettie and Jake sat across from each other attempting to finish their dinners, but his kisses in the hotel room earlier had ignited a burning fire inside her. She toyed with her food but tasted nothing. Lost in a heated, mesmerizing glow, she found it difficult to think of anything but being held in his arms and feeling his hard body against hers.

Her mouth felt as dry as the desert sands. And she enjoyed many more sips of the wine he'd ordered. All the while she imagined them together, upstairs in her darkened hotel room, twisting and moaning in the sheets on her bed.

Jake chewed slowly, tasting very little as well. His eyes seldom left her face and his body sang with the tightness of his desire. He'd tried to fight his wild attraction for this woman, but when he'd seen her tonight, standing there, waiting for him in that filmy green dress, his innate reserves had fallen away and he no longer held back what he felt for her.

He wanted time alone with Hettie. He needed her and wanted her. Feelings of deep, burning desire washed over him in a wild tide of need that nearly overwhelmed him. He'd see what she'd allow from him. He had no right to anything from her, but he wasn't a man to be put off for long.

The dinner ended. As he paid the bill, the waiter asked, "I haven't seen you in here for a while, Sheriff La Force. Been out of town?"

"No, just mindin' my own business," he drawled, hoping the man would take the hint to do the same. He stood and reached down to assist Hettie to her feet.

She took the proffered hand and, by the way she'd felt all through dinner, she needed it. "Thank you for a nice dinner, Jake."

She murmured it so low he had to lean close to hear her words and his nearness set her heart racing ever more furiously. She fought the feelings even that small thing aroused in her but she'd lost the battle. Passion filled her thoughts of the night ahead, and those wild imaginings kept her in a smoldering glow of heat.

"I could see you to your room right now or would you care to walk about town for a bit?" He knew what *he* wanted, but he gave her the option of a choice to delay the rising tide of passion that had risen in them both. He'd seen her distress and knew the cause of it. She wanted him as much as he wanted her, and it'd been a long time coming for both.

She fought her desire-laden thoughts with all she had. *I can't be such a fool. This man is trying to arrest me for murder!* But the glow of desire washed over her all over again when she looked into his eyes and caught the heady male scent of him. Yet, from some recess deep within, she found the strength to remember why she'd come to Flagstaff, and it brought her a moment of sanity.

"Jake, I came to town because I've had a very disturbing letter from a friend of mine. Could we walk a bit and discuss it?"

Hiding his feelings with a good bit of effort, he replied, "Why, sure, if you like, Hettie. It's nice outside tonight. Let's do that."

He took her elbow and they walked out of the hotel together. He contented himself just being by her side. Even that small thing gave him the feeling of completeness long denied.

People watched them as they left. Jake hadn't taken a woman to dinner in all the years he'd been sheriff. There were whispers and murmurings, but he heard none of them, nor would he have cared if he had. It felt right to have this woman beside him.

Once outside in the bracing, high mountain air, he asked her, "What letter and what are you worried about, then?"

"You know the black horse I ride, Diablo? My friend Cherry gave him to me of out of the blue, saying she never wanted to see the horse again. She wouldn't say why. But recently, I had reason to write and ask her for the horse's history."

She clung tightly to his arm. He wondered if it was because of fear, but hoped it was something more.

"What was in it that's got you in such a rub?"

"You ever heard of a killer called, *El Tigre?*"

"Got himself killed a year or so ago, south of here, I heard tell."

"My friend wrote to tell me this black stallion had been *El Tigre's* horse, which accounts for the fancy saddle and tack that came with him. The man's name was Matìn Maldonado." She took a deep breath. "Jake, about four months ago, I hired a man named Miguel Maldonado. Outside of the man showing an unusual amount of interest in the horse, I've no reason to suspect him of anything. But I worry now that he may be related to that killer and is looking to revenge his death?" She clutched his arm a bit tighter. "That's partly what I'm worried about. Is that horrible killer really dead? How can I be sure he won't avenge himself on me for having his horse? This Miguel never says much of anything, and whether he understands much English, I don't know that, either."

"I see what you're worried about. I'll find out what I can. It'll be damned tough finding out anything, but I'll contact the sheriff in Parson's Grove. He'd know for sure. As far as Miguel goes, if he came across the border on his own, the way a lot of them do, he could be related. Most of them think this is their country anyway, and everything in it belongs to them, or so I've heard." He uttered a small laugh and squeezed her arm against his body.

"It *is* very nice out here, Jake." She still burned inside from his kisses. *I've got to get this feeling out of my head! If I don't, I'll get myself in so deep, I'll never get out. Maybe walking around out here will help.*

Remembering the letter from her friend, she wondered, Did she really have a reason to worry about the Mexican who worked for her? "Maldonado is a common enough name. Isn't it?" she asked.

"Still worryin' on that letter, are you?" He brushed his knuckles across her cheek. "It's mighty nice walkin' about like this with you, Hettie." He stopped and looked into her eyes. "I think you know how I'm feelin' right now. It's damned hard to be a lawman and worry about anything besides what I want to do with you." His arm went around her and squeezed her closer to his body.

"I know what you're feeling, Jake." She took another deep breath, almost a gasp. "I dare not say how things are with me right now. If I did, you'd have me up in that room in the next few minutes." She looked into his eyes and saw his aching desire burning there. "Oh, Jake!" Her voice had become a smoldering whisper.

He didn't need any further answer and with his arm tight around her, they turned around to head back to the hotel. She offered no defense against him as they walked rapidly, retracing their steps, back the way they'd come. She realized she'd be opening a door that could never be closed again and made the decision to leave it to whatever the fates decreed for her.

He stopped. "Hettie, go on to your room alone. There's enough gossip about us already, and we don't need any more talk spread around. I'll be along right soon."

He sent her on alone, but before she reached the front of the hotel, she stopped at the sounds of loud, piercing screams. They echoed across and down the street. Hettie turned back to look where she'd left Jake.

"Someone's in trouble," he called to her. "Sorry, I've got to go!" And he sprang into action. "Wait for me, Hettie," he cried, as he sprinted away toward the screams.

People rushed out from saloons and homes nearby. Hettie stood there in shock, watching Jake reach the small crowd that had gathered. In a few moments she saw him struggling with someone on Front Street. She quickly changed direction, away from the hotel, and ran toward the struggling pair.

Dark though it was, there was enough lamplight beaming out of store windows that she could see Jake trying to subdue a frantic, screaming woman. She also caught a glimpse of blonde curls in the scuffle.

Hettie ran across the street to help. Reaching the scene, she stopped in horror. The blonde curls belonged to Annabelle Nellis and the ragged, torn clothes twisted about her small body were stained with what looked like blood.

"My God! Jake, what's happened to her?" She reached out and touched the girl, to comfort her, but quickly pulled back her hand—covered in wild, bleeding scratches.

"Don't touch me! Oh God, don't do that to me again!"

Annabelle screamed out her terror and fought them in un-reasoning fear. Jake held her struggling body against his chest and did his best to keep his face away from her flailing hands.

"Oh, please don't do that to me, anymore!" she cried un-til, suddenly realizing it was Jake, she slumped in his arms and became a sobbing dead weight for him to support. "Help me, oh, please don't let him do that again."

Hettie saw blood stains smeared down the front and back of the girl's tattered dress. "Jake, I think she's been attacked by a man." She pointed to the dark stains smeared on her dress. "That looks like blood."

He nodded at Hettie as he held the sobbing girl. "See if you can find the doctor. She needs one right now!"

People crowded around and Jake heard someone say, "Doc's on his way, Jake, guess he heard the screamin'."

Hettie stayed, then knelt down to face Annabelle and tried to speak with her. "My dear, who did this to you?" she asked but, looking into the girl's distraught face, saw only a blank, unthinking stare. She told Jake. "She's not hearing anything right now—too upset or in shock." She looked around in frus-tration. "Where's that doctor? Someone said he was on his way."

In a few more moments, she heard pounding footsteps coming along the boardwalk. A portly man in a suit shouldered his way through the crowd and knelt beside the distraught girl. "Anyone know what happened here?"

"We'd just left the hotel and heard her screaming," Jake said. "She's not answerin' any questions right now." He turned to Hettie. "Would you go see if you can find her parents?"

"I will, Jake," she replied, and turned toward the hotel. Reaching it, she ran inside and asked the first person she saw, "Do you know where Mr. Nellis might be? I need to see him."

"Don't know, ma'am, wasn't here tonight."

"What about his wife? It's very urgent we find either of them." She tried not to sound overly frantic, but the man realized something was very wrong.

"I know where they live. I'll find them. What should I say?"

"Tell them their daughter's been attacked and is in serious condition. The doctor's with her right now."

"Oh, no, not Miss Annabelle!"

His face turned pale and he left on a run to find the girl's parents. Hettie stood there in shock, trying to get her feelings under control. Her first thoughts were of Miguel. Did he come to town to finish what the saucy little Annabelle had started with him out at the ranch? She didn't know, but it made cold shivers run down her spine to consider such a fate for that poor young girl.

"I did warn her but, even if it *was* him, he had no right to do that to her or any other woman, flirt or not."

She'd tell these things to Jake when she saw him again. She realized her feelings for the sheriff had vanished after seeing the plight of the unfortunate girl. *But there'll be another time and it won't be long in coming.*

CHAPTER 14

Doctor Gentry had the men carry Annabelle up the steps and into his office. His wife acted as nurse when female patients were involved. She gently shooed the men away and closed the door so the doctor could attend the girl. Jake sat in a handy chair outside the door, listening to the moaning, sobbing cries of the ravished young woman. Relieved that the doctor and his wife had the care of Annabelle, he sat with Hettie and waited.

They heard the pounding of footsteps as Annabelle's parents came rushing up the stairs. The mother, pale and hysterical, looked at the sheriff sitting there. Her jaw was clenched tight, and her face had gone ashen. To Jake she appeared frozen in shock.

Angry and on the attack, she began babbling hysterically at Jake. "Some protection the citizens in this town have, allowing a mad man to run about attacking lone females! What have you got to say for yourself?"

"I had no idea she was out and about, ma'am. No decent woman ought to be out at night without an escort in any case. I don't say it's right, but an unprotected young girl running about at night can mean trouble." He looked the hysterical woman in the eye. "Just what was she doing out alone?"

Rebuffed, the distraught woman answered meekly. "She went to the restaurant to see who was there, said she'd be right back." She broke into deep sobs for a few moments then raised her tear stained face and demanded, "I want to see my daughter!" She stepped up to the room where the doctor treated his patients and banged on it with a clenched fist. "Let me in. I've got to see my child!"

The doctor's wife opened the door a crack and said, keeping her voice low, "Yes, what is it?"

Mrs. Nellis grabbed the door, shoved the doctor's wife aside, and went in. Jake heard her crying loudly, "Oh, Lord above! Look at all this blood!" Her voice, loud and obnoxious, must have brought Annabelle out of her trance.

Soon, Annabelle sobbed loudly with her mother. With both of them going at it, Jake felt relieved the girl had come to her senses enough to begin mourning what had been done to her. He needed to question her, if she could hold her hysteria down enough to answer his queries.

After a time, the doctor came out and took Jake aside. "She's been ravaged by some man who forced her off the street and into some dark place against her will. She called him, Miguel. I fear, in addition to her other injuries, he poured enough strong drink into her to make her deathly sick. It's very possible she has alcohol poisoning."

Of course, he couldn't detail her female injuries to Jake. That was woman's talk as far as both men were concerned. "Her mother is extremely upset and demanding that the man be caught and hanged."

"Of course, he ought to be, and he damned sure will be," Jake said. His jaw was clenched so hard it hurt. "I'll leave now and be in my office with Lin for a while if you have any more information for me."

Jake and Hettie left the doctor's office and went into the street. It had grown colder. The night breezes off the high peaks that sat close to Flagstaff, drifted across town, scattering dry leaves across the street as he escorted her to the hotel and ushered her inside.

"I have to go to the office for a while, tonight. With all that's happened, it wouldn't be right for us to go any farther, if you get my meaning." His voice grew heavy with emotion. "Dearest Hettie, we need time alone. Can we manage that?" he queried, his mind fraught with frustration.

She sighed. "Yes, Jake, we do need time to talk about…things."

He shrugged. "Of course, with a rapist to corner, it might be a while. She named Miguel so I believe he could be your man. You say she flirted with him, and more than once?"

"Yes, it certainly could be. Miguel Maldonado. Annabelle has been out to my place twice, and just yesterday she flirted outrageously with him. He responded to her and looked mighty interested. I tried to warn her that he was not a young boy to fool with. Yes, it could be him, Jake."

Her heart sank, thinking the poor foolish girl had met the man at her ranch. "I believe she planned to meet him along the trail when she drove back to Flagstaff this morning," she added. "I spoiled that for them by riding along with her." She grimaced. "She wasn't too happy with me on that ride. But I'm thinking this terrible thing would have happened that much sooner if I hadn't been along with her on that trail."

"I'll be coming with you in the morning when you head back to your place. I'll be arrestin' Miguel, if he's had the gall to return there."

Hettie frowned, puzzled. "If I know that girl, she'll find some way to blame it all on me. Do you suppose she saw us together and ran out of the hotel?" She thought for a moment. "If she did, it may have made her go running out on the street so late like that." She raised her eyes to Jake's. "The timing's right, and from what the mother said…"

He shook his head, but Hettie knew intuitively that Annabelle had seen them holding hands across the table. And that had sent the girl running into the street.

They parted then, Jake to his office and Hettie to her hotel room.

෧෨෧෨

The doctor came to see Jake after a couple of hours. "She said it was a Mexican man. She named him, called him Miguel. It might help your investigation. She was most certainly raped, Jake, and violently so. What kind of bastard would do that to a young girl like Annabelle?"

"I have someone in mind, Doc. I know the man and where to find him. Will you see if she'll speak with me? I need to get the name for sure, and if she'll positively identify the man who did this to her when we arrest him?"

"Assuredly, I'll certainly ask her, Jake."

After the doctor left, Jake decided to leave the office himself. Nothing more could be done tonight and Lin, his other deputy, was set to man the jail and the office for the night. The three of them were kept pretty damned busy some times. He sighed with regret. *Too bad it had to be tonight.*

Jake headed to the doctor's office and waited to see Annabelle. When the doc said she'd see him, he entered the room. The girl, resting in a small bed, face washed and hair brushed by the doctor's wife, opened her eyes and looked at Jake. He saw the bruising and discoloration and anger filled him.

When the girl saw him, her eyes took on a soft glow. "Oh, Sheriff La Force, you've come to see me."

Amazed at the silly simpering in her voice, he held his surprise and gently asked, "How are you, Annabelle?"

"Oh, Jake, he's ruined me for life!" She broke into hysterical sobbing, yet between sobs, he saw a sly, devious look in her eye that told him she wasn't hysterical anymore and knew exactly what she was doing.

"Would you be able to tell who did this to you?" He kept his voice as soft as possible, wondering what raced through the girl's mind.

"It was that Miguel Hettie has working on her ranch. He couldn't take his eyes off me and flirted with me every chance he got." She broke into a fresh wave of weeping. "When Hettie and I went riding that night, he...touched my leg when he shortened my stirrups!"

"I'm heading out that way to arrest the man if he's to be found. If not, I'll find him."

"Th–thanks, Sheriff–Jake." She stopped sobbing and eyed him. Realizing he'd be seeing Hettie, she asked, "Do you have to ride all that way?"

Jake saw the calculating gleam again. "'Fraid I do, miss. It's my job and I intend to do it." He saw her sudden start beneath her blankets as he rose from his chair.

"Do you have to go so soon, I haven't told you everything," she said in whining tones.

Jake almost felt her tentacles sinking into his flesh. He'd heard enough and didn't want her going into further detail about what Miguel had done to her. He had the doc's word on that. "Yes, Miss Nellis, I need to tend to a few things. I'll say good night now. I hope you'll be feelin' better."

That sounded trite, and useless, after what the girl had suffered, but he wanted out of her presence and the sooner the better. He saw her hand come out of her blankets in a vain effort to detain him, but he left the room, heaving a sigh of relief as he walked on down the street to his own, lonely quarters.

His mind quickly went back to Hettie and the night together they both had wanted and needed.

CHAPTER 15

Hettie prepared for her long ride home after a breakfast she'd happily shared with Jake. Due to the heated events of last evening, she wondered what things she'd left undone, what supplies she needed and hadn't bought, things neglected because of her feelings for Jake. Still, she'd informed him of the letter, so she hadn't forgotten everything.

Worried about Annabelle, she decided to visit the doctor's office to see her. It wouldn't be right to leave town without checking on the unfortunate girl.

"I'll see if she'll see anyone," the doctor said. "So far it's been the sheriff, last night, and her mother. Wouldn't let her father in at all." He ushered Hettie into his main office. "Wait here, I'll see." He tapped slightly on the inner door and entered. He soon returned. "It's all right for you to come in."

He led Hettie into the room where he had a bed in case he needed to keep someone for a spell. The room was painted a creamy white and the movable curtained panels created privacy where needed.

Hettie saw the crumpled figure of the girl lying quietly under several blankets. She approached the cot. "Annabelle, its Hettie, come to see you."

The girl turned her head and looked at her. The accusing look in her eyes and the intensity of her angry glare made Hettie back away from the bed.

"It's your fault," the girl cried out. "You know it is, all of it! First you introduce me to that scoundrel at your ranch, and then you bring him here to attack me," she snarled in her hate and anguish. "I'm ruined forever, after what he did to me. What man will ever look at me now? Who, Hettie?"

Her voice soared to an even higher tone of hysteria, as she kept on and on. "I came into the restaurant and saw you playing up to that sheriff! The sight of it upset me so much I went outside and ran as fast as I could."

She shook an accusing finger at Hettie. "It was seeing you two together, cozying up to each other the way you were. That's what made me go out on the dark street unprotected!" she sobbed, her shoulders shaking. "That's when that monster caught me!" She sat up and grabbed her knees, rocking in the bed, trying to ease her agony. "Oh, why did you do it? Why for God's sake? You know Jake wants me, not you!"

The doctor stood back in amazement at the girl's wild accusations. When he tried to sooth her, she turned on him, gnashing her teeth and cursing in vile words few cowboys ever used. Hettie had often observed how the men used especially foul words when they drove cattle. It seemed to be the normal course of events. She wondered where Annabelle had ever heard words like that.

The doc took her arm. "You'd best leave. She's hysterical again." They left the girl sobbing alone in the darkened room.

"Doctor, I can't believe what she's saying!" Hettie gasped. "Has she gone mad? What she said about the man at my ranch could be true. She came out there twice and flirted outrageously with him both times. Jake will be hunting for Miguel and will arrest him when he finds him." She shook her head. "It must have been him, since she identified him, but we won't know for sure until he's caught."

"She's suffered an extremely traumatic attack for any woman, and certainly, we'll do what we can for her. I suspect she's been given her head all too often by her mother. She's their only child, you know." Doctor Gentry shook his head at the sad turn of events for the Nellis family. "It's too bad."

"I'm leaving for my ranch now, Doctor. If there's anything I can do to help, please send word." She shook his hand and patted his arm.

"Thank you, Hettie. Don't pay any mind to her ravings. She may not even remember having said those things later on."

"I certainly hope not." She left the office and went down the stairs to Diablo. He nickered softly to her as he stamped his hooves and tossed his shimmering head. Hettie took special notice this morning of his saddle and the rest of the fancy gear. "So this fanciful rig belonged to a notorious killer. No wonder Cherry didn't want me to know the history."

She mounted and kept a tight rein on Diablo. The animal was ready for a good run after a night's rest and plenty of hay and oats. Would Miguel be there when she got back? She'd fire him if he was the man, but Jake was the one to handle that situation.

ଏଓଏଓ

Hettie left the environs of Flagstaff and headed down the trail toward her ranch. After about two miles, she gasped in surprise at seeing Jake move toward her from the side of the trail. "Jake! What are you doing out here? I thought you'd be out hunting for Miguel or another of his description."

"I'll see if he's at your ranch first, bein' the best place to begin, and find out whether or not he'd been gone for the night." He looked at her, joy shining from his pale blues. "How was Annabelle this morning?"

"Not good. She keeps raving and saying all sorts of ugly things. Of course, she blames me for introducing her to Miguel but does name him as the man who attacked her." She shook her head. "Doctor says she may not remember all the ugly things she's said when she comes out of it, but I wonder."

She looked him in the eye. "She has a case on you, Jake. She raved on and on about seeing us together in the hotel dining room. Claims she was so upset she ran out in the street because of it. Somehow, that makes it my fault, but not yours—imagine that."

"Hell's bells, Hettie. I don't care for her in any way. You must know that. I've never given her any encouragement. I'd never noticed the girl. Good Lord, she's just a kid!"

"I know that, but she doesn't. She so spoiled, she thinks if she wants something, it'll fall right into her lap. I doubt very much, the mother has ever told the girl no."

"Well, let's get movin'." He turned his horse onto the rough wagon-rutted trail. "I'll enjoy this ride along side of you, I know that much and come to think of it, Hettie, I believe I could use a little spoilin' myself."

He rode close to the black and nudged his knee against her leg. The nearness of the other horse irritated Diablo, making him squeal and nip viciously at the buckskin. Hettie ignored the horse's complaint. Jake's nearness sent thrills deep inside her. The intense feelings they'd roused between them last night were barely held in check and she wondered how this ride would end. The trauma of last night's events had definitely cooled her passions, but Jake riding along beside her didn't help at all. She fought against it, but the inner tides of heat and wanting were rising at a rapid rate.

They said little as they rode and Jake stayed as close as the black stallion would permit. Diablo continually squealed and bared his teeth to nip at Jake's horse when he came too close and it made them laugh as they traveled through the trees, shrubs, new growth, and heat of the encroaching summer season. They forgot their worries and troubles in the deep joy of being alone together, away from Annabelle's troubles and wild accusations.

About high noon, Jake pulled his buckskin up. She recognized the spot where they'd lunched on the day he'd first come to the ranch. "Why don't we rest the horses a bit and have a bite ourselves?"

His voice was so low she barely heard it, but his meaning sent her blood racing. She nodded, saying nothing. *Can I fight this*? *Do I want to*? The rise in her pulse threatened a complete betrayal of her own senses. She hadn't thought to bring a lunch from the hotel. Did he?

He helped her off her horse. As she slid down he caught her against his long, hard body and kissed her, hungrily and thoroughly, before they took their horses' bridles and led them down into the familiar grove beside the trickling spring. Once there, he took her in his arms again.

"Oh, God, Hettie!" he cried as his tongue urged her lips to open for him.

She weakened. The small bit of resolve she'd clung to melted in the heat of him, and she met him all the way.

He finally let her go long enough to tend to the horses. He watered them and staked them where they could reach a little grass. Hettie sat on a rock, her inner turmoil such that she was unable to move. She watched him spread out a soft blanket on one remaining, shaded patch of thick, soft grass, his movements, quick, easy, and efficient. She kept her eye on the tall, spare-built man, completely mesmerized by his strong, loose-limbed body, and if she believed in magic spells, she'd have claimed he'd put one on her.

He came to her, helped her up from her seat, and led her to the blanket he'd prepared. Together, they sank down on it.

"Hettie?" He looked into her eyes, met her burning gaze, then kissed her again and again before his hands went to her blouse. Finding no protest, he opened the small buttons and ran his hands down to cup and mold her firm, full breasts. He rubbed her twin nubs gently and saw, by her rapid intake of breath, his effect on her senses.

They took the time to remove a few things. She removed her boots as did he then they worked off the rest of their clothes. The cool air reminded her how open they were to everyone and everything.

As she sought to cover herself, he said, "No, dearest girl, no. It's all right. We're alone here, well, except for the horses, and I'm sure they won't mind anything besides finding enough grass."

He grinned as he said it. "I've long wanted to see all of you and, my darling sweet woman, you're even more beautiful than I ever imagined." He moved his body over hers, pinning her to the soft blanket. "I've spent a lot of time thinkin' on this, my darlin' Hettie. Haven't you?"

Amazed at Jake's confession, she was in a daze of disbelief as she heard his soft chuckle of joy. The heavy weight of his body lying over her, pressing on her, gave her a feeling of safety and rightness. She welcomed it.

"Oh, God help me, Jake!" She looked into his eyes. "I think you're beautiful, too, and I want you so terribly. I'm ashamed of my behavior, but I don't want to wait any more."

Tightening her grip on him, she pulled him closer and tighter over her writhing body and moved her thighs apart for him.

He settled against her. "Hettie, I never thought to find a woman to love again!"

His lips found her swollen nipples and suckled gently. She moaned in pleasure as he went over her tender skin with his tongue. She pressed ever closer to that special firmness she felt rising against her. Feeling all of him sent burning thrills that enveloped her entire body, making her seek relief from the deep ache that possessed her.

"Please, Jake. Oh, please."

He moved a bit, nudging his knee gently between her legs, then felt downward over her belly. Thrusting his swollen member deep inside her, he cried out, "I love you, Hettie!"

He whispered soft words into her fragrant hair as he moved slowly to claim that warm, willing haven for his own.

She gasped and clung to him as he filled her with burning heat. Together they moved slowly, in a rhythm as old as time itself, and one of their own special making, until at last, they reached the final, earth-shaking end.

As they lay gasping and laughing in each other's arms, she heard him murmur in his softest voice, "My God, what a woman you are!"

"I'm not sure I dare trust you, Jake, but I love you with all I am. I can't believe this has happened to us."

"Hettie, you're a wonderful, brave woman. For me, I've been alone for so long, I gave up on ever finding a woman to love again. Never bothered to look, and right now, I can hardly believe this, either. But, darlin', sometimes, something good comes along."

He held her close for long moments, but said no more regarding his past. She believed he held onto a deep sorrow and hoped he'd tell her about it one day, when he felt he could.

Jake helped Hettie get herself together, fussing over small things like buttons and ties that set them both to laughing. They ate no lunch and didn't care, as they climbed up to the road and continued on their journey.

They said little, but touched each other when their horses allowed. Exulting in these new feelings, Jake's heart swelled in his chest and it felt uncommonly good. His past had faded and nearly left his mind whenever he watched this exciting, strong, and handsome young woman riding next to him. He reveled in a fine glow of happiness he hadn't known for many years.

It was nearing dusk when they arrived at the ranch yard. Jake hadn't forgotten his mission. It lay heavily on him. If the guilty man was indeed Hettie's hired hand, it'd be hard for her to accept. He swung down off his big buckskin and led him to water while Miguel hurried out from one of the barns to take the black horse from Hettie. Jake saw Hettie's face pale as the young man approached, but she gave nothing away.

"Thank you, Miguel," she said, her countenance serene. She didn't want to alarm the man if he was guilty. That was Jake's business.

As always, the Mexican took the stallion's bridle and led the horse away, crooning to him in soft, Spanish words.

Hettie looked at Jake to see if he'd noticed. His quiet mien and barely perceptible nod told her he was very much aware of the Mexican's attitude with the horse. Jake put his own horse in the corral, tossed him an armful of hay, and said to Hettie, "I'll check things out around here and see you in a bit."

She caught his meaning. "Won't you join me for dinner, then?" As if they barely knew each other, she left him and went into the house.

Jake entered the bunkhouse to find Handy Bates boiling potatoes on the old iron cook stove and setting out items for the evening meal. "Howdy there, Handy. Yeah, it's me again. If you have the time, I have a few more questions."

"Why, shore, Sheriff. I got time enough. Rest of the boys won't get in fer a while yet." He scuffed his way across the floor, and sat down at the table. "What's on your mind, then?" The nervous way he picked at the crumbs left on the table told Jake that something wasn't just right.

"If there isn't anything more you've got to say on the Greenup killin', I'd like to know if that Mex out there was around here last night. I guess you'd know everybody's whereabouts, wouldn't you?"

"Why, he was right here all night, Sheriff. We even played a few hands of cards. Man's a devil at Fan-Tan. Most of his people are, you know." He squirmed slightly in his chair but managed to look Jake in the eye. He glanced at the meat he'd left laying out. Flies buzzed about it and he appeared overly anxious to get on with his meal preparations

"Thanks, Handy. Anything else going on around here? You boys ever find the cows old Elmer was after that day?"

Jake didn't like the evasiveness he felt in the pudgy cowhand and decided to press him for a few more answers. It had become increasingly difficult to take the man at his word.

"Never seen hide nor hair of 'em a'tall. Looks like we got us a rustlin' problem on this ranch, Sheriff. One of the neighbors to the south, on the Bender Ranch, had some of theirs missin' too, so their man claims." He cleared his throat and continued. "Ain't been any more gone lately, though."

Jake noticed his trembling hands and the way he twisted his fingers when he forgot to hold them still.

"Well, thanks again, Handy. It helps to know what's happenin', or what's not. Appreciate it." Jake rose to leave the bunkhouse and then turned back. "How long you say that Mex kid's been here?"

"Aw, he ain't no kid, sheriff, not the way he sounds if he ever opens his mouth, that is." Handy remembered the question. "Why, yes, he's been here, oh, maybe five, six months by now. Damned good worker, especially with horses."

"Yes, I see that. He's sure taken a likin' to that black horse of Miss Hettie's." Jake went outside. He saw Miguel brushing the gleaming hide of Diablo and approached the man.

"Nice animal," he offered.

The man looked at him and squinted his eyes, gleaming with black shades of obsidian, but he said nothing. Jake looked him over carefully, his clothes were soiled, and a few darker spots stained the man's trousers in the front. It could be the man had something spilled there or it sure as hell could be something else, like blood from the savaging of an innocent young girl. *Could Handy be lying to protect the man? If so, why would he?*

Someone, sure as hell, was lying, he knew that. The girl said it was Miguel, but Handy said he was here all the time. *Could the Mexican have something on Handy? Was Handy involved in the missing cattle and had to shut old Elmer up?* Jake had lots of questions and damned few answers.

When the dinner bell sounded, he entered the house. He looked for the woman he hadn't seen for a short while, though to his hungry eyes, it'd seemed like hours. He grabbed Hettie in his arms, hugged her, and kissed her in joy rather than passion. "Smells good, darlin'. I could eat a bear."

He couldn't escape the feeling he'd gone back in time, coming into a house where his woman cooked his dinner and awaited him with open arms. After haunting him for many years, it was real again. The sudden fear that he'd lose it all again came over him, the cold chill of it freezing him in his tracks. Miguel, and any crime he'd committed, left his mind for the moment.

"Jake, what's the matter with you?" Hettie exclaimed seeing the pale, frozen look on his usually stern face. "You see a ghost?"

"Sorry, Hettie. I had a sudden memory that sort of took me by storm."

"Will you tell me about it someday, Jake? I know you've known trouble. I've seen that much in your eyes. You know my losses, and I could handle knowing yours, too." Not wanting to push or pry, she wondered if his secrets might be too painful for him to speak of. She'd wait until he was ready, if ever.

He got himself in hand and smiled at her. "What's for eats?" he asked and laughed, a faint little chuckle to break the terrible tightness in his heart.

"Nothing much, but I hope it suits you." How easy it was to fall back into cooking and doing for a man. It felt right to her, and doing it now gave her real happiness, for the first time in years. Remembering his quest, she asked, "What'd you find out, when you asked about Miguel?"

"I found a pack of lies, to begin with. Annabelle identified the man. She knew him well enough to be sure, if what you say is the case." He tossed his hat in a corner. "Someone out there is lyin' his head off." He went on to explain what made him feel that way. "Nothing rings true when I talk to Bates or the Mex either."

He looked at her. "Have you noticed anything going on around here?" He paused then added, "Something worth killin' a man?"

Hettie's first thought was of the gold she'd found in Elmer's possessions. She should tell Jake, but her natural reticence kicked in and she didn't. She only hoped he didn't detect the lie on her lips.

"I've always trusted my men to do their job. Until the mining claim money came in, I was about to lose this place. With Del around, we seemed to make a go of it." Her voice softened. "Of course, we did lose some cattle before Elmer was killed. We thought they'd gotten off the range and wandered away. That's why he went out that day, looking for them." She put her head down. "Never found them…"

Jake noticed Hettie's frown. He thought she had more to say and wondered if she held something back from him. He glanced around the large sitting room. His eyes narrowed, passing the guitar hanging on a peg, the pictures, he's seen before, and the old rifle her husband had prized so highly. *A lot of unanswered questions around here, too.* He turned to her again. "Where do I sleep tonight?"

CHAPTER 16

"Why don't we have some dinner?"

He figured she was thinking about that very thing as she led him to her table and pulled out a chair for him. But he took her by the waist and sat her there.

"You sit first, Hettie." He seated himself and they began the meal. He poured the coffee, and she passed the potatoes. They said nothing, as each of them gave thought to what the night ahead had in store. He ate in silence, but his mind raced ahead considering this new event in his life.

Finally, he faced her. "Hettie, would you consider marrying me?" He knew his heart was in his eyes as he waited for her answer.

She looked at him in surprise, knowing he waited for an answer to a question she believed she'd never hear again.

"Jake, can you forget what happened in your past and go on to a new life with me?" Tears sprang into her eyes. "I know it must be very painful, and you don't need to tell me what you hide so deeply inside yourself. And I'd never ask."

"I'll tell you someday." His voice was so thick, he almost whispered. "Until that morning when I looked into your beautiful face and those gold-shaded cougar eyes of yours, I'd lived as a dead man in more ways than I can name. Never looked at a woman or had any interest that way, all these years." He halted, shook his head in wonder. "When I laid eyes on you, girl, somethin' changed inside me. I can't explain it, but after knowin' you…yes, I can go on. In fact, I wouldn't want to live the rest of my life without havin' you for my wife. I wouldn't, Hettie darlin'."

Her eyes misted at the endearments. "You hit me near the same way, Jake. I have memories, too, all good ones. I loved my husband terribly and mourned him for years. And now you've come along and I feel alive all over again. I've never known any man like you, sober and threatening, yet caring and protecting. I can't explain how you make me feel, but I know I'd die, too, if I didn't have you in my life." She smiled into his eyes. "Yes, if you'll have what's left of me, I'll be your wife, Jake."

He came around the table, grabbed her in his arms, and kissed her for long moments until he looked in her eyes. "I love you, Hettie."

He still wondered where he'd be spending the night, and she saw it in his eyes.

"Would you like to stay with me tonight?" She laughed and tried to escape his arms but couldn't manage it as he overwhelmed her with laughter and long, hot kisses.

"No you don't! You're not getting away from me ever again." They laughed together and cleaned up the supper table, living in the glow of the love they shared. "What will your men think?" He had to bring it up.

"I'll let them know we'll be married as soon as we can get things together. Besides, it's really none of their affair, now is it?" She knew they had a lot to work out. Where would they live, for one thing? He was a sheriff, in town, and she had this ranch to consider.

He went about the house snuffing out lamps, but she kept a small one lit as she went into the bedroom and pulled the bedding down to make ready for him. "Sure beats a patch of grass." She laughed as he approached her and together they stood looking at her open bed.

Jake hugged her hard. "I'll go check on the horses. Be right along, my darling." He put on a jacket and walked outside. The horses were munching hay in their corrals. The lights had dimmed inside the bunkhouse. Monte and Windy hadn't been around earlier, and he wondered if they were in the bunkhouse now. He needed to hear them say Miguel was at the ranch to corroborate Handy's story, though he knew without a doubt that Handy had lied about the Mexican's whereabouts.

No evidence was stronger than identification by the victim, and it bothered Jake that he hadn't taken Miguel under arrest when he'd first arrived. He decided he'd ask them in the morning and went to the horse trough to wash as best he could before going in to Hettie. Thinking of the night ahead, he forgot Miguel and all the lies he'd heard.

Jake entered the house, caught the faint drift of a gentle fragrance drifting through the rooms, and saw Hettie standing by her bed dressed in an old worn nightgown, so thin it hid absolutely nothing from his seeking eyes. He felt his lips go wide in a grin of appreciation. "Oh, girl!" He choked on the words as he snuffed out the lamp and went for her.

ᔕᓂᔕᓂ

They laughed over a leisurely breakfast and continued to bask in the glow of their newly found union. But Jake had business outside and finally rose from the table. "I'd best get myself out there, got work to do." He hadn't told her what he planned, but hauling the Mexican off to jail was his first duty. And shucking off the glow of their night of passion, he knew he'd better get at it.

Stepping out the door, Jake automatically looked at the corrals. Bucky waited impatiently for his morning hay and stamped his hooves at the sight of Jake. He saw no sign of the black stallion and alarm bells went off in his mind as he raced to the bunkhouse and whipped open the door. Handy stood inside cleaning up after breakfast.

"Miguel around?" Jake asked.

"Ain't seen 'im this mornin'." Handy busied himself setting the clean plates back on a shelf. "None of the other boys even came in last night."

He began wiping crumbs off the table next, but Jake wasn't having it.

"Handy, you're sure as hell a damned liar, a poor one at that, and we both know it!" Jake stepped close. "That bastard, Miguel, raped the hotel owner's daughter night before last. You've lied for him and like a damned fool, I believed you! The girl spot on identified him as the one, and she was too hysterical to do any lyin' right then. Said she met him out here, and more than once, so I hear." He grabbed Handy's shirt front in a tight fist and pulled the man up tight against his chest. "This makes you a party to what happened to the girl. You know that?"

"I wasn't a lyin', Jake. That trouble makin' girl, now she's the liar!" His voice took on a whine while he denied Jake's claim. "It's the God's honest truth! I swear what I'm tellin' you is true!"

"Where's that filthy bastard gone to?" Jake pulled the shirt closer and twisted it until he saw Handy's neck getting red. His eyes bulged out a bit and Jake tightened the twist a bit more. "If I have to choke the truth out of you, it won't bother me a hell of a lot." He twisted again.

"Dunno, Jake! He wasn't here fer breakfast this mornin', nobody was."

"Why'n the hell you washin' all those plates then?" Jake rasped in anger at the chunky man. "Ghosts for breakfast, you lyin' son of a bitch?"

"He lit outta here on that black horse, Jake, and that's the truth! I seen 'im goin' off," Handy admitted, gasping for breath.

"Right after you fixed the bastard a nice breakfast, that it?"

"He's threatened to kill me if I talked!"

"How long ago?" Jake released the man. "He say anything?"

"Just said that horse was his. Sure couldn't figure his way of thinkin' on that," Handy babbled on. "Always had his eye on that horse, since he come here, talkin' to him, brushin' him all the damned time." The man tried to sound indignant like he'd been taken in by Miguel, but Jake had no time to waste on his lying tongue.

"You'd better be here when I get back with that horse. You hear me?"

Handy straightened his crumpled shirt. "Yeah, you bet, I ain't goin' nowheres."

Jake left the bunkhouse and hurried toward the ranch house. Hettie met him at the door, her eyes wide with anguish. "Where's my horse, Jake?"

Her eyes met his but she already knew the truth. Her fine black horse was gone, and Miguel with him.

"Looks like Miguel escaped and took Diablo with him. I'll get on his trail soon's I get my gear together." He took her in his arms. "Sorry as hell about this, Hettie."

"He did attack poor Annabelle and rape her, didn't he?"

"I'd say he did. And your man Handy, out there, lied through his teeth for him." He made a rueful face. "Wonder what else he's been lying about. Be careful while I'm gone, won't you?" he cautioned.

Enough had happened to make her realize she had a real problem with some of the men she'd hired.

Jake took the time to study the black's hoof prints from the soil of the corral. "Need to know what I'm trackin'," he said to himself as he threw his pack and gear on behind the saddle. Once he had it tied snugly with the long latigos on the saddle, he turned to Hettie. "I don't know how long I'll be gone but, Hettie, last night was...I don't even know how to say it. I love you, woman. God help me, I do." He held her close for a long moment then released her and stepped into the saddle.

He rode out of the yard a short distance then carefully circled the perimeter of the ranch until he saw what he looked for. One of Diablo's shoes had a curious defect that left a crooked V-shaped mark. In areas where the soil was loose, he caught enough glimpses of it to determine that Miguel had headed in a southerly direction. "Bastard's takin' that horse to Mexico, that's for damned sure."

He continued on Miguel's trail hour after hour, making good time, but not enough to catch the man he pursued. He kept on until the darkness of encroaching night began gathering. Yet there was light enough to spot something shining in the last fading rays of the sun.

He dismounted and quickly discovered that the horse ahead of him had thrown a shoe. The shining object was a well-worn, curved bit of metal with an identifying crooked V.

"Too bad for Diablo. Miguel will ride him till he can't hobble another step. Tough on the horse, but damned good for me." Jake relaxed. All he had to do was be careful when he started seeing blood from the horse's torn, bloodied hoof, and he had his man.

Miguel might keep on after dark, but not for long. The rocks were just as sharp at night, and his horse would suffer greatly as the man sought escape. Jake knew he'd not get far after Diablo's foot gave out and from now on, he'd play a waiting game.

Finding a snug hollow, Jake made a camp. Not wanting to be discovered by a desperate Miguel, he made a scant fire of very dry twigs and broken bits of bush. They would burn with little smoke and the general direction of the night breeze blew easterly. What smoke there was would not alert Miguel. He made a bit of coffee, ate some jerky, and drank from his canteen.

He wasn't very hungry, only angry and upset that he'd allowed his love for Hettie to divert attention from his duty. Disgusted at this turn of events, he was hurt that while he'd spent a blissful night with the woman he loved, the rapist had taken the chance to run. Jake's shoulders slumped as he gazed into his fire. He ought to have the right to have a private life, the same as other men, but his sense of duty ran deep and failure wasn't an option. He rolled into his blanket to toss and turn on the rocky ground for long hours before sleep found him.

かへかへか

Before the sun made enough light to see well, Jake had a quick cup of strong, black coffee and a biscuit. He began trailing Miguel again by going back to where he'd found the lost shoe. He carried it along in his pack and followed what tracks he found throughout the day without seeing a trace of blood marking the jagged stones. He decided Diablo had excellent hooves. Perhaps his Arab heritage served him well.

Nearing dusk, his patience paid off. He'd gotten close enough to see a figure outlined against the distant sky, only for an instant, but he knew the chase neared its end. From now on, he'd have to be doubly careful, knowing the man ahead of him would lie in wait when Diablo went lame. Miguel would need to steal Jake's horse to continue his escape.

Jake found a place to stop for the night—a box canyon that had plenty of water, grass, and firewood. This time, he felt free to make a fire and have a solid meal. With so much ahead of him, he needed the rest and should be safe enough for this night but maybe not after.

He assembled cottonwood twigs, branches, and other deadwood. The dry stuff would burn hot and make little smoke, and that suited Jake. He made his evening meal of coffee, bacon, and biscuits. "Not as nice as yours, Hettie, but it'll have to do." He made his rude bed while murmuring his thoughts of how her thick, ropy hair curled around his fingers and the good way she smelled to him, all woman and sweet as honey. Remembering her warm smile and willing body, he chuckled softly. "You sure got me off the track, darlin', but it was worth every damned bit." He fell asleep with a smile on his lips, his head pillowed on his saddle.

ക്കരു

The next morning, he returned to his trailing of the stallion and, around mid-morning, saw the first few drops of blood on the trail.

"Won't be much longer," he muttered, keeping a sharp lookout for an ambush. Soon Diablo wouldn't be of much use and Jake didn't think the man ahead of him wanted to walk the remaining hundred miles or so to Mexico. Without a horse under him, he'd seek a way to finish the trip on Jake's big buckskin, but Jake planned to be ready for him.

He stopped often, listening for sounds but, hearing nothing, moved slowly on. Another two hours gone, he dismounted and followed the bloody trail on foot. Jake was certain that taking the black stallion to Mexico remained uppermost in Miguel's mind. But he'd soon be forced to relinquish that dream if the horse couldn't walk any farther. The Sonoran Desert, though beautiful with its plentiful and varied desert growth, was a deadly place for a man without a horse or water.

Along about noon, the deep groaning of a horse could be heard from a quarter mile away. Jake stopped to consider his next move. He heard no more and saw nothing, but if a man had hackles, they'd be up and his senses on full alert. His prey was near enough that Jake devised a plan.

He led Bucky, not daring to leave him tied somewhere unguarded for a desperate Miguel to find. On foot, the man faced an impossible task, reaching Mexico across the terrible desert to the south. Jake knew Miguel's only recourse was to steal his horse, Bucky. And if he had to kill Jake to do that, he would.

After finding an inviting, green glade, Jake tied Bucky to a handy tree and left him standing alone. Miguel knew by now he was being followed and, desperate for a mount the way he was, might not recognize that a horse tied so conveniently was a trap. After securing the big buckskin, Jake crept into the brush nearby.

Long moments that turned into an hour or so tried his, patience but as a lawman, he waited with a resilience gained from long years of practice. When he saw the big butter-hided horse lift his head, sniff the air, and give out a soft nicker, he knew someone approached. A twig snapped, far off. Someone moved about in the periphery of the grassy glade as the sun moved far to the west and began to sink.

After many more moments, Jake saw Miguel slip furtively from the underbrush and move quietly toward Bucky. Creeping slowly, looking from side to side, he edged toward the buckskin.

When the man got close to the horse, Jake stepped out, his gun drawn. "I wouldn't. Lift your hands, Miguel. You're under arrest."

"I no see you, *Señor* Jake. Why you come for me?" He turned to face Jake and stood with his hands above his head. His face smooth and dark eyes smiling, he so easily portrayed the picture of innocence.

Jake stepped behind him, brought both arms back, and slipped a set of handcuffs on him. With the metallic click, he felt satisfied he had his man safe for the moment. He pushed Miguel away from the buckskin, removed the man's gun belt, and tossed it toward his horse. He'd hook it onto Bucky's saddle when he could. He looked Miguel in the eyes. "Where's Diablo?"

"I no understand what you say, *señor*." Miguel scoffed. "I have no horse with me." His look, innocent as a newborn babe, served to make Jake angry enough to chew nails but ever more cautious. He had the feeling he was dealing with a deadly snake—one who'd turn and strike if he found the slightest opportunity. And he knew without a doubt, Miguel waited for that chance.

CHAPTER 17

Jake pulled Miguel's arms up higher behind him until he winced in pain. "Where'd you leave him? Answer me, or you'll get more." He gave another strong jerk. "We'll start back in the morning, but tonight, I must find Diablo and get him down here where he can eat. Where is he?"

"*Aiee, señor*, he *mucho malo*...feet go bad." The man knew how to whimper if he thought it would help. "*Por favor, señor,* you hurt me." He slumped to the ground.

Jake figured Miguel looked for a chance to strike at him with his feet and was careful not to give him an opportunity. He hauled him to a good-sized tree, opened one manacle to wrap Miguel's arms around the trunk, and snapped the handcuff back on. The cuffs were a bit too tight, but he couldn't take a chance the man would escape and take Bucky. He used his lariat to rope him even faster to the tree. He wanted the man right where he was when he found Diablo and brought him to this small canyon to grass and water. He took Bucky off a ways to another good bit of grass and staked him before setting out to find the injured stallion. He felt bad for any suffering beast, especially Hettie's horse, but he didn't give a damn about Miguel's comfort.

He back-trailed the Mexican's route across sharp, rocky terrain, following every imaginable sign he could see. He'd find the stallion and bring him back where the hoof could heal and grow back, in safety. Diablo would have water and grass enough for a good while. Jake would have to leave him there to re-grow his hoof, hopefully enough to re-shoe him and bring him back to Hettie.

After two hours of careful backtracking, he heard the sound of a horse groaning in distress. He quickly found the beautiful black standing with one hoof only partially touching the rocky place where he was tethered. The horse nickered to him as he approached. He gently ran his hands over Diablo's head and down along his belly, seeing blood where Miguel had used his spurs.

He cursed the man. "Son of a bitch has misused this poor animal. Hettie'll want a piece of his hide for that and she's welcome to it."

He grabbed the bridle and led the horse back along the way he'd come. It was hard for him to watch Diablo limp so severely. He saw the blood left on passing sharp rocks, but down in the steep pocket where he held Miguel, the poor creature would have water and grass. The black limped along behind Jake, his proud head lowered.

A tedious hour later, they entered the small box canyon. Miguel remained tied to the tree and, when he heard Jake return, whined in his cramped misery. Ignoring the man's discomfort, Jake turned his attention to caring for the horse. He removed the tack and bridle then led him by his halter to the tiny trickling stream. After the horse drank his fill, Jake took him to the nearest grass and let him loose.

He pulled out a tin of salve he kept handy, went to Diablo, and lifted his hoof for a good look. It would heal in time. He plastered it with the ointment, knowing it wouldn't stay on the hoof for long. He had no linens to wrap the bleeding mess.

He found a fair sized indentation in the canyon wall, and stowed the black's things inside it, covering it with the saddle blanket and what he could find to keep the fine leather goods out of the weather.

He returned to Miguel. "You bastard, you'd have left him for the buzzards!" he snarled. "I know all about that killin' brother of yours, *El Tigre*. Didn't make out too well against a real man, did he?" He hadn't heard the full story, but in his anger over the horse, he didn't care about details. It made him feel some better to throw the biting remarks at his prisoner.

Miguel snarled the cat-spitting hatred he'd likely held inside for many months. The heated vitriol gushed forth in staccato Spanish. Fortunately, Jake didn't know enough of it to understand, or give a damn. It'd been a long day and he was tired.

He scooped up a cup of water and offered it to the man. "Here, drink, you bastard. I'm not like you." He gave the man a drink but didn't untie him. Miguel suffered in his bent and cramped position, tied around the tree that way, but remembering how Annabelle had screamed and cried hysterically, Jake didn't give two damns in hell about seeing the man suffer a little.

He brought Bucky closer, took off his tack, and set a fire big enough to cook a good sized dinner for both him and his prisoner. He made biscuits and jerky gravy and filled a battered tin plate for Miguel. He went to the tree and untied the lariat, then removed the cuffs long enough to take Miguel to a spot where he could sit. He put them on in front and bade him eat. He gave him the coffee left in the pot, grounds and all, keeping the cup for his own use. He ate his own chuck from the frying pan.

Miguel ate a hearty supper. Jake noticed the man hadn't packed himself a bedroll, and decided he could sleep on the ground. He generously allowed the Mexican Bucky's saddle blanket to lie on. After tying his prisoner's feet to the nearest tree, Jake settled himself for the night. He didn't plan on sleeping, unable to trust the fugitive enough for that.

ℰ∽ℰ∽

Morning saw them on their way. He made Miguel walk for the first part of the day and did some walking himself during the heat of the afternoon with his prisoner in the saddle. He kept the reins in his own hands, leading Bucky over the rocky trail while his prisoner seethed with hatred. Hopelessness burned and raged in his eyes, but to Jake, who'd handled hard men before, it made no difference. Ignoring the occasional nasty remark from the prisoner was easy. He didn't give a damn.

Bucky might allow two people on his broad back, but sitting that close to his prisoner didn't strike Jake as a good idea. He chose to walk some and made Miguel walk plenty until it grew too dark to travel. He made a dry camp in the rocks and if the rocks were hard for Miguel, they were hard for Jake, too. He couldn't chance real sleep, only a short cat nap or two, and after nearly two days of inadequate sleep, his eyes burned with fatigue and sweat.

The Mexican snored loudly at times and Jake envied him his rest. Walking tired the man and helped keep him under control, but Miguel was a man who waited for one weak moment when Jake wouldn't be watching. That made sleep impossible for him.

About dusk the next day, they arrived at the ranch with Jake in the saddle and Miguel staggering along in front. Hettie rushed out to greet him. "You've found your man, Jake." She looked for Diablo, raised questioning eyes to him while gazing with distain at Miguel.

Answering the query in her eyes, Jake told her, "He's all right, Hettie. We'll go out in couple weeks and get him."

"I'd like to know what happened, but it can wait. You look plumb worn out."

Jake made no immediate reply, knowing his red-rimmed eyes and growth of beard told her enough for the moment. His clothes were sweat-stained and dirty. He felt gaunt from hunger and worn with fatigue. Miguel looked even worse.

Seeing her look of distress, he added, "I'm tired Hettie, but I won't rest until this man is behind bars." He dismounted and led his horse to water.

Miguel, dispirited and exhausted, slumped to the ground and waited.

Windy and Larry came roaring out of the bunk house to help. Jake, seeing no signs of Handy, looked to Hettie in question.

"Handy left here a couple of days ago for parts unknown. He just disappeared. Wasn't here two mornings ago." She wanted to know about her horse, but it had to wait. He'd tell her everything, shortly.

She nodded at Miguel then turned back to Jake. "You all right? You look like you've been riding forever, Jake. The boys can keep an eye on your prisoner while you get some rest, can't they?" She hesitated, worried about him. "I'll take care of Bucky, just go sit on the porch for a spell."

He laughed. "I'm tired as hell, but I'm not dead, Hettie. Miguel's got to be taken to jail, but it'll wait until the morning." She looked all soft and wonderful to him, but his prisoner took precedence. He looked at Windy and Larry. "Boys, Miguel here, is my prisoner, and I sure as hell could do with some rest. Can you watch him for a while?" If they handled the prisoner, he'd be free to take care of Hettie, too. With a sly squint in his eyes, he gave her a look of heated meaning.

"We shore can, Jake," Windy replied, his chest puffed out a bit. "What you want us to do with him?" Both men looked at Miguel like he was a stranger, though he'd once worked and ridden with them. "Just what'd he do, anyway?"

Jake didn't want them taking the side of the prisoner and explained the charges against Miguel. "Remember the little blonde girl who came out here to visit?" He nodded at Miguel. "He savaged the poor girl several nights ago, and got Handy to lie for him. Said he was right here when he sure as hell wasn't." He shifted his stance and, through narrowed eyes, informed the men further, "Then the bastard ran off with your boss's horse, makin' his escape. I've brought him this far, and he'll go to Flagstaff tomorrow, under arrest for rape and horse thievin."

Larry's eyes were filled with concern. "Horse all right?"

"Will be. Threw a shoe and got his foot banged up. He's in a good spot for healin' right now." Not too tired to throw a scare into Hettie, he went on to say, "If a cougar don't get him, he'll be right enough in a while."

Jake watched currents of alarm rise in Hettie at the mention of a cougar, but getting Miguel to jail took precedent. She knew that. Tough choices had to be made and Diablo couldn't walk enough to get home.

Larry gestured at Miguel, slumped on the ground in fatigue. "We'll keep an eye on this gazebo. Where'd you want 'im?"

"You'd best tie him to a bunk for the night, but one of you two has to stay awake." He faced them, wondering where their sympathies lay. "He'll likely face hangin' for what he did to the girl. They won't go easy on a man for that, and stealin' a horse is a hangin' offense, too."

"We'll handle it." Larry shook his head. "Too bad. Miguel was a good hand, and now with Handy gone, we're runnin' mighty damned short." They hoisted the Mex to his feet and dragged him off to the bunkhouse. "We'll feed him a bite of vittles, too. Don't worry, Jake, we got 'er under control."

Windy grabbed a length of rope to take with him and Jake was satisfied his prisoner was in good hands since neither man held with mistreating women. And a horse thief deserved hanging around these parts.

Hettie had Bucky in hand, already unsaddled and turned into the corral. He watched her toss him a big armful of sweet, cured hay. They had a field that grew decent grass during the summer and the boys made hay off it. Every man he knew hated that kind of work, but the feed was nice to have around when you needed it.

She came to him and led him into the house. "Let me fix you something to eat, Jake."

His steps lagged from fatigue, but seeing her all fresh and catching the sweet, clean smell of her caused his waning strength to return.

"I'll have at least one kiss before I eat." He kissed her, knowing his scruffy beard scratched and tickled. "Sorry about that, but I had to have a kiss. I might be dirty and tired, but I'm sure not dead."

"Eat now, while I fix a nice bath for you." She sat him at the table and he waited while she bustled around frying bacon and eggs, something easily fixed in a hurry. She sliced bread and put out a pot of thick jam.

After she served him, he ate ravenously and found the coffee revived him enough to watch her with utter amazement as she brought in a large, round, tin wash tub and set it on the kitchen floor. She had water heating on the stove and hauled in more to fill the tub.

When he'd finished his food, she came to him. "Let's get these filthy clothes off, Jake."

He was nearly in a trance of disbelief as she removed his shirt, his boots, pants, and disgusting socks. She held his soiled clothes out from her and, with the other hand, pinched her nose as she carried them away. They both enjoyed a good laugh until she stood looking at his naked form.

"You really are a beautiful man, Mr. Jake La Force."

She poured the heated water in to the tub and bade him sit in it. His legs hung out but the heat of the water felt wonderful. Her movements, washing his back and chest, had him in a heated glow, the like of which he'd never known in his life.

Hettie knelt beside him, brought a cup and brush near, applied a thick lather, and began shaving his stubby growth of beard.

"My God, woman, what the hell are you doing to me?" He closed his eyes in bliss but managed to move his mouth as she requested until she finished the shave, washed his face, and dried it with a towel. After he felt the coolness of a splash of Bay Rum across his clean-shaven face, he tried to grab her.

She evaded him and handed him a cloth. "You can finish things down there." He opened his eyes to see where she indicated, her face flushed red. "And I didn't get to your legs."

She disappeared into another part of the house and finally returned with a pile of clothing. "If you like, these have some wear left in them. That is, if you'd consider wearing these things of my husband's."

He felt a moment's hesitation in accepting them, but saw in her eyes, it'd be all right if he did.

"Thank you, Hettie. It'll be real good puttin' on something clean. I want to sleep soon so won't need much right now." He looked deep into her eyes and waited for her answer.

"Yes, Jake," she murmured, not to the clothing, but to being with him in her wide, inviting bed. When he remembered he had to check on the prisoner before he went to sleep, he cussed. "Hell, I have to get dressed. I'm still the damned sheriff." He dug into the pile and selected underclothes, heavy corded pants, socks, and a worn, faded blue shirt. "Not a bad fit. Thanks."

He pulled on his boots and went out to check on his prisoner. He felt refreshed, renewed, and completely aglow. "Bless that wonderful woman!"

At the bunkhouse he found Miguel asleep, his handcuffs around a solid bit of iron that supported the thin mattress where he lay. When Jake saw the man's feet were tied with rope, he relaxed. "You boys've got him well in hand. I'll turn in then."

Before Jake left the bunkhouse, Windy gave him a look. "Uh huh! Looks like the boss's got *somebody else* well in hand, too." They smiled quietly and went on playing the hand of cards. As he walked away, Jake heard them laughing aloud. "Lucky son-of-a-bitch! Looks like we'll either be havin' a new boss here, or a new owner one of these days."

Jake entered the house to find the kitchen gleaming in the lamplight and Hettie waiting for him.

"Jake, you were gone so long I'd begun to fear I'd lost you."

She stood there in the dim lamplight looking like a tawny goddess in that thin, revealing rag she called a nightdress. He was in a burning haze as she led the way to her bed. Numb with fatigue and desire, he shucked off his borrowed clothes and followed her.

                              ℰↄℰↄ

Jake shook himself awake. The softness of Hettie lying asleep beside him filled him with a heartwarming sense of completeness. He lay quietly for a time, listening to her soft breathing, remembering how she'd been in the night.

Having this woman lying beside him in a warm bed was as close to paradise as he ever hoped to get. But nature called, he needed to get up and take care of things before getting his day started. He slipped quietly from the bed.

As his feet hit the floor, his heel landed sharply against a hard round object so near the bed it lay partially out of sight. He nearly cussed aloud before he remembered the sleeping woman. He bent down to pick the offending object off the floor. As he brought it up the rounded brass of an empty shell casing gleamed in the early light of dawn—the very thing he'd searched for at the murder sight.

Finding it under Hettie's bed shocked his senses. His heart went spinning off into an endless void. Empty casings were a good part of the evidence he needed to clear up Elmer Greenup's death. He hurriedly slipped on his borrowed trousers and knelt down to slide his hand beneath the bed. He found two more of the damning things. He didn't want to know what they meant and fought against himself—there had to be an easy explanation.

Remembering her reaction when he'd questioned her before, he wasn't going to bring it up just now. He had his prisoner to handle and there was time enough in the days to come for him to destroy those wonderful feelings that had grown between Hettie and himself.

Jake grew sick inside with the agony of it. If these were the right caliber for the rifle hanging over the fireplace, he'd have to give some credence to what Handy Bates had said, yet he knew the man for a liar. He'd proven that already.

Finding spent shells under Hettie's bed didn't exactly incriminate her, but it didn't set right with him. And because of the suspicion it aroused, his mind sank into a numbing, sick turmoil. The mere thought of bringing this lovely woman to justice made his blood run cold with dread.

Could there be some other reason for those casings to be where he'd found them? Unless she'd lost them there carelessly or while undressing, but he didn't think so. It wasn't her style. *Killing a nice old man isn't her* style, *either.* Torturing himself with such thoughts, he knew the casings comprised a strong bit of evidence he had to consider, along with where he'd found them.

CHAPTER 18

Jake shoved the brass shell casings in a pocket of the borrowed clothes and, feeling the onus of those spent shells in the pit of his stomach, trudged to the back of the house and the small building kept for such needs.

When he returned Hettie was awake, smiling at him. She wore the soft, languorous look of fulfillment on her gentle features, remembering their passionate night together. He'd been tired, but not enough to dampen his desire for her willing body, and sleep had been long delayed.

"Good morning, Hettie." He kept his voice normal, but the caring and love of last night had been replaced with an uncertain coolness and a trace of suspicion. Her face stiffened at his tone and he hated seeing it.

"I'll make you breakfast before you head out, Jake."

He instantly noted her sudden change of tone and mien. A cool one, she'd never let on. And though she knew something had happened to chill things between them, she went on as though it hadn't. Saying nothing more, she laid a fire in the big, flat-topped cook stove and pulled out things for a hasty breakfast.

Jake completed dressing and stepped out into the morning air. It was a beautiful day with a fine breeze, birds singing high in the trees, but his heart felt like those chunks of river ice that floated down the Tonto in early spring. Frozen all the way through. Feeling he'd fallen into a bottomless pit, he headed to the corrals and bunkhouse, never seeing the sunshine.

Inside, Windy did his best to put together a breakfast, but he was no cook and did a lot of cussing as he worked. "Son of a bitchin' spuds. Can't slice the damned things worth a steer's patoot." He worked over thick slabs of bacon while the prisoner and Larry sat there grinning.

"He shore don't take to cookin' none," Larry observed with a smirk.

Miguel sat where he'd been all night, and Jake figured his bladder was about to bust. Worrying about the shell casings, he knew he was distracted. He hoped the horse-thieving devil wouldn't see his momentary weakness and use it to his advantage.

"I'll take this yahoo out for a bit." Jake removed one cuff from the bed frame and refastened it on Miguel's wrists before leading the man outside.

Miguel grinned as he reached down to relieve himself. *"Muchas gracias, señor."* He groaned softly as the yellow stream ran down the backside of the bunkhouse.

"De Nada," Jake responded and hauled the man back inside. They sat at the table to eat with Miguel manacled to the bunk, his hands in front. Jake nodded to the boys. "Go ahead and finish your chuck, I'll be right along."

He re-entered the ranch house. Hettie had set a place for him, but not one for herself. Tight lipped, she said nothing and didn't look at him. Her grimly set jaw spoke for her. His heart ached, but this wasn't the time to get into that shell business with her. She wasn't going anywhere. He ventured a query, "You don't know what's on my mind, do you?"

"I'm not sure I want to know with the way you are. I love you. I can't help that, but I sure as hell don't trust you, Jake La Force."

Her voice held a tone of bitterness he'd never heard from her before this morning, and it hurt like hell. He wanted to take her in his arms and caress away her fear and hurt. He couldn't. He had to leave it this way until he figured it out.

He left the house after a terse, "Thanks, Hettie. Fine breakfast."

The boys had Miguel settled on a horse and awaited him. "Any of you boys have an idea where Handy might have got to?" Jake asked. When he had his prisoner safely stowed in jail, he'd hunt down that paunchy liar.

"Didn't know much about his dealings off the place," Larry answered. "But he had a friend down Prescott way. I heard him say that, once."

Windy said nothing and Jake, seeing the tight smile Miguel wore across his face and the secretive shine in his eyes, realized the man no doubt had enough answers to straighten everything out—if he'd speak up. Getting it out of him would be tough as hell. During the ride to Flagstaff, Jake had an idea about how to pry it out of him.

Miguel sat trussed up and mounted on Patches for the ride into Flagstaff. Jake held the lead rope on the pinto Hettie had loaned him for the trip. She'd had no words for Jake aside from that. His chances with this woman had just slipped away like water into the thirsty sands of the vast Sonoran Desert. He hurt like hell inside but kept it off his face. She stood in the ranch yard, a forlorn figure, growing smaller as he led off, the lead rope of Miguel's horse in his hand.

After no conversation for several miles, Jake patiently began his quest for answers. "Matin was your brother?"

Miguel hid his surprise at the question and wore a look of total misunderstanding. "*Que, señor?*"

He shrugged his slim shoulders. But the wily glow in his eyes told Jake the man enjoyed having certain knowledge the sheriff wanted and needed. If he could bargain for his life with what he knew, he'd do it without revealing a thing.

"I know Handy lied for you," Jake said. "I need to know why, *comprende?*"

"*Señor* Sheriff, I know English quite well, but *your* Spanish...*por Dios, muy malo.*" He laughed, said nothing more, and rode with his head held high.

"I may be able to help you with the girl's case and could forget to mention the horse stealin'," Jake said, making a tentative offer.

"I am innocent, *señor.* That horse belongs to me. I have no need for your help."

"Maybe of horse stealin', but you were identified by the girl as the one who attacked her and will be again when she sees you in court. Around here that's a hangin' offense."

Miguel laughed again and said nothing, but Jake saw a sickly pallor steal across his face. They rode in silence for a time. It had grown hot and Jake stopped to offer the man a drink from the canteen hanging on his saddle.

They looked at each other, and Miguel's faint smile of disdain set Jake's tightly held reserves on fire. It took all he had not to lash out in frustration, but he capped the canteen and they rode on. The man knew what had been offered so Jake would have to bide his time for answers. What choice did he have? With that in mind, his thoughts took a devilish bent and he decided on what to do. In time, Miguel would be only too happy to spill what he knew.

They entered Flagstaff and stopped in front of the jail. Jake hauled his prisoner unceremoniously off Patches and half dragged him inside to Lin.

"This is Miguel Maldonado, accused of raping that young girl a few nights ago." Jake hesitated a moment then nodded at Miguel. "Lock this sick bastard in with old Vonokovitch back there. The cell ain't all that big, but it'll have to suit the two of them." He held a smile back as best he could in the face of Lin's surprised stare.

"You really want that, Jake?" Lin muttered, keeping his voice low to prevent the prisoner from hearing the fateful news.

"You damned right I do." Jake nodded for Lin to go ahead, and the deputy hauled Miguel off down the corridor between the cells. He heard a few comments from some of the other prisoners as they moved toward the back of the row of iron-barred cells.

"Poor son of a bitch, won't last out the night," floated across the fetid air of the locked cells.

"Aw that damned Roosian only beats up on his women folks," came a return comment.

After Jake heard the heavy sounds of the iron-barred door slamming shut, Lin came back. "I took off his handcuffs. Poor bastard'll need both hands, bein' in with that monster." Lin looked a little green in the face as he contemplated what would happen to the young Mexican. "I don't like it, Jake. It ain't right, no matter what he done."

"He's asked for that and more. If he begs for a change of scenery, tell him he'll have to ask me."

⌘

Hettie sat at the kitchen table, pondering Jake's sudden change in attitude. She certainly knew there'd been one. "What did I do? What on earth is that man thinking? Something has made him suspect me all over again, and I can't for the life of me imagine what it could be." Her voice echoed the heaviness of her heart. It felt like lead, and so did her feet. Unable to take action about Jake, she sighed. The ranch was still there and work had to be done. She had no time to mourn the loss of her horse or that damned Jake La Force either.

She felt her temper rise and got up from the chair. "Well, that suspicious son of a gun can go to hell and take that big buckskin horse of his right along with him!" Glad now that she hadn't mentioned finding the gold nuggets among Elmer's things, she snorted in disgust. "If Hodges comes back again, I'll ask him. Being a mining engineer, he'll have sense enough to know."

She went out to speak to Windy and Larry Potter. They hadn't left for any of the usual work, except taking care of the animals at the ranch that needed daily care. She met Monte bringing up the milk from the cow.

"Howdy, ma'am, sure quiet around here, ain't it?"

She wondered if he had any opinions about her allowing Jake to spend the night in her house, but even if he did, it was none of his business.

She set her jaw firmly. Things had to be done. "We'll need to hire another man or two. Any ideas?"

The man scratched his head. "Well, can't think of one right off, ma'am. The cattle are well in hand right now and so far, there ain't been no more rustlin' since we lost that bunch Elmer went lookin' for. We'll be all right for a while and might be, Handy'll come back. Never knew why he left, anyways."

He scuffed his toe in the dust and flushed a bit as he faced her. She wondered if he knew what new evidence Jake found to use against her, but she wouldn't ask.

"I'll have to leave things in yours and Windy's hands for now. I don't know where that sheriff left Diablo." She frowned, her face tight. "I'm worried about him, too, being left out there for the coyotes."

"It has to be off to the south somewhere, that's all I know. Miguel was headin' for Mexico and takin' the horse along, accordin' to what Jake said."

She decided to tell him about the horse. "Larry, I've received word that Miguel may be related to the man who once owned this horse. A man by the same surname, Maldonado, was a hired killed named *El Tigre* and was killed last year, several months before Miguel came to work for me."

"So that's it!" He whistled. "No wonder he had an eye for the horse. Maybe that Mex had plans all along to steal your horse. Suppose that killer ain't dead and he's sneakin' around here somewheres?" Larry scuffed in the dirt and slapped his gloves against his leg. "You say you don't know where they left Diablo? Jake didn't say?"

"No, not for sure. He said they left him somewhere to the south with his foot all torn up and in a canyon with enough water and grass to keep him until his hoof grows out. He can't walk now and needs time enough to heal." She hesitated then added, "My friend Cherry wrote that *El Tigre* was dead for sure and buried on their ranch." Uncertainty lay in her mind, but she was praying it was true.

Now, with that to worry over, as well as Diablo, she felt the frustration of her situation. "I'll have to wait until Jake shows up again before we can go get him." Thinking of Maldonado, she agreed with Larry. "That's why that man came here in the first place. Had his eye on the horse. I'm guessing Miguel is that killer's brother."

"Sure sorry for what happened to thet little blonde girl you had out here, ma'am. She was a terrible little flirt. Looks like Miguel thought she wanted him." He shrugged. "No reason to attack the girl that way, though. No reason at all. She was just a kid." The man walked away, shaking his head over a dreadful crime like that.

"You're right about that, Larry," she called after him but she wasn't sure he heard.

In frustration, and remembering the traumatized girl, she returned to the house. Going into her bedroom, she looked at the unmade bed. "Something happened here. What could it have been?" She couldn't begin to imagine what had gotten Jake's tail in a twist, anyway. In her misery, she decided to straighten things up.

As she pulled on the bedding a pillow fell to the floor and, in retrieving it, she saw an empty brass shell casing lying partially under the bed and nearly out of sight. It shocked her, but seeing that bit of gleaming metal let her know what Jake had seen. "There must have been another one or two under there and he thinks I put them there. He spots a few shell casings, and immediately believes I tried to hide them there. He's plumb loco!"

With a painfully sick feeling, she understood his change of attitude toward her. "Well, I've got news for that damned fool! He can take his stupid suspicions and stuff 'em where the sun don't shine." Her temper hit a new high. "Everything was so wonderful between us, yet at the first chance he finds, he's bound to hang that murder on me. I loved old Elmer. Jake's plumb crazy!" she stamped her foot, fuming about the house.

"My horse is gone; my men are half-gone, and now this!" She couldn't get herself settled and fought the tears that stung beneath her lashes, waiting to fall. She needed answers. "If Handy lied to Jake—" And she knew he had. "Why? And what's he guilty of to act that way?"

She began to believe he might have been doing a lot of things around her ranch that she was totally unaware of. Furious, she went outside to find Windy and Larry.

She found Larry near the corrals. "I need to talk with you boys."

"Windy's gone out to bring in some young stock for medical care, screw worms, he said."

"Maybe you'll have an idea." She went on to explain what she feared Handy may have done. "Why else would he lie to protect Miguel? That man must have him dead to rights over something."

"Wouldn't surprise me none. They's always gettin' together for one thing an' another, clannish, like," Larry said, with a frown. "I'd already done some worrying over it, an' wondered if they had a deal worked out. Maybe them missin' cows was part of it." He shrugged. "He kept Windy and me out of their way more than once, too. Don't know nothin' more'n that, though."

"Thanks, Larry. It helps me in trying to figure out what's going on around here. Maybe that's partly the reason the ranch has done so poorly the last few years." It gave her something to think on. "Maybe that miserable sheriff will sort things out instead of trying to hang me from the highest tree."

Remembering how tender he was when he'd made love to her and how deadly he was working on a case, she heaved a sigh. "It's like he's two men, and one of them—God help me, I can't get along without."

CHAPTER 19

L ate the next day, Jake went to the hotel looking for Andrew Nellis. He found a nearby clerk. "Nellis around?"

"He's right here, sheriff."

He beckoned to the older man sitting behind the reception desk. The man rose quickly and came to Jake, his face drawn and tense.

Jake raised his hand to head off the man's tirade. "I came to inquire about Miss Annabelle's condition."

"It's about time *something's* been done! You know our girl will never be the same after what that devil did to her. She nearly died from the alcohol he poured down her throat." Nellis stood there, his fists clenched tight and his face flushed red while he blustered at Jake.

"Mr. Nellis, I've arrested the man who attacked her. He's in jail. I'd like to speak with Annabelle if I may. Is she receiving visitors?"

"Well, she might see you, but she hasn't seen anyone else. She cries all the time. Won't come out of her room, let alone see anyone. She had a lot of friends in Flagstaff, being the popular girl she was, but she won't see them, none at all! She's ruined forever in this town and keeps crying about it. That man nearly ended her life, Sheriff." Tears brimmed in his eyes and his grim expression revealed his pain.

"Sure sorry to hear she's that bad off," Jake replied. "But, as I said, we did get the man she named, and I'd like to speak with her about it. She'll need to appear in court against him. You realize that, don't you, sir?"

"It'd be exceedingly cruel for her to have to do that, sheriff." Nellis's voice held a warning, but to Jake it was a father's protective instinct talking. For himself, he had to follow the law. Sometimes it was painful.

In his own case, considering what he'd found under Hettie's bed, Jake understood. He'd hate testifying about that in a court of law, bringing suspicion on the woman he loved.

"Let me know if she'll see me, then." Jake left him and went into the dining room for a bite to eat. He looked at the menu. Nothing looked good to him, nor would it taste good when he got it. His mind was on Hettie. He knew damned well she wasn't a killer. So why'd he make her feel like a guilty miscreant, with him hunting for some way to arrest her? He shook his head, disgusted with himself.

He had a lot of fence mending ahead of him and wondered if he'd ever manage it. Hettie wasn't one to put up with his wild accusations. And didn't that woman have one hell of a temper? What did those damned shell casings mean anyway? Her husband could have left them there long ago, but she'd have swept the floor under her bed before three years had passed, as clean a housekeeper as she was. For whatever it meant, he'd better find out how they got there and why. The way things looked to Jake, he'd lost everything. The desolate look on Hettie's face before he'd ridden away let him know she hated his guts, and he didn't blame her. She sure as hell had every right.

His supper half-finished, he got up to leave the dining room when Nellis came to his table. "She'll see you sheriff. Seems rather anxious, too." He motioned for Jake to follow him.

They left the hotel and turned up Beaver Street for a couple of blocks. "We live right here."

He led Jake to the front door of one of Flagstaff's nicer homes. The knocker was of thick, shining brass, and the other door hardware looked to be the same fine quality on this large solid home, two stories high and spacious. As they entered, Jake saw Mrs. Nellis waiting, twisting her hands together in agitation and anxiety as she stood in her nicely appointed living room.

"She's real poorly, Sheriff La Force...won't speak to anyone else, but said she'd see you" the mother informed him as she headed up a wide staircase, indicating that he was to follow. "She's up here in her room."

Jake trailed the short woman with a broad back and lumpy hips, a harbinger of what Annabelle's little figure would become in later years. Seeing the mother, he knew Annabelle's tiny form would change into that of a mature woman in short order. Maybe it wasn't right to compare other women with Hettie but the evidence was before him and he took notice.

They reached a white painted door. Mrs. Nellis knocked softly. "Annabelle, dear, the sheriff is here to see you."

Hearing a murmur of assent, she and Jake entered. He saw her propped in her bed against several, thick, stacked pillows with blankets and a nicely embroidered coverlet pulled up to her chin. Her face looked pale, her blonde curls disheveled. He noticed her eyes were reddened and puffy from crying.

Jake moved closer to her bed. "Hello, Annabelle. I hope you're feelin' some better these days. I'd like to speak with you for a bit if you're willin'."

Mrs. Nellis said nothing, but watched and waited.

"Yes, it's fine, but..." She turned to her mother. "You can leave us now, Mother."

Mrs. Nellis wanted to protest, but Annabelle's tone was adamant. Her look became hard, and her icy voice matched her gritted teeth. Jake watched the mother turn pale at the girl's command.

Mrs. Nellis left the room but left the door ajar and Annabelle shrieked, "I said, leave us!" To Jake, she ordered, "Go shut that door, please."

"I'd rather not, Miss Nellis. I'd prefer your mother be present in the room while I'm in here with you." He stepped to the door. "Mrs. Nellis, would you please come back in?"

She came, but by the woman's sheepish look, Jake realized the girl totally controlled her mother and, despite the trauma of her recent rape, remained the spoiled young woman she'd always been. Mrs. Nellis seemed completely terrorized by her demanding and manipulative daughter. Jake planned never to be alone with this young woman and gave Annabelle a look that said he'd have no more of it.

She settled back against her pillows. "How've you been, Jake?"

He couldn't miss the light of joy and victory in her eyes at having him in her bedroom, even with her mother present.

"I'm just fine, Miss Annabelle." Already tired of her nonsense, he went on with his questioning. "I have some business I'd like to discuss with you. It'll be some painful, I know, but we have to proceed with things if we're to get this case taken care of." Taking a handy chair, he sat close to the bed and addressed the girl, his tone formal. "If you haven't heard, we have taken Miguel Maldonado in custody."

Her face grew pale and she sank down in the bed, clutching the coverlet until her knuckles turned white. Fear widened her stricken eyes as her memory of the assault returned to her in full force.

"What we need from you is this: Your testimony against him in a face to face identification is by far the best evidence. Of course, we have other witnesses who saw your condition that night and heard your accusations. They saw your torn clothing and, of course, there is the doctor's report. Otherwise, though we have your word on what you screamed out that night. You were upset and out of your head. Maldonado could claim you were hysterical and only named him because you happened to know who he was."

Watching her expression turn from fear to anger, Jake wondered what was racing through her mind.

"Oh, God, no! You want me to go into a courtroom and admit in front of the whole town what that man *did* to me?" She gasped at the horror and reality of such an event. "I'll be the laughing stock of everyone in Flagstaff! I'll never live it down! My life will be ruined more than it already is!"

She continued to rave until she became almost incoherent. "Oh God. I'm ruined, my life is over! Who'd ever want to marry me now?" She pounded the bedding with clenched fists, her tears and sobbing increasing with her rising hysteria.

Jake looked at the mother. "Should you get the doctor?"

"He's been here every day. He says she's got to come out of this, or she may lose her mind." Her fear-filled voice was low, so Annabelle wouldn't hear what she said, but the girl wasn't in such a bad way that her devious little mind failed to pick up her comment.

"Don't you dare make me go into that open courtroom. If you do, I'll kill myself, Jake. I can't face that awful man," she sobbed. "And I refuse to disgrace myself in front of everybody in this town!" Screaming her rage at Jake and her mother, she repeated, "I won't do it!"

Jake turned to leave. He heard her say in a voice, suddenly changed to low and seductive, "Oh, Jake, how can you leave me like this? You know how much I need you now after what the monster did to me."

Her wheedling tone froze him clear through with the insanity of it.

"I need you, Jake."

Her mother, mouth agape, cried, "Annabelle! Remember yourself!" She moved toward the bed to comfort her daughter.

"Stay away from me, you bitch!" the girl screamed hysterically. "You don't care what happens to me. You never have!"

Nellis, hearing the mad raving, raced up the stairs and into the room. Standing over her bed, he warned, "Annabelle, if you speak to your mother again that way, sick or not, you're going over my knee. And I'll use a belt on your bottom like I should have done years ago." He glowered down at her, his embarrassment plain. "You hear me?"

Annabelle slunk down under the bedding. "Yes, Daddy."

She said nothing more but glared at Jake with hatred in her eyes. He already knew she'd hate Hettie as long as she lived, and now, she included him. He didn't mind that one little bit, as long as he got the hell out of this room and this house.

If she wouldn't testify against Maldonado, the man might go free to rape again, and he'd have to bring up the horse stealing charge. He hated the thought of that. He'd promised to withhold that hanging charge if Miguel would help him convict Handy.

The feeling against Maldonado ran high enough around Flagstaff to bring out a lynch mob. Jake knew he'd be lucky to find a jury that would let him escape the hangman's noose in any case. He said to Nellis, "Let me know what she decides. A lot depends on her testimony."

He bade them good night and left the room. Making his way down the stairs, he stepped and out into the clean, fresh, mountain air. He drew in a big breath and let it out before heading for the jail.

He wanted to check out Miguel's situation after being put in the same cell with Vonokovitch. Everyone in Flagstaff knew the man as an inhuman brute who frequently beat his wife and children. He'd been in trouble before with the law for violence against his family, but this time he was in danger of the hangman's noose. At the moment, the life of one of his children hung in the balance from a severe beating. Should the little boy not recover, Vonokovitch faced his own end.

He was a huge, thickheaded mongrel of a man with a heavy black beard and thickly accented speech. His ancestry was old Middle-European, and his beliefs and methods were old country as well. Sick old bastard or not, Jake hoped the ornery cuss would aid him in getting the information he needed from Maldonado. He entered the jail and his other deputy, Mel Smith, rose to greet him.

"How'd it go with the young lady? She ready to testify?" Mel queried, his brown eyes filled with curiosity. He nodded toward the back of the jail cells. "It's getting' real excitin' down there."

"Oh yeah," Jake said, nodding in reply. "Had a visit with Miss Annabelle, right enough. But don't know if she'll testify for us, though, bein' she's still in a real bad way." He looked down the corridor between the cells. "Things getting rough for Maldonado, are they?"

"It's not so good for the Mex in that cell." Mel frowned. "If your man wants to live much longer, he might just want to help you out, Jake." His worried look also carried a sly grin with his wrinkled brow.

"That bad, eh?" Jake stifled a laugh. "I'll just go have a talk with him." He walked down the corridor between the barred cells, receiving several comments, some friendly, others just surly grunts.

He approached the last cell and saw his man sitting on the top bunk with his feet curled beneath him. "How're you makin' out in here, Miguel?"

"Fuck you, *bastardo.*" He spit out the words slowly, scowling and gritting his teeth.

"Shaddup, fool, I keel you, no shaddup."

The big bear of a man came to the bars, grabbed them in his meaty hands and shook. The entire building trembled a bit and a trail of dust and plaster trickled down. The man's black eyes were bloodshot, and his nose ran with yellow mucus. Jake felt sorry for Miguel living in the same cell—almost.

How the authorities had ever allowed a man like that to immigrate into this country puzzled Jake. Maybe he'd come as a child. As bad as things were in that cell, he easily saw that Miguel wasn't close to spilling what he knew, not yet.

He walked to the front, stopping to hear one inmate's complaint. "Sheriff, if you don't take that damned Rooshan out an hang the bastard, you're gonna have a goddam revolt in here. He's filthy, belches all day long from that devil's brew his wife hauls in ever day fer the son of a bitch to eat, snores like he's rippin' lumber, and farts so loud we're all a goin' deef." It was old Shorty Dykes, a frequent inmate from drinking, fighting, and smashing up the bars.

"Sorry to hear that, Shorty. I'll see what I can do." Jake, smothering his glee, nearly stumbled up to the front desk.

"What the hell's got you grinnin' like that?" Mel asked.

The look on Jake's face said a good deal. "Maybe it won't be so long before Miguel gets set to have a confab with me with that business goin' on back there." He muffled a healthy laugh in his scarf.

Jake helped himself to a cup of the strong black coffee Mel had brewing. "Guess I'd better get Mrs. Jamison's horse back to her before she accuses *me* of horse thievin'."

He went out into the night, knowing it was more to catch sight of the woman than returning a horse. He figured she wouldn't have anything more to do with him after the cool way he'd treated her. He'd hurt her and it'd made him feel like hell down deep inside. The shell casings added a new twist to things, and he hadn't got that worked out. Maybe she had nothing to do with those stray rifle shells, but he didn't know for sure. He did know she was no killer. Being sheriff could make life hell at times, and this was one of them.

For years he'd kept buried the kind of feelings he'd known in the past, but all that had fallen away when he'd met Hettie Jamison. He had a lot to straighten out with that lady and wondered if he even could. A rock lay in his path and he gave it a vicious kick, sending it off the boardwalk in to a pile of horse dung that lay in the street.

CHAPTER 20

Hettie sat at the kitchen table, her head in her hands. "I'm sick and tired of sitting here waiting for that man to come and arrest me for murder. I've heard nothing from him or what he's working on, and it's driving me plumb off my noggin." She stomped into her bedroom and pulled out her riding togs. "I don't have my horse and right now, thanks to him, I haven't even got Patches. He ought to be hung for being a damned horse thief, right along with Miguel."

Easily overlooking the fact she'd loaned Patches to Jake for Miguel's ride to jail, she went to the corral and caught up a small bay mare. She had a rough gait but was sure-footed in the rocks and arroyos. "Come on, Bessie, I've got to get out of here." She flung an old saddle on the mare's willing back. She'd used it in the past before having the fancy one that came with Diablo and it was no pleasure to ride in. "I wonder if he's safe where they left him. Jake mentioned cougars before he rode off with another of my saddle horses."

She filled her canteen and put a slicker over the back of her saddle, but gave no thought to taking food. Her gun rested in the holster belted snugly about her hips. She'd learned long ago not to venture out in the rangeland without it.

"I won't ride far today, but if I head south, maybe I can find the trail he rode to arrest Miguel. Diablo has to be out that way somewhere." She rode away from the ranch and kept her head bent to see if a trail became visible. It took time to get her vision adjusted to that particular task, but she worked at it until she saw a hoof mark she was sure belonged to Jake's big buckskin.

"Here we go, Bessie," she said to her horse as she followed that trail for long hours until she found where he'd camped that first night. "I wonder how close he was to Miguel when he stopped here that night?" She stopped to let the horse graze and took several long pulls from her canteen.

Off under some low bushes lay the pile of branches where he'd fixed a rude bed and she imagined herself lying beside him in the dark of night. "Stop your ridiculous notions, you silly fool," she exclaimed aloud. "It's all over with that man. All you'll ever see of him now is when he shoves you inside his stinking, filthy jail." Hettie felt her tears flowing and didn't try to stop them. There was no one around to see.

She rested in the shade collecting her emotions before she mounted up to turn back. "Del, I've missed you for so long and thought I'd finally found someone to love again," she mused as her old mare picked her way carefully over the rocky trail. "You'd have liked Jake, I think."

She sat in the saddle, feeling lonely and wondering how things would play out. No need to guide her horse, the old girl knew the way home. All animals did.

Going through a narrow pass, a rockslide began and Hettie hurried Bessie to escape it. Nearly out of the narrowest spot, the mare squealed with pain and lunged against the rock wall, nearly unseating Hettie. A huge rock had rolled down to strike her hind leg and Hettie heard the sharp snap as the leg fractured. Sitting astride the mare, she felt the horse's entire body tremble with pain.

She dismounted. Not wanting more rocks to hit the horse, she carefully led the hobbling mare out of danger before inspecting the leg.

"Oh, Bessie, you poor girl," she crooned and patted the horse while smoothing her mane. Knowing what she had to do, she felt sick, hating the thought of it. But by the deep groaning of the mare, and the way her head hung low, Hettie knew she suffered terribly.

She removed all the tack, and laid it aside. Then she patted the mare and hugged her head before she drew her pistol. Gritting her teeth, she put it to the mare's head and squeezed the trigger. "I'm sorry, Bessie. You were a good horse."

She cried as the faithful mare's knees buckled and she slumped to the ground. Tears blurred her vision. All cattlemen, male and female, knew not to let an animal suffer. Hettie had never had to do this terrible thing before, but her husband had and so had her father.

She'd ridden too far to go to make it back to the ranch and walking about in strange territory after dark was a poor idea. "I'll have to make a camp some way, but not right here by poor Bessie." She took what she could, the saddle blanket, slicker, and the canteen and set off toward the ranch, looking for a protected spot to spend the night. Hunger pangs had started but she easily ignored that. She had water and her pistol. She could make out for a night.

❧❧❧

Jake rode his buckskin and led Patches along behind. It was late in the day when he'd started and it would be long after dark when he reached Hettie's ranch. He hungered for the sight of her, but with the tenseness between them, thought he'd just leave the pinto in the corral and head on back to Flagstaff.

"I'd better light out of there before she takes a shot at me." But he grinned at the thought of seeing her again, even if she did pull a gun on him.

It was after dark when he hit the ranch yard and saw there were very few horses in the corrals, the place looked nearly empty. He went to the bunkhouse and found Windy there alone. "Where's everybody?"

"Don't know. The Missus was gone on old Bessie when I got in, but she ain't come back yet." He scratched his head. "Larry's still out, too. He went out north this mornin'. Didn't expect to be back, though." His face looked pale in the lantern light, his features tense.

"You don't know where your boss has gone?"

"No, cain't figger it. Unless she went out to the south, tryin' to find that black horse of hers. She's been real worried about him."

"Damn, I'll bet that fool woman did just that." Jake wasn't sure what he ought to do, but he wanted to hunt for her, he knew that. "I'll just ride out that way, and see if I run into her, then." He headed for Bucky, gave him a good drink, and rode off. He knew the trail, he'd been over it.

It was dark but the moon had come up bright enough so he could make his way. He worried about Hettie being caught out like this. She knew her way around and should be safe enough, but he felt unsettled about it. Something might have happened to her. So he kept on.

Hours later, with enough light from a setting full moon to aid him in following a dim trail, he spotted the glow of a small fire, reflecting off a low canyon wall just ahead. He was sure he'd found her but wanted to avoid frightening her—and get a bullet for his pains.

He dismounted and tied Bucky to a small Mesquite tree. Creeping slowly, he rounded a boulder and saw Hettie crumpled in a tight figure next to the fire. She wasn't asleep. He knew that when she reached for a small bit of wood and tossed it on the lowering flames.

Not seeing her horse, he wondered what'd happened. She'd obviously met with trouble. He felt his heart pounding—and a glow of pride, knowing she'd handled the situation. He called out, his voice soft. "Hettie, been looking for you. All right, are you?"

At the sound of Jake's voice, she felt a rush of joy before she remembered why he looked for her. She called back to him. "I'm not lost, Jake, so why are you out hunting for me, anyway?" she asked, managing to keep the happiness and relief from her voice.

"Windy and I were worried when you never got back." He couldn't keep the crooning tones from his words and hoped it wouldn't set her off. He moved out from behind the huge boulder and edged closer to her fire.

"You can go straight to hell, Jake, and take that damned buckskin horse with you!" Her voice dripped with venom. She was stuck out here because of him, now he'd come hunting her down.

"I was worried you met up with trouble. Windy was, too."

"My horse broke a leg."

"Where is she?"

"I took care of it. I'm not some helpless ninny," she replied quietly. "Bessie was old, but a good mare and I hated to lose her. All my other ones seem to be missing these days." She hoped he caught her accusing tones.

"Aw, come on, girl. You've got me all wrong."

"Don't I know about *that*." Her temper flared, and her many losses didn't help. At the moment, she felt like she'd lost everything and couldn't see the end of her troubles. She put her head down against her knees and began weeping. "I've lost my beautiful black horse, now this one, and you want to hang me for murder. Don't tell me I've got it all wrong."

Jake crept close and sat beside her. The rock he found was a bit jagged and hurt like hell, but he wanted to comfort Hettie right now more than anything. "I never wanted to hang you, darling. Where'd you get an idea like that?" He slipped his arm around her, but she didn't fly off the handle—yet.

"Why are you torturing me? And I'm certainly not *your darling!*" She sniffed back her tears, trying to hide her elation at his tenderness. She was very glad not to be stranded alone in the darkness of these wild canyons, but she didn't plan to make it easy for him after the way he'd treated her. "You can take that arm off me, mister." Her voice, filled with ice and as much anger as she could rake up on short notice, made her feel like she'd edged him a little, and she enjoyed every second of it.

"Sorry, Hettie."

She knew another loss when the coolness of the night air replaced the warmth of his arm. "Jake, what happened to make you change toward me the way you did?" She didn't want to ask but she needed to know. Holding her arms around her knees, she rested her head on them.

"When I came out before and you had the fancy Eastern dude here, I was searching for spent shells from that gun of your husband's. I never found a one. But that last night when I stayed in your bed all night long—you remember that, don't you?" he asked softly and nudged against her.

"Just get on with your story and leave off talking about what you think you remember, Jake."

He'd tried softening her fear and hatred of him with his soothing tones, but she wasn't having it.

"That morning, I slipped out of bed and went to pull on my pants—well, your husband's pants, and I stepped on one of the shells I'd been looking for. Then I reached under the bed and found another." He let his shoulder touch against hers and again, she didn't lash out, so he continued. "Remembering what Handy had said, I have to say, it came as a bit of a shock to find those shell casings right under your bed, Hettie."

"Handy said…what'd *he* have to say? Why won't you tell me?" She couldn't stop the rise in her voice.

"I'll tell you. He said you were plannin' to get rid of the old man because he couldn't get his chores done anymore." Jake waited to hear what she had to say on that, but all he heard was a quick intake of her breath. "That's why I decided to ask you how you felt about him. I'd already got the feelin' you were planning on makin' his work a bit easier on him."

"Yes, I had planned on that." She looked at Jake. "I should never have sent him out that day, but no one else was around."

"Anyone else ever go inside your house?"

"No, but no one around here locks their door, and we've never had one on ours, either." She raised her head. "Did you believe me, then?"

"You bet I did. By then, I couldn't get you out of my mind and already had feelin's for you that I'd never thought to have again. Hettie, you've got to know how I feel." He put his arm around her again and she leaned into him.

"Things have gone so wrong for me, Jake. I'm losing everything, it seems, and I don't know how to stop it."

"I'm here, Hettie, and I always will be if you'll have me. We've talked about this before. I thought it was all set that you'd be my wife."

"Yes! Right up until you made me feel like a hunted crim-
inal."

"I don't blame you for sayin' that, but I *am* a law man and
tryin' to do my job. It gets tough sometimes." He pulled her
closer. The rocks he sat on were close to torture right now, but
he wasn't moving.

She enjoyed his closeness, but could she trust him? Or
was this more sweet talk? "Let's not talk about it anymore. It
makes me feel hunted and mad as hell." Hettie wanted to
change the subject. "How was Annabelle after what happened
to her?"

"I went to see her, needin' her testimony against Miguel,
now that he's in custody, but it looks like she might not testify.
The girl is worried what the town folks might say if she has to
come out and tell in court what happened to her. She hasn't
changed as far as being spoiled, and she was downright nasty
to her mother. That girl is loco it seems to me." He didn't want
to relate how she so slyly had tried to get him in her room
alone or the evil words she'd flung at her mother.

"Poor, foolish girl," Hettie said. "I warned her about Miguel, especially after that letter from Cherry, but she wouldn't
listen to me. She flirted outrageously with the man both times
she was out here." She uttered a hopeless laugh. "But she really came out here to see if I was after you, Jake."

"Did you tell her yes?" He squeezed her shoulders again,
and when she didn't protest, he pulled her into his arms and
kissed her lips over and over. When he came up for air, he
whispered, "I love you dearly, Hettie. I truly do."

"Oh, Jake, where do we go from here? I can't trust my
heart to you after what's happened. How could I?"

"Nothing has happened, Hettie. I'd give up my job if I
thought you were really guilty, and I'd sure as hell never arrest
you." He held her in his arms, believing he'd lost the battle for

her heart. He'd already lost the battle for her mind. She'd never trust him again and it hurt like hell. But she couldn't see it or feel it.

They sat together during the remainder of the darkest part of the night. She slept, leaning against the warmth of his body. He felt good, holding her that way, even as he realized his future with her had slipped away. Sitting on sharp rocks didn't help and shifting around for comfort didn't either.

His backside and legs had grown numb and when the light became bright enough, he struggled painfully to his feet and left to find Bucky. The big horse had spent the hours trying to reach sufficient grass and he needed water now, too. The area where Bucky spent the night was trampled and bare. Jake realized he'd completely forgotten his horse while holding Hettie.

He led the horse to where she waited. "We'll have to double up. I hope Bucky won't mind it. Never tried it before or had a woman to do it with."

His double meaning was not lost on Hettie and she flushed red hearing it.

He mounted and helped Hettie get up behind him. Bucky bunched up under the saddle, disliking the extra body astride him. His instinct was to dislodge the extra weight but a few words from Jake settled him and they started for the ranch. She clung to him with her arms around his body. She didn't really need to hang so close to him since they moved at a leisurely walk. Jake grinned to himself, knowing her need was as great as his in wanting to be close and feel the touch of the other.

"What are you planning to do next, then?" she asked.

"I figure to go to Prescott and find Handy. He's got a lot of the answers I'm lookin' for. If Miguel is still alive after being in the same cell as that mean, bastard Russian, maybe he'll be ready to help me out. He gave me the idea he knows the answers to everything."

"I wonder who might have put those shells under my bed. I found another one there, myself." She hated to bring the shells up to him, but it lay between them and they had to discuss it.

"You never told me that. Keepin' secrets yourself, are you?"

"No more than you, Jake. You have a past you never speak of. Whatever it is, it's so painful, it haunts you every day of your life, yet you don't trust me enough to tell me about it." She was very tired and laid her head against his back as they moved along.

Hettie was the first person he'd ever considered telling his personal sorrows to, but not yet. Instead of answering her question, he stroked her arms. "If you keep makin' up to me like this I'll have to do somethin' about it, missy." He felt his passion burning with the way she kept her body close against him. He wanted to dismount, pull her off that damned horse, and do all kinds of things to her wonderful body. It burned on his mind and reached the point he could barely sit his horse.

"You can just forget that stuff, mister. I've gotten more involved with you already than I should have. I pray to God you haven't gotten me in a fix I can't get out of."

She hadn't given much thought to what may have already happened, but she considered it now and felt overwhelming regret and worry at what she'd done. Having a child with Jake had become a very real possibility. She hadn't conceived during her marriage to Del and, over the past few years, had convinced herself she couldn't, but maybe…

"Hettie, if something like that happened, I'd be the happiest man on this whole damned earth," he said, squeezing her arms tight against his chest.

"Don't talk that way! I'm fine as far as I know." Alarmed, she drew away from touching him, balancing her tired body behind his saddle. Already, she missed the warmth, feel, and smell of his shirt, jacket, and the good way his arms felt holding her. She was exhausted and had no one to lean on now.

"Looks like we're almost there, Hettie."

Looking around his broad shoulders, she saw the familiar ranch house sitting right in front of her and had to fight back tears. It was midday and the gnawing hunger in her gut had become acute and demanding. She needed a cup of coffee in the worst way.

When they neared the corrals and watering trough, she said, "Let me down, Jake."

He reached an arm around to help her slide off Bucky's side to the ground. Her feet stung from being up so long, but she walked it off quick enough and looked at the empty corral.

"I wonder if Diablo is still alive." Her voice came wistful, and she wondered if she'd ever see the horse again. She heard the bunk house door open and her hands, Windy and Larry, rushed out to meet them.

"Glad to see you've made it back, ma'am," Windy said. And right behind him, Larry nodded in agreement.

"I lost Bessie. Got her leg broken in a rock slide." The tears came and she turned away to the house.

The men watched her go. Jake stood there knowing Hettie had reached her lowest point. His arms ached to hold and comfort her, but she'd have none of it right now.

"Looks like she's about worn out," Larry said. "Must be tough on a woman, being caught out like that." He went to a corral and caught up a horse for himself. "I'm headin' over to the east ranges today, Windy. They's been some coyote activity agin' after the young stuff."

"Why shore, pard, catch up with you later." Larry turned to Jake, gestured at the ranch house and Hettie. "She all right?"

"She will be." Jake led his buckskin away and unsaddled him. After watering Bucky, he turned him into a corral and took the time to toss several armloads of hay in after him before heading to the house. "Wonder if she'll let me in?"

He knocked and waited. Hettie came to the door and opened it. "Yes?" She stood there, her face expressionless, her eyes dull.

"I'd like to come in for a while, if you don't mind." He had his hat in his hand while he waited. He worried about her, so pale and distraught.

"Why? Need to look under my bed for more evidence?" He couldn't miss the fear in her voice and hated it, yet he wanted to laugh at her accusations.

"Hettie, why not try to see my side of it?" He stepped inside and she didn't stop him, not yet. He went close to take her in his arms.

"Don't you touch me. I know your tricks!" She turned away from him, went into the big room, and sat down solidly in a chair. "What're you doing in here, Jake?"

"Tryin' to help you, Hettie. You've got things all wrong, somehow."

"Have I? I saw that look on your face and I'll never forget it. Not a word of explanation from you, so I'd know what'd happened. Never bothered to ask a question I could answer or maybe explain." She glared at him. "You found it easy enough to believe the worst of me, didn't you?"

"You know I looked all over when I was around the murder scene for evidence. I couldn't believe I'd find it under your bed that way. I admit it set me off on the wrong trail for a bit. But in thinkin' it over, I knew you couldn't have done a thing like killin' Elmer. Not the gentle way you are." He wondered if she heard him, she looked so frozen sitting there with her arms tight against across her chest.

"I'm hungry and makin' supper. You're welcome to stay and eat if you've a mind to." She got up, went into the kitchen, and started putting kindling in the stove. "But don't get the idea you'll be sleeping in this house tonight, because, mister, you won't!" She flung the words at him as she went into her pantry to pull out the makings of a meal.

Jake sat in the big room, gazing around at all the gentle, feminine touches of a woman's home. Lace on the back of a chair he knew she used frequently; flowers in a vase, all dried up, yet attractively arraigned with twisted red Manzanita to add color and effect; a colorful dyed rug before the fireplace; and everything neat and kept up. But it was the old guitar hanging lopsided by the cords that struck him deepest of all. The mere sight of it brought back way too much. He swallowed the huge lump in his throat and fought back the tears.

He left the big room. He'd missed all those familiar things through the years, and Hettie's home brought them back to his mind, along with other memories he'd tried to forget.

CHAPTER 21

He went into the kitchen to watch her work. Maybe he'd tell her the things of his past, but he couldn't figure how to begin. He loved this woman, he wanted her, and again, some small, misplaced thought and expression had taken it away. He hurt inside from the pain of it.

"Hettie," he began. "You said I had secrets from the past, and I do. You're the only person to ever make me feel able to speak of it. I guess you have the right to know everything there is to know about me."

"You don't need to tell me anything if you think it's because we have a future together. After all this, I don't see how that can happen." Her chin was set so firm, he feared for her teeth.

"There is no 'all this,' girl. If you think that, it's all in your head. I'm innocent of all charges that way." He stood his ground, his arms crossed over his chest. He was starving, same as her, and hoped she wouldn't run him off before he got something to eat. She looked wonderful, all huffy and working in her kitchen. He had to ask, "Whose guitar is that?"

"It was Del's if you must know." She turned away from him and he saw her wipe a tear away. "Don't try to get me off track, Jake. You're making me crazy with what you say. I want to know how my horse is, too, if he's alive or if the cougars have gotten to him." She slapped a hunk of meat into a heated frying pan, grabbed a bowl, and started mixing flour, lard, and things for biscuits. She busied herself trying to shut him, and that lanky body lounging around in her kitchen, out of her sight.

Jake didn't plan on being shut out of Hettie's life. Always charmed by the sight of her, the sound of her voice, and how her body felt, he wanted this woman for the rest of his life. "We'll go out and see him in the mornin' if you like. It'd take two days each way, though," he said to let her know she'd be in close company with him all that time.

"Can't you just tell me where he is?" She didn't look at him while she rolled out the biscuit dough, used a water glass to cut them into rounds and fit them into a baking tin. She shoved them into the oven and the heat of it flushed her face to a rosy glow as she turned to face him. "Where *is* my horse, then?"

"He's two days out and I'll have a hell of a time finding him myself. I can't say exactly where he is, Hettie." He met her eyes and tried to smile. "It's a small box canyon some-where to the south of here. Don't worry so much. He's got wa-ter and grass enough for a while, and he needs time enough to grow out that hoof." He hesitated then added, "Hettie, he can't make it back here until it grows out a bit."

She shook her head at him and clucked her tongue in frus-tration as she set the table with two places. He felt relief that she wasn't planning to chuck him out before she fed him.

After a bit, she nodded toward the table. "Come and eat, then."

They sat across from each other. He got up to pour the coffee. She handed out the biscuits, meat, gravy, and fried potatoes. There were no greens, she hadn't had time to get any, but what she'd made was tasty and he ate with relish. She did the same. She hadn't had anything for nearly two days and he was almost as hungry.

"This is sure good chuck, Hettie."

She kept her eyes on her plate. "Thanks."

"If you'd wait a bit on goin' for Diablo, I need to ride back to Flagstaff and on to Prescott to find Handy Bates. He knows what went on around here and so does Miguel. He might be willing to talk when I get back to town." He tilted his head down a bit, trying to catch her eyes. "We could go after that. His hoof was pretty banged up. Might have grown out enough so he could make it back here by then."

"How long are you speaking of?"

"A week for sure. I don't know exactly where I'll find the man, when I get there." He held his breath and waited for her answer.

"I really don't have a choice, do I?"

"Sorry, Hettie, but I have to clear up Elmer's murder. You must understand that. Of all people, I'd think you'd be glad of it. Handy's the one who tried to set the law on you. I didn't know you at the time. I found it hard enough to believe even then, and now I know you better, I know you'd not be capable of killin' a man."

"Then you wouldn't want to know what I'm thinking right now, would you, Mr. Jake La Force." She got up and left the table. He was right behind her and caught her hand.

"Hettie, you can't go on hating me like this. I can't handle that! You know how I feel about you, and you can sure guess how I'm feelin' right about now."

He grabbed her into his arms, but she held herself stiff and unyielding, her lips firmly together. He kissed her gently, one hand caressing her back, the other in her hair, and his lips were ever so soft against hers. He felt her softening, moving slowly closer to his body. He kept on until she melted into him.

"Oh, Hettie, darling, I love you more than my life!" he cried into her hair and kissed her ever deeper.

She let him move her into the bedroom and onto her bed. "Jake, I haven't had a bath for two days!" She drew away from him. "There's no way you're sleeping in my bed like you are, nor me, either." She wanted him, but her fastidious nature wouldn't allow it in their travel-worn state. She felt utterly confused and angry with herself. "I can't believe I'm thinking about it. What are you doing to me?"

"It's just that we belong together, and you know it." He stepped toward her. "If we're both so dirty, why not us have a bath together, then?" He grew wild at the thought of seeing her that way.

"Jake, such an idea!" Her face flamed bright as she gave thought to it, but finally, she said with a sly smile, "You'd better go out and do the best you can at the horse trough, and I'll manage in here alone."

She meant what she said, and the realization he'd spend another night with her in that nice soft bed made him accede to her wishes. He headed for the horse trough.

Hettie cursed herself for being a damned fool and took enough water from the reservoir of the cook stove to give herself a decent bath. Her hair would have to wait for another day. She gave thought to locking Jake out of her house, but he'd set such a fire inside her body, she was mighty glad her door had no lock.

He returned and went right to her, taking her into his arms. They both nearly cried with happiness at being together again. His hair was wet and cold, but she never felt it against her flaming body as he took her to the bed and began moving his hands and lips over her.

"Hettie, my wife, I love you now and will for as long as we live." He moved over her and joined their bodies together in a passion deepened further by their fatigue and near exhaustion.

❦❧❦

After a lengthy breakfast with Hettie, Jake saddled his buckskin and headed for Flagstaff. As he rode, he went over the way he'd left things. They'd formed a thin sort of truce between them, but she'd let him know she still didn't trust him.

"As much as I love you, Jake, until this is straightened out, I'll never be able to trust you." His heart ached at the tears in her eyes. "Sorry, I can't change how I feel," she continued. "Even after the way it was between us last night, and I wouldn't have changed one moment of that for all the worries I have with you. You say I'm in your blood, well, I'd have to say you're in mine just as much."

Her soft, flushed face still bore the traces of her passion. Jake resolved to get things squared away regarding the killing of Elmer Greenup, and the sooner the better.

Hettie wasn't a woman to put up with this uncertainty much longer. She doubted him and would until the case was solved. Those thoughts lay heavy on his mind and he saw no mountains, pink-flushed morning sky, or long purple morning shadows across the faraway peaks—nothing but the trail he rode, deep in thought.

CHAPTER 22

His first step was a talk with Miguel, if he was ready for it. When Jake reached Flagstaff, he stopped at the jail and went in. Lin, his face tense and nervous, jumped up from behind his desk, as he came through the door.

"God, Jake, where'n hell you been? The place is comin' down around my ears." He chuckled a bit. "That damned Russian is about to kill that Mex back there and the rest of the prisoners are going loco!"

"Sounds quiet enough in here to me. Better go see him, then." Jake headed down to see Miguel and as he neared the cell, the huge black haired man rushed the bars. "I keel heem!" His eyes wild, he shook the bars, making the surrounding structure rattle once again. But in surprise, Jake saw an unreasoning fear in the huge man's eyes along with the rage.

"Maldonado, what'd you do to that man?" Jake hid his feelings of mirth and surprise, though his curiosity ran rampant as he saw how thin and sick Miguel appeared.

"You like *hablar, señor*? You know the way to hell? You go there!" He spat the words.

Jake believed Miguel was ready to talk, but his pride, and hatred wouldn't allow it, not yet. He chuckled. "Well Miguel, as you like. Check you later, *mi amigo*." He returned to the desk. "I'm plumb worn out and starvin', Lin. I'll be goin' to my quarters." He left, walked his horse down to the stables and left him in the man's capable hands. Hearing the welcoming whinnying from the other horses stabled there, he chuckled. "My horse's got more friends than I do."

He walked back and went into his small, spare quarters. His three rooms included a small cooking area, a bedroom, and sitting area. It was all he needed and it suited him. He washed up and changed clothes.

Later, when he went to the hotel for dinner, he found Nellis looking pale and agitated. "How's your daughter makin' out?" Jake asked the man.

"She'll never be the same, Jake." His worries were essentially the same as before. "That monster took the life right out of her. Won't come out of her room, and we can't get her out of the house. When is that bastard going to trial?"

The man looked worn with worry and Jake felt pity for him. They'd spoiled their girl. Maybe being an only child, it'd been easy enough to do. He went into the dining room, took a table, and ordered.

After he'd eaten, he went back to the office and found Mel holding down the place. Worry creased his thin face. "You know, that damned Russian's gonna kill the Mex."

"Hell, he will. I saw fear in the Russian's eyes. Miguel's got him scared out of his mind. The only thing that'll help us might be the sounds and smells from the man. If that won't do it, nothing will." Jake laughed, enjoying a light moment as he hadn't had many of them lately.

After talking with his deputy and checking into the progress of other cases, Jake had a feeling. "I'm goin' down to his cell again, back in a minute." He grabbed the keys.

Lin leaped to his feet. "I'll back you." He walked down with Jake. "If that door's open, you can't turn your back on that damned Russian."

Jake approached Miguel's cell and knew immediately something had changed. The young man came close. "Señor, I weel speak with you, when you like."

Amazed at this sudden change, Jake took quick advantage of it. He slid open the door and Miguel made his way to it.

"*Por dios, muchas gracis, señor,*" he said. To the big Russian, he sent a flaming glance and snarled low, tone threatening, his eyebrows raised over an evil, leering smile. "I do something," he muttered to the huge man.

Jake saw that the Russian looked relieved. He might be losing his entertainment, but it was something more.

"I keel heem. He take my vife!" The Russian roared the words as his voice reached a fevered pitch of worry. His face had turned pale, and Jake realized the big man quailed in fear of the young Mexican.

He led Miguel to another empty cell and went in with him. "This'll do for you." They sat on the bunk and Jake narrowed his eyes, finding it difficult to believe how easily the Mex had put the fear of God into the Russian.

Miguel shrugged and grinned slightly in huge enjoyment. For some reason he was ready to spill his story and got right at it. "*Señor,* I see Handy kill *el hombre, viejo.* For Handy steal cattle from *la señora.* I see him do this, but he help me and I help him." He shrugged and heaved a sigh of obvious relief not to share the befouled space with the brute any longer.

"Will you tell that in court?"

His dark eyes held a sly glitter. "I will if you help me."

"Only with the hoss thievin' part." But Jake added, "*Gracias,* Miguel." He left the cell, locked it, and went up front.

"Well Lin, things are quiet enough around here, I've got to go to the Prescott area tomorrow. That's where I'll find the answers to the Elmer Greenup murder." He was tired. He'd not had a lot of sleep for two days, but a smile spread over his face remembering the last night spent with Hettie.

"What the hell's goin' on with you, these days, Jake?" Lin had a quizzical look on his face. "What're you up to, anyway?"

"I just might get married, Lin. Once I get shut of this case." He paused then added, "Well of course, we've got the rape case, too."

"Not the old bachelor you've always been?" Lin frowned. "You're talking of Hettie Jamison, aren't you? Been out there enough times, so I noticed." Lin took on a serious look. "You know, that Annabelle's been spreadin' it around town as how the whole rape thing is that Jamison woman's doin'. She's tellin some of her friends that's where she met Miguel and some of the townspeople are listenin' to her wild ravin's."

"Her pa told me she wasn't seein' anyone to spread stuff like that around. The girl's off in the head, Lin." He shoved his hat back on his head. "She may refuse to testify at Miguel's trial, the way she was ravin' on, when I saw her." He sighed. "I won't pay her gossip any mind. The fool girl's been after me and set her traps a few times." He shook his head in disgust at the stupidity of a spoiled young girl. "I never gave that fool girl any reason to think I'd be lookin' at her."

"Her daddy listens to her, Jake."

"I saw the other side of that business, too, Len. He knows damned well what she's been up to. And I don't give a damn in hell about her talk, anyway. I got work to do gettin' this murder case put away."

Jake left the office, visited the stable, gave orders for extra hay and grain for Bucky, and ordered another horse to use for his trip. Then he went to his very modest quarters and went to bed. It was early, and he hadn't had supper, but he wanted time to sort things out. The dining room held no interest for him, and he didn't want to talk to anyone right now. Going to the Prescott area was painful for him in more ways that anyone ever knew.

ཙ◦ཙ◦

He left at dawn after taking a quick breakfast at Ma James and had a lunch made up to eat along the trail. He'd find Handy around Prescott somewhere and had to make the trip. He rode the other horse. Bucky needed a rest after his grueling trip through the rocks and narrow passes on Hettie's ranch. He missed his own horse, but this big bay-spotted pinto, Hytone, was a decent ride for a long trip. It'd take two days to get to Prescott and, as he set out, his mood was grim.

He rode for nearly two days without much sleep, but before he neared the Prescott area, he turned the big pinto onto a washed-out, faded trail leading off to the west. He followed it, knowing what he'd find. The end of this trail was always the same. It'd been a long time, but it was there and it drew him if he came anywhere near.

After another two hours, he came to a small ranch house, long abandoned. The gaping, ghostlike windows and a door held by one rusted hinge spoke of a life once lived here, but long since forsaken. No livestock graced the environs or any other living thing aside from gophers, mice, and flitting birds. He rode up to the house and dismounted.

Inside, he stepped carefully over the warped and sagging floor as he walked about the empty rooms. In one of them, he caught sight of a small rag doll, worn and faded, the face, partially eaten by insects or worms—he didn't know which. He wiped a tear away at the sight and went out back where he made his way to a small knoll. He came to a halt before three solitary graves.

The markers were bent and the wording was dim, but Jake knew well enough who lay there. He stood for a long time, looking at the larger grave of a woman. Martha La Force, the date of her death, 1883. The two smaller ones were unreadable, but he knew those dates well enough, too. Here lay all he'd held dear in the past, along with a deep pain and loss he'd tried to forget and never could. After muttering a few soft words of a prayer heard only by God, he turned away.

❧❧❧

About sunset, Jake rode into the small town of Prescott situated beneath a great outcropping of rock called Thumb Butte. It made a nice landmark to welcome weary travelers and he already had his eye on a small hotel he'd noticed. After seeing to his horse, he planned to head for it, take a bath, eat a good meal, and hit the hay.

Hettie had described Handy's horse for him. He kept his eye out for a dark blue roan with a good-sized notch in his left ear, and while at the stable he checked over the horses in the stalls and corrals. He didn't see a horse like the one she'd mentioned.

He went to the hotel, took lodging, and later, sat down for a meal. His dinner came and it looked decent enough. Ravenous after his long ride, it made him think of Hettie's fine cooking. He ate and did some looking around then went to find the local sheriff's office before turning in.

He passed several saloons laid out in a row along one street. Loud music and laughter flowed out into the streets, making him remember this was Prescott's famous or infamous street, called Whisky Row. He noticed it had nearly doubled in the number of bars and flophouses.

He looked over most of the horses tied out front but didn't catch sight of the blue roan. Passing one of the saloons, he heard a loud argument going on inside. Just now he needed the sound of human voices, whether they'd be soft or loud and raucous, and decided to enter. He took a seat in the corner, ordered a whiskey, and kept his hat on, pulled down.

A fist fight broke out, and in time, the sheriff or one of his deputies came in and put a stop to the outburst. The man didn't arrest anyone and after things died down he came to a table nearby, sat down, and tipped his hat to Jake, saying, "How do?"

"Howdy yourself, Sheriff. Glad to know you." Jake moved his chair closer. "I'm Sheriff La Force from up Flagstaff way, down here huntin' a man wanted for a murder."

"Don't say. Lookin' for him around here, are you?" He introduced himself. "I'm Harvey Butler."

"Yes," Jake went on. He described Handy Childs. "Wonder if you might've seen a man like that." He saw the sheriff's brow furrow, his eyes change and narrow in thought. The end of his hunt lay in the sheriff's eyes.

"Just might have," he said. "A man like that was here a while back, flashin' a wad of money around. Never said how he come by it." He frowned. "We got some real good poker gents working the players here on our Whiskey Row—well, maybe a little too good, and the man didn't hold out for too long against 'em." He thought a minute before continuing. "Ain't seen him around for a few days, but I'll ask around. Might find a few hombres who'd know or remember him."

"Thanks, Sheriff Butler. I'll just be right at the hotel there." He gestured down the street from the direction he'd come. "You might forget to say who's lookin' for him, and if you see him, I'll do the arrestin'."

"Sure thing, La Force. You'll be at the Pioneer, then?"

When Jake nodded, Butler got up and left the saloon. Jake wasn't far behind.

He entered the hotel. Dog tired after a long two days in the saddle, he mounted the narrow steps to his room and closed the door. The place wasn't much, but the bed looked mighty good. Still tired from his jaunt with Hettie, he needed sleep, but worn though he was, that compelling woman was never far from his mind.

Deep down, he wondered if he tempted fate by taking a wife again, but knew he'd jump at the chance. He'd fallen in love with Hettie and didn't want to face the rest of his life without her. He'd already lost too much of it to loneliness.

He lay on his bed, thinking of being with her, knowing he was guilty of inventing damned thin reasons to find ways to see her. In fact, he barely tolerated his time away from her. And after their jaunt when she'd tried to find the horse, they still had a long way to go to get things sorted out between them. "You're a damned lovesick, boob, Jake!" he told himself.

He didn't know why he felt so strongly about her and imagined a magical thing like that could just happen between a man and a woman. With Hettie he'd found a love filled with a kind of lightning and passion he'd only guessed at.

With his Martha, they'd grown up together and getting married was a natural thing for them. But with Hettie, this wild craving and burning had come out of nowhere and hit him square between the eyes. Different and exciting, these feelings had taken them both by storm. He believed it was the same for Hettie.

After he'd gotten things smoothed over pretty well from their earlier misunderstandings about Elmer's murder, he'd found those damned rifle casings and things had gone south again. If she'd allow it, he planned to marry her and take his chances. Hettie had already given him more happiness than he'd known in the past ten years. He hit his pillow, longing for sleep.

CHAPTER 23

Sitting in a saloon, near the end of Whiskey Row, Handy sipped his drink. Nearly down on his luck, he'd lost the pile of cash he'd gotten for the cattle he'd rustled off Hettie's ranch.

"I can't go back there to get more," he grumbled into his glass. "I got to get shut of this gamblin'. I had me a nice grub-stake, coulda gone to San Francisco or someplace like that."

Disgusted with himself, and angry at how things had turned out, he cursed, bemoaning his rotten luck. "Damned Miguel had to go and savage that girl an' throw our plans into a damned sink-hole after I had everythin' all worked out. Mrs. Jamison woulda been sent up for murder and I'd be the one left to run the place and have free rein over all the damned live-stock." He shook his head. "That was a sweet deal we had set up."

Tossing off his drink, he wandered back up the street looking for a game without some slick, card playin' devil, like that one at the Sourdough. "That cheatin' bastard liked to rob me blind, but that fancy little two-barrel Derringer he carries has done away with too many losers like me already." Handy didn't have the guts to brace the man. "I had to walk away and leave my pile a layin' right there in front of God and ev-er'body."

His rotten run of luck had him burning inside as he walked. Along the boardwalk, he noticed a small saloon, the Greenhorn, and went in.

Sometime later, Sheriff Butler, wandering past the place, caught a glimpse of a heavyset gent well into a poker game and recognized Handy. The man from Flagstaff would want to know, so Butler hurried across the street and into the hotel.

Jake was roused from a heavy sleep at the knock on his door. He climbed out of bed and opened it to see the sheriff standing there.

"Found yer man."

Butler was man of few words, but what he did say had just made Jake's trip that much shorter.

"I'll be right along, hang on a bit." Jake pulled on pants, shirt, and boots, stuck his hat on his sleep-tousled hair, and strapped on his gun belt. Following Butler down the stairs, he was elated at the thought that he'd get this business over and done with. Getting back to Hettie, and that two day ride out and back to find her black horse, held a world of fine possibilities, and Jake was more than ready to take that trip.

They located the Greenhorn Saloon and walked in. Handy sat at a card game. He had a sizable pile of chips in front of him.

"Some places are usin' chips. Keeps the money off the table," Butler informed Jake. "Just started that recently. Don't stop fights or shootin's though."

Jake walked over to Handy and tapped him on the shoulder. The man looked up to see who stood there and, at the moment of recognition, his face went white as a sheet.

"Howdy there, Handy. I'd like a word with you." Jake nodded toward the open door. "Outside, if you please."

"Aw hell now, Jake. How's about I get this here hand played out?" His voice had a begging tone. This'd be his last winning hand outside of hell, and both men knew it.

Jake nodded in assent. "All right, get it done then." He stepped back and waited.

The hand ended quickly when one of the other players slapped down four kings. "Reckon you cain't get around these." He waited, giving Handy a smug look, his chin out and a victorious smirk across his face.

Handy laid down four aces. "Reckon I can, Newt. How's that?" His grin spread the width of his face. In his rapture over a winning hand, he forgot Jake for the moment. This had to be the best hand he'd ever held in recent memory. But his elation rapidly plummeted to a new low as the realization set in. He was up for hanging and already knew it'd be his last good hand.

The loser, Newt, cursing softly, gritted his teeth, and shoved his pile of chips toward Handy. Handy eagerly scooped his winnings into his hat. To Jake, he said, "Thanks, 'preciate it, man." He cashed in his pile to the barkeep in charge and faced Jake. "You had something' you wanted to say to me?"

"Right, Handy, we can do this outside if you like." After the men reached the boardwalk, Jake said, "Miguel told me what happened with Elmer Greenup out at the Lazy J, and I'm arresting you for the old man's murder. Sheriff Butler here will keep you overnight in his jail, and we'll be startin' back to Flagstaff in the mornin'."

"He's a damned liar, Jake. Ever'body knows that!" Handy flushed red in the face, but his shoulders slumped in defeat. Jake, on watch for signs of a fight, saw none, as Handy ranted on. "That damned Mexican just come here to fetch that black horse away from Hettie. Said it belonged to him if his brother was dead. Heard the brother was shot to death on the Bender Place over a year ago and Miguel just got word of it a while back."

His voice had taken on a whine and that didn't set well with Jake. "So why'd you want to throw the blame off on Mrs. Jamison?" he asked as they neared the Prescott Jail.

"'Cause she's the one who done it, just like I said. She was gonna fire the old codger. He told me that." Handy was adamant on that subject.

"You're askin' me to believe that, after you said Miguel was at the ranch all night when you knew damned well he was in Flagstaff savaging that young girl?" Jake demanded, feeling himself getting riled. "My God, man! He had the bloody evidence all over his clothes and now he's admitted he did it." Miguel hadn't actually admitted his guilt in the rape, but it didn't matter to Jake. "How come you lied for him like that?"

Handy muttered something inaudible as they entered the jail. Jake followed as Butler led Handy to an empty cell, put him in, slid the iron barred door shut, and locked it. The heavy metallic click and finality of the lock made Handy shudder and grasp the thick steel bars. He went quiet and pale. The reality of his situation had apparently set in.

The rotund man slumped down onto the narrow bunk. "I was afraid of that hombre, Jake! You don't know the things that man has done, an' he told me a hell of a lot. He speaks better English than any of you know, said his brother sent him money for schoolin' down in Mexico."

"So you say, Handy." Jake looked at the heavy set man, not only down on his luck, but out of it, too. "I'll be back to pick you up in the morning. Got a horse around here?"

"Naw, gambled the nag away. I'm afoot, Sheriff." Suddenly having something to hold over Jake, he managed a smug look. "If you want me in Flagstaff, looks like you'll have to fix me up with a ride."

"Maybe you can get yourself a new one with that nice pot you just won. You'll need one unless you fancy walkin' all the way back to Flag." Jake left Handy sputtering and walked away.

Before he left the jail, he met with Butler. "Much obliged for the use of your cell back there."

As he returned to the hotel, a man came sidling up to him. "You the feller arresting ol' Handy, there?"

Jake was dog tired and didn't have time to talk. "What's on your mind?"

"He sold me some cattle. I knowed they wasn't his. Well, I didn't when I took 'em, but when I saw the brand, I knew they wasn't from 'round here any place."

From the self-important way his chest puffed out, Jake knew him for a weasel, but he had to pay him some mind. He might need the man's testimony later on. "Will you testify in court about it?"

Hearing that, the man's face turned pale. He backed off. "No sir, won't I be as guilty as old Handy, then?"

"Maybe so, if you're just now tellin' the law." Jake saw the man waver, then turn away, and hurry down the street.

"I'll come back later, Sheriff. I will!" He tossed the words over his shoulder as he skedaddled away. His gate resembled a crab scuttling away through the rocks on the bottom of a creek.

"Why'n hell did the man bother me with it, then?" Jake muttered. Then he chuckled. "If I need this man's testimony, I'll find him." This day's work done, Jake went to bed and slept soundly.

ℰↃℰↃ

In the morning, Jake took breakfast at the hotel and ordered a good lunch packed before heading for the jail. Butler had Handy in cuffs and ready to ride.

"You got a horse in mind?" Jake asked.

"No I ain't." He was staunch in his refusal to spend his money on a new animal. "You want me in Flag, you get me there."

Jake didn't miss the small bit of victory gleaming in the man's eyes. He also saw a twinkle in Butler's eye. "We got one you can borrow and no hurry gettin' the nag back, either," the sheriff said and sent his deputy running to the stables.

He came back in a short while with a bony nag, sporting a worn out rig. The horse had to be near twenty years old by the looks of him.

"Ain't much is he?" Handy muttered.

"You're up for murder, man, no need to spend your time worryin' over a horse. Ridin' into Flag on a fancy horse won't be any help to you." Jake helped Handy get aboard. They had a long two-day ride ahead.

After a short few miles on the rough-gated nag, Handy began whining. "This damned horse's got a short step and a gait like a box of rocks. He'll like to kill me before we hit town."

Jake was sick of listening to the man's complaining. "You're ridin' him for two days, so shut the hell up and get along with you."

They headed north. It was a decent day, with only a few clouds, and looking far ahead, the long, thin blue line of the far mountains beckoned with their cool, tree-covered heights. Jake smiled. Hettie was up there somewhere, too.

The ride was long and they only stopped long enough to eat the packed lunch. Jake was in a hurry to get home.

Handy's backside was in pain by the time they stopped for a night's rest in a small swale with a sluggish stream running through it. He moaned and complained, but Jake took little notice of it.

He took care of the horses and shot a rabbit to roast over the coals of their campfire. Handy had quieted but remained sullen and whiny. Jake really didn't give a damn.

They slept on the ground with only saddle blankets for comfort. Handy was handcuffed with his feet tied to a tree. The rope lay over Jakes legs. If it moved, he would know.

CHAPTER 24

The next morning saw them on their way without much of a breakfast. They finished off what was left of the plentiful lunch of yesterday, and Handy whined for something more to eat. "You tryin' to starve me to death on this ride?"

"Not a bad idea, Handy, and it won't kill you, so quit your whining. You've got enough damned fat on you to last clear to San Francisco."

Later in the day, they made the climb into the high Ponderosa forests surrounding Flagstaff. Jake took Handy straight to the jail. Lin, holding down the front office, sprang up to meet them.

"I see you found your man." He took in the bedraggled looking Handy, trail worn and saddle sore to boot. Jake didn't look too happy, either. "How was your trip?"

Handy opened his mouth to whine, but Jake cut him off. "It was just fine. Give this man a cell and get him some supper." His answer was terse and short enough to let Lin know he'd had a rough trip and enough of his big-bellied prisoner as well.

"Right away, Jake." The deputy grabbed Handy by the arm and dragged him down the row of cells until he found an empty one. "Here you are for now. Supper'll be along soon's I can get someone to go for it."

"I'm near starved to death and ain't had a drink of nothin' for a month of Sundays. This ain't no way to treat a man." Handy's whine set off the rest of the men in there, including the Russian. He heard a deep-throated rumble that passed for a laugh.

"Dey keel you in ziz place, har har!" The huge man rattled his bars hard and they felt small tremors of the building, again. The other prisoners had comments and grunts, too, but Miguel sat quietly alone in his cell. It adjoined the one chosen for Handy and Lin saw a look pass between them.

"Oh God, this place is hell," Handy whined.

Lin left him and walked back to Jake. "He's in."

"Anything happen while I was gone?" He was tired and didn't want to hear any more bad news.

"Well, I hear Annabelle has left town, either that or disappeared." Lin told him. "Her folks haven't come in to tell us anything. I just happened to hear she was gone. The talk is, she was complaining she couldn't hold up her head around here. 'Spose she's run off somewheres, maybe?"

Jake grunted in reply. "Who knows about that dizzyheaded female an' if I never lay eyes on her again, it'll suit me fine." He hesitated a moment. "I need to go back to the Lazy J, Lin. We had to leave a very fine horse way out. Damaged his hoof. He threw a shoe and that Mex kept right on ridin' him up in those rocks until his foot ran blood. I had to leave him in a canyon out there."

But thoughts of riding out with Hettie lay uppermost in his mind. Being with her held his interest far more than the horse, fine animal though he was.

He walked down to Miguel's cell and spoke to him. "I'll be goin' out to find that horse in the next few days." For some reason, he respected the feeling the Mex had for his dead brother's fine stallion. "He's had nearly two weeks to grow out his hoof."

"*Gracias, señor.*" It was his only answer, but the timber of his voice spoke volumes. No matter what a devilish killing machine his brother, Matìn, had been, Miguel, had loved him.

The next morning, Jake set out for Hettie's, his heart singing in his chest. "I'm a damned lovesick fool." He sang the words out into the air. The sky was clear, birds wheeled gracefully about, darting here and there, and there was no one to hear his plaintive cry.

Arriving in the early afternoon, the sight of the familiar ranch yard warmed him all the way through. He looked about for the woman he loved but saw no one. He got off, watered his horse, ground hitched him, and headed for the door.

Hettie came around the side of the house with baskets full of greens and freshly dug potatoes. Seeing him, she stopped in her tracks, a look of alarm over her face. "What now?"

Relief and joy swept over him at the sight of her. "Nothing new, just thought we might go find that black horse of yours."

He smiled, hoping to disarm her suspicion of him. But it was alive and well, and he saw it in the darkening of her eyes and the stiffening of her stance. He had a long way to go with this woman, a lot to make up for, and he was ready to try.

"Oh. I wondered if you were out here with more of your idiotic made-up charges against me."

Her voice held the accusations, yet she laughed at what she'd said, and he felt better. Hettie could get so damned mad.

"There's some news. I've arrested Handy Bates for the murder of Elmer Greenup," he said and hoped hearing that news would settle her a bit.

"Handy? How do you know he's the one?" Her tone held her suspicions of him, but he saw the relief in her eyes.

"Miguel spilled the beans on him," he told her. "Do you know, in spite of the heavy charges against him, his worry is over that black horse. It had belonged to his brother, just as we figured." Jake began to relax as he told her his news. "Handy was behind your missing cattle and sold them in Prescott to pay for his gambling."

"And Handy tried to lay Elmer's death on me."

Jake nodded. "Miguel came here in the first place to get that black horse, and if he planned to kill anyone here, we don't know."

"Do you really believe his brother Matin is dead?" Hettie still worried about that.

"Sheriff in Prescott seems to think so. I didn't go to Parson's Grove where it happened."

Hettie sighed in relief. "I'll fix supper, but I've been thinking things over, and you'll be sleeping in the bunkhouse tonight. There's plenty of room out there these days. I've taken too many chances with you already." Her voice was firm and Jake went along with it. He looked forward to four days alone with her on the trail to find and bring Diablo home. He'd wait.

She kept her reserve during the supper meal, and he enjoyed freshly dug carrots, newly cut spinach, and potatoes, along with the fresh meat she'd fried. She had a knack with cooking, and the thought pleased him. "Nice meal, Hettie. You're a wonderful cook. It's a lucky man, gets to eat at your table."

"You can keep your sweet talk, Jake. I've heard it all before from the likes of you." She bustled around cleaning the table and heating water to do up the dishes. She stacked the dishes and wiped the table. He loitered about, looking for an opportunity to help, but more to feast his eyes on her.

"You won't need to help me with my work, Jake. It's woman's work. Isn't that what you men always say?" She kept her back to him while she worked. Her nicely rounded arms were deep in suds as she cleaned the dishes.

"We need to take something to wrap Diablo's foot with, for the trail back. His hoof's probably grown out some, but not enough to make it back here without more injury. Couldn't put a shoe on him this soon."

"We have some lanolin grease from sheep hides around here, out in the supply shed or where they do the horse shoeing." She paused a minute then added, "Maybe take some padding and some hide to bind up that hoof?" She turned around and faced him, her hands dripping with suds. "Instead of hanging around the house bothering me, you could be out looking for things to make a nice boot for him." Thoughtful for a moment, she said, "You could tie it on him, Jake, couldn't you?" Her mind saw him trying to work with a half-wild horse's hind leg. "Is it a hind foot?" He'd go flying from those hooves, and she laughed as she pictured it. "You could try."

Jake thought he'd never seen anything so wonderful as the picture she made, standing there, hair escaping from the ribbon that held it, dress wet in places, and those yellow cougar eyes snapping like golden fires. "Hettie, do you know how good you look right now?"

"No, I don't, and you *are* sleeping in the bunkhouse. You'd best get yourself out there right now." She barely held her glee at his disappointment. She had plenty to work out with him. The way those seeking blue eyes and big, lanky body made her feel, her arguments against him would disappear like smoke in the wind, and they'd never get things sorted out. She needed more time.

"All right. Good night, Hettie."

His eyes held a sparkle that warned her he wasn't going to be put off for long. Hat in hand, he left the house.

In the bunkhouse, he spent time with Larry and Windy. They easily sensed he was having difficulties with the boss. As they laughed and played cards, Windy finally said, "Jake, that Hettie's worth goin' through all the hell a woman can dish out."

Jake grinned and nodded agreement. "She sure as hell is."

They doused the lantern and went to sleep in their narrow bunks.

𝒆𝒔𝒆𝒔

Hettie finished her cleaning, pulled out clothing for the days she'd spend on the trail in Jake's company, and washed herself for bed. She looked forward to spending that time with him. She loved him but hated knowing he'd ever harbored a belief she could commit murder. He had that solved with Handy's arrest and was certain he'd killed Elmer.

Knowing that, she ought to be rid of the hunted feeling she had when Jake looked her way. So why wasn't she?

She went to sleep in her big, lonely bed, dreaming of a tall, lanky body that chased her slowly, constantly. Yet he never caught her. Salty tears soaked into her pillow as she moaned and twisted.

𝒆𝒔𝒆𝒔

They put everything together in the early morning and had a couple of large packs to tie on behind their saddles. Hettie rode Patches and Jake rode Bucky. The horse's shoes had been checked before they set out to make sure they didn't have another incident.

As they rode away, Hettie heard the boys talking. "Looks like a weddin' comin' this way, an' pretty damn soon. He's a good man, that Jake, and tough enough to handle her." Larry laughed. "If she don't run him off, afore they get things settled."

∽∾∽∾

Jake rode beside Hettie when he could, but the trail got rougher and narrower. Snakes, that often lay close in bushes and shrubs nestled against canyon walls, were hard to spot and quick to strike without the usual warning rattle.

"Watch those bushes for snakes," he warned.

"I've ridden through here before, Jake." She didn't need any instruction from the likes of him. Following him, she figured he'd best keep watch for snakes himself since he'd be the one to rouse them up.

Along about noon, he stopped where he'd been before. "Right here's a good place to eat a bite, if you're hungry." They dismounted near a tiny stream that still trickled from the spring run-off. Hettie went to it and knelt down for a drink. The snow fed water was cold as ice.

The picture of her kneeling there reminded Jake of the first time they'd ridden together when he'd come to see about Elmer's murder. He took in the sight of her at the water's edge, looking graceful as a young doe, taking sips of water from her cold-reddened hands. He ached to crush her in his arms, but for now, she'd never allow it. He'd wait, but she'd not get away from him for another night. A smile crossed his lips.

She set out the lunch for him. Cold meat sandwiches, biscuits with a small jar of honey, and an apple each.

He ventured a more personal comment. "Nice lunch there, girl."

She slapped his sandwich in front of him. "I'm not your girl, Jake."

"Aren't you?"

His words came so low and heavy with need and longing, she flushed to hear it. He looked at her, his eyes burning with desire. She knew he'd take her right now and knew full well he could, aside from her putting up a fight.

She didn't reply, just got up, re-wrapped the remainder of the lunch, and stowed it back on her horse. She knelt at the stream for another drink. Her hair came loose and hung in a shimmering curtain about her face.

"Do you know how you look right now?" he crooned to her.

"Just you never mind that sweet talk! We ought to get going. You know very well I'm worried about Diablo. He could be dead or starving out there while you're going on with your nonsense." She twisted her heavy, ropey, tresses into a knot and shoved them beneath her hat.

She had his heart racing like a trip hammer with her defiance, but he complied, and they got back on the trail to cover more of the rough, rocky ground heading into the Rincon Mountains which lay to the south. Miguel had done his best to cross them, trying to reach the Sonoran Desert that led into Mexico. Jake knew it was a lucky thing Diablo had thrown that shoe.

He had read somewhere that this was the only desert in the world with such varying and lovely kinds of growth. This ride could have been a wonderland in many ways if their cause was not so worrisome.

As it grew late, he drew to a halt where he'd spent the night previously. She saw the same pile of branches he'd cut to make a bed of sorts. Dried and leafless now, he broke them up and set up a campfire. When a few coals began to form, he dug out a small coffee pot from his pack, scooped water from the nearby stream, measured the coffee, and set a pot onto boil.

She watched his sure movements, his ease in any environment, and totally loved the way he looked—tall, lean, and wiry. Watching him, a heated glow of desire filled her, numbed her senses, and sent the familiar wild thrills coursing through her taut and tired body. She'd tried to fight how that man made her feel, but already without any overt movements toward her on his part, he'd sent her into a burning state of need.

Jake went on with his preparations for a camp-style meal. He walked off a ways and after a time, she heard the sharp staccato of a gunshot. He returned with the cleaned carcass of a sage hen. He cut green rods from one of the rangy bushes nearby, skewered the bird, and placed it over the glowing coals. He pulled out a sack and mixed flour, a bit of fat, and water from the creek. "I keep a mix like this for campin'. Works for me."

Breathless with wanting him and her growing need, she could only nod her head.

After a time, it grew to be pitch dark. The only light came from the glowing coals of the campfire. After tossing a few dried sticks on the coals, he set out the food on two battered tin plates and poured coffee into equally poor tin cups as the sticks flared up. She was starving and, in spite of her inner turmoil, ate with a hearty appetite.

Hettie sat immobile while Jake made short work of cleaning up. The sky was clear, and stars spread across the night sky as he led the horses to a better spot for grazing. When he had them hobbled for the night, he turned to spreading what few saddle blankets and bedding they had, making a small sleeping area. She noted he made one bed.

"I can't go another night without you, Hettie."

He went to her, pulled her to her feet, and led her to the bed he'd prepared. She made no protest as he took her into his arms.

"Oh, Jake, what am I to do with you?" she moaned as she melted against him.

She looked up at him, but he only saw the reflection of stars shining in her eyes.

He held her so close she could scarcely breathe and kissed her so deeply she nearly fainted.

He opened her blouse and began his search of her body. His hands moved over her breasts and on down over the rest of her. He never tired of how she felt. Yet, somehow each time was like the first. They sank together onto the blankets as he slowly removed the rest of her clothing. The air was cool and she shivered.

"We'll be warm enough," he murmured.

He kissed her until she became a mass of fire. When she began to moan aloud for him, he moved his long body over hers, went slowly into her, then held her still.

"Oh, lordy, girl, don't move just yet! I love you so damned much!"

Then together they began the eternal dance of love, until she screamed out his name and heard it echo against the canyon walls.

CHAPTER 25

After a breakfast, during which she barely looked at him, they set off again. He watched her, tried to figure out what she was thinking, and shook his head in utter frustration, guessing he never would. No further words were spoken until around noon when they'd neared the small canyon where he'd left the stallion.

Confused, he finally confronted her. "Hettie, what's got into your craw, anyway? How's a man supposed to know where the hell he's at when you treat him this way? What've I done that's got you in such a damned fix!" Angry in his desperation, he was sick of her nonsense.

She was near tears. "You know very well what you've done. A woman isn't safe when you're around. I can't fight a man like you!"

"Why'n hell would you want to *fight* me?" His voice rose. He shook his head in disbelief at the imaginings of a female. "Woman, this man standing right here loves you and wants to marry you. What do you mean, you can't fight me?"

She glared at him. "You know every way there is to get around me and get me to do what you want."

"You didn't want to make love with me, last night?"

She flushed but said nothing. He got off his horse and went to her, helped her off, and took her into his arms. "Is this what you mean?"

He kissed her lips and down into her blouse until she pressed her body against him and moaned aloud with her need of him.

She had tears in her eyes. "Yes—yes, I can't control myself around you."

He laughed and pulled her tightly into his arms again. "Hettie, don't you *ever* stop feelin' that way about me. Don't you know how *right* it is?" He didn't want to know, but he had to ask. "Wasn't it this way with Del when you two were married?"

"Not like it is with you," she admitted. "I've never known anything like the way it is when we're together." She studied him, trying to understand. "Is it supposed to be this way? Where your whole world spins around and you become so weak-willed you don't know how to stop what's happening?"

She relaxed in his arms and finally began to laugh. "I never knew of anything like this going on between a man and a woman, Jake, I never did."

"I didn't, either, Hettie, but I sure know it now. I'd say we were two very lucky people to have found feelin's so special. Maybe it's meant to be this way and makes some marriages a whole lot better than most." He held her out and they gazed into each other's eyes with a new realization.

"Oh, Jake, do you think so?"

When Bucky snorted and raised his head, Jake stiffened. "We're near your black horse. My horse smells him, or a cougar's prowled close, sniffing us out. Maybe we're found Diablo, Hettie, darlin'." He held her by the shoulders. "Stay here with the horses. I'll see if Diablo's right close. Might be, by the way Bucky's carrying on. Keep your gun handy and fire if you need me."

"You don't really think it's a cougar do you?" By now, she knew him well enough to know he couldn't resist trying to put a scare into her.

"I don't know, darlin'. I'll go look for your horse."

He walked away into the underbrush and Hettie waited, hoping to see her horse again. She treasured that beautiful creature.

Jake climbed over several rocky ridges until he heard the snort of a horse on alert. He worked his way down into a small canyon that looked familiar. After a bit, he spotted the shimmering black stallion. He faced Jake and pawed the ground with his good hoof. His magnificent head reared up in defiance. Jake saw that he used his injured foot with a heavy limp. He couldn't get near the snorting, defiant horse, but he figured Hettie could. He headed back the way he'd come.

Hettie heard him crashing through the underbrush and drew her pistol. She hoped it was Jake but stood ready if it wasn't. When he appeared, she heaved a sigh and holstered her gun. "Did you find him?" Relief flooded over her. By the smile on his face, she knew he had.

Jake approached her for a long, deep kiss. "We'd best go to where he is. I couldn't get near him but maybe you can. I'd hate to have to rope him." He grinned and grabbed her again for a great bear hug. "He looks great, Hettie."

Together, they worked to find a passable way to the horse, a better trail that Diablo could hobble out on. They spent several hours, careful to make the rocky ground as easy for the horse as possible. When they finally reached the small canyon, Diablo whistled to the other two horses and Hettie cried out in joy when she saw him.

"Thank God. He's still here, and oh, he looks fine, Jake." She slipped off Patches and walked toward her black horse. He snorted and reared. Jake stood ready to act, worried the stallion would trample her.

"Be careful, Hettie," he warned.

But she kept on until she came close. The horse nickered softly, limped to her, put his head against her chest, and stood there while she stroked him and talked to him in her soft voice.

She looked back at Jake. "Where are his things?"

"I'll find them." Relieved at the way she handled the stallion, he went to the small crevice he'd found in the canyon wall. "I know just how that horse feels when she touches him," he murmured, grinning. "Takes the fight right out of a man."

He tore away the brush and branches he'd used to hide the fine leather goods and pulled out the elaborate trappings. It hadn't been rained on, and he saw no damage. Brushing the worst of the dust and twigs off, he returned, loaded with the tack. He handed her the halter used beneath the bridle. "Diablo won't need the bridle on the return trip, and he'll carry the rest on his back."

The stallion snorted and tossed his head at Jake's approach so Hettie slipped the halter on him and led him around a bit. "He's still got a limp but maybe enough healing's taken place, he can make it back. He'll be a lot safer at the ranch." She bargained with her own feelings about the pain this trip would cause—her horse's misery now against his safety at being in the big front pasture.

Jake came close, leaned against the black's shoulder and picked up the damaged front hoof. "It's grown out some. He'll make it if we pad him well enough." He looked at Hettie. "You've got this horse eatin' out of your hands, haven't you?" He chuckled softly. "I know how that is, bein' you've got me the same way, girl." The sun had edged down enough to forewarn of darkness. "We'd best spend the night right here and start back in the morning, then."

Together they set up a rude camp. Jake went out and brought in a small turkey. "We'll have fried chicken tonight, darlin'."

Hettie busied herself, making their bed and bringing in fire wood. Diablo wore his halter as he grazed what grass was left with the other horses, content at being part of a herd again.

They ate well. Sitting beside each other with a new understanding of the way it was between them. Jake no longer saw fear or mistrust in her eyes.

He sat in the firelight, using the pieces of rawhide to fashion a boot for Diablo's foot. He showed Hettie his creation and she nodded approval. "It'll wear out pretty fast on that rocky trail. Got enough to make another?"

"Good idea," he said, grinning with joy at their newly-found harmony. He leaned into her, nudging her with his arm. "I'll see what I can do." He used what he had left to make a spare, wondering how Diablo would take to having that contraption wrapped around his leg.

It had grown completely dark. They needed some rest, and again, he burned with a heated desire for her slender body. He drew her toward their bed beneath the stars, thinking, *I've never been this kind of man. What has this tawny-eyed woman done to me?*

೧೨೬೧

After a scanty breakfast, they caught up the horses, saddled them, and packed their few supplies. Jake put Diablo's tack on him, and fastened the odd looking boot on his front leg, padding the damaged hoof with a thick bed of grasses inside the boot. He tied it on as snug as Diablo would allow while Hettie held the stallion's head and soothed him. The horse was restless, but they managed.

"I hope that holds, for part of the way at least." Jake said, wiping the sweat from his brow. He rose up and stretched his back. "Damn, that's near as bad as horse shoein'.'"

They started slowly up the rocky trail. Jake kept a close watch on the boot he'd made. It wouldn't last the entire trip, but it would help and it was the best they could do. They reached level ground and all went well for several hours. By the time they reached the first campground. Diablo's limp had increased, and Jake took a look. He tore the old bindings off and replaced them with the last one he'd made. "Won't make it all the way, Hettie, but so far the hoof hasn't started bleeding again."

They stopped for another night, and spent some time planning their future, to further cement their relationship.

In the morning, the horses were rested and they hit the trail again. Hettie had found sufficient bunch grass to further pad the remaining boot.

"If we can get him home, he can spend a few months in the big front pasture. We just have to make it, Jake." She suffered for her horse, but he'd be safer near the ranch. The new boot helped, but his limp grew steadily worse. Hettie had tears in her eyes, but they kept moving. There was no other way.

Near sundown, they emerged into the wide space of the ranch yard. With a sinking heart, Hettie saw Annabelle's fancy rig sitting there, her small brown horse stood hitched and uncared for. The scheming little baggage sat in the shade on the porch, waiting for—most likely Jake. Yes, definitely, Jake.

Hettie looked at him. "She hasn't given up on you, not yet. That's why she's out here. She doesn't care two hoots in Hades for me. I know that."

"Well, let's get this horse doctored and we'll take the rest of as it comes." His mouth set in a tight line, he ignored the little blonde, dismounted, stripped the saddle off Diablo, and led him to the shed where the supplies were kept. "What've you got around here for doctorin'?"

Hettie indicated a smaller shed off to the left. "What we have will be in that one."

Hettie left Jake and turned her attention to Annabelle. The girl was a guest and, welcome or not, Hettie extended greetings.

"My goodness, Annabelle, how are you feeling? Well enough to travel about the country this way?"

"I certainly am, as you can see." But her eyes were on Jake. "My, what a nice horse that is!" She looked at Hettie, her eyebrows narrowed. "Where have you two been?"

"When Miguel tried to escape, he stole my horse and left him crippled. It was two days to the south of here and we had to bring him in." She hoped the mention of Miguel would quiet the girl's disgusting attempts at Jake.

"You were out there alone—together?" Her accusing eyes and tightly compressed lips betrayed an intense jealousy and anger.

"Yes, I couldn't find him on my own. I didn't know where Jake left him after he captured Miguel," Hettie explained, her patience wearing thin. "That man tried to take my horse to Mexico, but he threw a shoe and went lame."

"Oh, I'll just bet you didn't know where he was!" She huffed, nearly in tears. The mention of Miguel never touched her consciousness. The girl had no cause to be angry at Hettie, but when did that ever stop Annabelle Nellis?

"What brings you out here today?" Sick of the girl already, Hettie wished her gone but it was too near dark for that, the little baggage would be staying the night.

"I missed seeing you, Hettie," Annabelle simpered, intently watching Jake take care of the stallion.

At the forge, he removed Diablo's other three shoes and applied heavy lanolin to the damaged hoof. After tying a freshly made boot onto the injured hoof, he led him to the big front pasture and turned him loose. Watching the man's rangy form, Annabelle appeared to have forgotten Hettie was standing there.

"Come in the house, and I'll fix you something to drink. Jake will take care of your horse, Annabelle," Hettie added in disgust, noticing the girl had given no thought to her animal at all.

Hettie was dead tired and wanted to be alone with Jake again tonight, but with Annabelle around, that wouldn't happen. Would he be safe in the bunkhouse with the predatory blonde girl on the scent? she wondered, angry at needing to accommodate a person who did her best to get between her and the man she loved. But hospitality came first and she obliged her guest.

Reluctantly, the girl followed her into the house and flopped in a handy chair. "What were you two doing on that long ride? Such a long time, two days, was it?"

"Actually, it was four." Hettie's answer was short, matching her temper. "Miguel got quite a ways before the horse threw a shoe. Which reminds me, how *are* you after his terrible attack on you?" she asked, looking for signs that the girl had changed her ways after being violently raped.

"I suffer terribly, Hettie. I've lost all my friends. They laugh at me now if I see them." Her look didn't match her words. The girl had a one track mind. After her rape, and the utter brutality of it, she appeared to have been hardened in some sinister way and, seeing it, Hettie felt a chill.

A shadow passed through her. It was clear as day to Hettie that Miguel, for all the violence he'd committed against her, had merely brought about some sort of carnal awakening within the girl. If Annabelle had been after Jake before, she'd now become a predator with her sights set exclusively on the sheriff. It made Hettie wonder if the attack had affected Annabelle's sanity.

"I wouldn't call them friends then," Hettie told her, fighting for control of her emotions. "A real friend is one who stands by you in times of trouble." She paused then questioned, "Have they actually said those things to you, or do you only believe they'll turn against you now?" Her own feelings ranged from pity to disgust.

"Well no, I haven't given those brazen hussies a chance to run me down, but I know how they are, not like you and Jake." Deepening her gaze, Annabelle narrowed her eyes. "You two were alone out on that trail all that time, is that it?" Her mind had quickly returned to her primary interest, Jake La Force. She couldn't get her mind off him for ten minutes, and her raging jealousy was barely controlled. "For four days?" she added.

"Yes. It was absolutely beautiful, camping out under the stars, except for worrying about my horse. Jake's a real good cook, too" Twisting the knife came easy for Hettie right now. She was tired, near the end of her rope, and sick of the interfering jealousies of this conniving little snip.

Annabelle turned away, her face white, her lips bitten between rows of little white teeth. "I don't think it's very proper for a woman to do things like that," she sniffed.

"Things like what?" Hettie found herself enjoying the conversation.

Annabelle turned her face to Hettie, her eyes blazing. "Don't think I don't know what you're up to with Jake! You know very well I care for him, and you're doing your best to get in my way, aren't you?"

"Has he ever done or said anything to make you think he's interested in you? At all?" Hettie asked, fearing again for the girl's sanity.

"We had dinner in the hotel once, and he asked me to dance, too. I saw that eager look in his eyes when he held me in his arms and waltzed me around the floor."

Hettie remembered it, too, but it wasn't the way Annabelle imagined it. Discussing it wasn't an option. Hettie would never get through to the little snip.

She smiled. "What shall we have for dinner, tonight?" *Besides Jake La Force, that is.* She watched the change in Annabelle's face.

Annabelle's voice changed to sweetness and cunning. "Is Jake invited?"

"He's welcome, if he wants to come." Sounding as off hand as possible, she added, "I'll go ask him."

"Oh yes, let's."

The girl's pathetic eagerness made Hettie want to rip those damned blonde curls off her sick little head. Yet, pity welled up inside her. The poor girl would never know the wonderful heights of joy and passion Hettie had found with that lanky man. She had the sad feeling Annabelle wasn't the type to care that much for anyone but herself and no doubt would never know feelings like that.

They went to the bunkhouse to find Jake alone. "Windy and Larry aren't in yet?" Hettie asked with a note of alarm in her voice.

He gave her a warm, friendly smile. "They left a note sayin' the coyotes are real busy out on the north range, and they'd be out there for several days. You know, Hettie, you could use another hand or two around here."

"I know that. Thought I'd ask Windy to find someone." She gave him a look that told him what she really wanted to do with him tonight, but they both knew they couldn't. "Would you join us for dinner, Jake?"

He smiled at her, ignoring Annabelle completely. "I'll be right along."

They returned to the house, with the girl pouting and angry. She'd seen the intense interplay between them. "I guess I'll be going back to town in the morning, Hettie."

Saying nothing, Hettie set about putting a meal together. She'd been gone for four days, the cow had gone dry. No milk was available, the eggs hadn't been gathered, and there was only jerky for meat. She might as well have been out on the trail again but, this time, she wouldn't have a nice young wild turkey to make fried chicken with and no Jake beside her in that lonely bed at night.

CHAPTER 26

Hettie bustled about fixing supper while Annabelle sat in a chair watching her swift, sure movements.

"You sure know your way around a kitchen, don't you?" She fluffed her blonde curls. "I suppose Jake likes that about you."

Hettie didn't want to get the girl upset again. "He's never said anything about it, except, 'Thanks for a nice meal.'"

Annabelle didn't speak again, but Hettie saw her looking out the window, waiting to see Jake's tall form come walking to the house. When the food was ready, she asked the girl to go out on the porch and ring the dinner bell.

After racing to ring the small bell, Annabelle stood on the porch waiting for a sight of Jake. Hettie knew by the flutter of her small hands as she saw him leave the bunkhouse and come her way, that the girl imagined she was his wife waiting for him to come inside, claim her with his long sensual lips, hold her, and make love to her.

Poor little soul. Hettie understood completely how that felt and smiled sadly in pity for the troubled young girl, knowing she must burn inside with wanting him, and he'd never given her a passing thought.

Jake met her on the porch, tipped his hat, passed her without a word, and headed into the kitchen to Hettie. Annabelle's face turned red, and her fists clamped in to a tight knot. Hettie figured she burned with a fury only the devil himself could ignite as she entered the kitchen.

In the kitchen, Jake released her from his embrace, just as Annabelle entered to catch them. Hettie saw her lips tighten across her face, as she slumped into a chair at the table, waiting to be served.

Annabelle turned her nose up at the jerky gravy over potatoes, but took a fluffy biscuit with butter and honey, saying, "I'm just not that hungry." She drank some of the coffee and nibbled on the biscuit. Her tight little face reflected a burning hatred of them both.

Hettie watched Annabelle. Her devious mind was no doubt considering ways to get even with Hettie for stealing Jake. When she saw a small smile of victory linger across Annabelle's lips, Hettie shuddered.

After the meal, Jake said good night with a wink at Hettie and left to check the horses and then on to the bunkhouse for the night. He planned to return to Flagstaff in the morning, but most definitely not in the company of Miss Annabelle Nellis.

Hettie fixed a bed in the spare room for Annabelle, one she'd used before, and without further conversation, they parted for the night. Hettie worried about the girl, believing she'd completely lost sight of reality. It might be the aftermath of being raped. Hettie didn't know.

ⓔⓢⓔⓢ

Annabelle left the next morning. Her last sight of the ranch included the image of Hettie and Jake standing together solidly as a couple. As she whipped her horse into a trot, she gave them a look Hettie took to mean, *I'll show you both you can't do this to me!*

She nodded her blonde head, her eyes narrowed, and a tight smile crossed her lips as she drove. Hettie frowned, wondering what lay in store for Jake from the devious mind of Annabelle Nellis.

Hettie heaved a sigh. She and Jake stood close together, watching the dust settle after Annabelle's little rig disappeared through the greening sage brush. While they'd brought Diablo home from the lost canyon, they'd sorted out their differences and were at ease with each other.

Jake sighed as well. "Thank God, that's over with."

"Is it?" Hettie replied. "We haven't seen the last of that troubled girl, and I know it, Jake. She went awfully quiet after she saw you hugging me in the kitchen, just before supper. Never spoke another word to me for the rest of the night." She looked up at him, worry tightening her chest. "She's very spoiled, very stubborn, and used to having her way."

He laughed and pulled her by the arm. "Let's go look at Diablo." They walked arm in arm down to the big pasture and crawled through the fence. The sun was out and the warm breezes flowed softly against their happy faces.

"He's limping so badly," she cried as the black horse made his way over to her and nuzzled his finely formed head against her body. "Pretty boy," she crooned, playing with the spot behind his ears. "How long will his healing take?"

"Give him a month or more. Miguel rode him right into the rocks."

Together they walked about the ranch yard, enjoying each other, until finally, he heaved a deep sigh. "Well, darling, I've got work to do." After a long, deep kiss and tight hug, he moved away from her and caught up Bucky.

She watched him ride away and felt the loss immediately. She had things to take care of, but her worried mind stayed on Annabelle. She was spoiled and devious, with her heart fixed on Jake, and Hettie feared the girl meant trouble for him, as well as for her.

ℰↄℰↄ

Jake wasn't likely to get anywhere near Annabelle who preceded him on the trail. He made sure of it and reached Flagstaff just before dark. Hitching Bucky outside, he went into the jail and found Lin on duty.

"How're things in here?" he asked.

"I've heard there's some talk around town that Annabelle Nellis has run off somewhere. Her folks haven't said anything to us about it."

"She's been out to Hettie's place. Drove back this mornin'. They must know where she went." Jake scoffed. "If she never made it back, she's layin' in wait somewhere, hoping to trip me up."

"If she has run off, I'm worried she won't be around to testify." Lin feared the case going bad and turning a rapist loose.

Jake nodded, feeling a frown cross his face. "I'll wager she's playing games again. Just wish I knew which ones." He wiped the sweat from his brow. "It'll wait for next day. I'll be turnin' in, Lin." He left the office, took Bucky to the stable, and left orders for extra grain before heading out to his own quarters.

Tired, he headed to his small place for a clean-up and a nice dinner at the small, fleabag eatery, Ma James's. He entered his few rooms, lit the lamp, and went into the bedroom to find something clean to wear.

Stopping, he felt a shock pass through him at the sight of a small figure snuggled under the blankets. "What the hell?" He strode over to take a look.

Annabelle met his shocked stare with a seductive, eyes-half-closed look, and twisted her body suggestively under the bedding.

"What the hell's goin' on in here?" he thundered at her, angry as hell at seeing his blonde nemesis cringing under his blankets, right here in his own personal quarters, and in his own damned bed.

"Hi, Jake. What took you so long? I've been waiting for-ever and ever for you." She faced him, her blonde curls awry, a pout on her red lips, and in disgust, he saw a bare shoulder peeping from beneath the blanket.

She had to see by his face, he was mad as hell. She tried another tack and began to beg. "Please, Jake. I didn't have any place to go where I could hide. I'm so sick of being stuck in my room at home and Hettie doesn't want me around." She sat up in his bed, tucked her knees beneath her chin, and pulled the blankets up around her neck. Her sweetly entreating face had no effect on Jake.

"Miss Nellis," he snarled down at her. "You can't be here. You've got to get out of my place—and now!" He couldn't allow this girl to ruin his life with her wild accusations. If she stayed where she was, she'd have him in prison.

Waiting in the doorway for her to move, he realized the dreadful reality all over again. *Damn. This girl is pure poison*! He couldn't stand the sight of her and wasn't about to be trapped by her. Unmoving, she stared back at him, her red lips firm, and made no effort to get out of his bed.

He decided what he had to do. Trying to be kind, Jake said, his tone more gentle, "If you won't get out of here on your own, I'll go fetch your mother, then. She'll be worryin' about you bein' gone. Did she know you were out to Hettie's?"

"Oh please don't! She never understands how I feel." She nearly wheezed, until her frantic tone turned to a wheedling, seductive mewing that sent the ice roaring through his veins. "Not how I feel about you, anyway." She wiped her eyes. "She doesn't care where I go, either! No one cares about me." He thought he saw a tear.

Annabelle changed suddenly, her eyes narrowing into a calculating look. "You spend a lot of time with that *old woman,* Hettie, don't you? I know you do! But what you don't know is she's got a big secret, and she's hiding it from you. It might be the real reason she did away with that old man out at her ranch. She doesn't know I know about it, but I found it hidden in that old man's clothes while she was sleeping. If she didn't tell you about it, she's got her reasons." She stuck her chin in the air, with a knowing *I-told-you-so* look on her face.

"I have no idea what you're goin' on about, Miss Nellis. Hettie will tell me if she thinks it's important."

"You really think so? What she's got hidden out there could easily be worth more than a million dollars! You don't know about it, so she didn't think enough of you to let you in on it, did she? That old Elmer must have found that gold somewhere, and now it's hers. It looks like she killed him for it."

"I won't pay any mind to your wild ravings, but you're going to get your little backside out of my quarters, now. You won't ruin my reputation by being caught here in my bed. I'll burn the damned place down if you don't get out and right away. This has gone way in hell, too damned far!"

He gave her a stern, no-nonsense look. She stared back at him and never moved.

"Don't forget what I told you. She's hiding something big, Mr. Jake La Force." She wiggled her body under the blankets of his bed, exposing a bare shoulder, watching to see if he liked what he saw.

Disgusted and worried, Jake turned away from her, walked out into the night air, and drew a deep breath. He'd sleep in the barn or at Ma Jones place if he had to. But reason prevailed, and he headed to the Nellis home. It took some time, but he finally reached the place and knocked, using their elaborate brass doorknocker.

Mrs. Nellis came to the door. "Why, Sheriff, what can I do for you?" Her tone was ever so sweet and he detected no fear at having her daughter missing. Something wasn't right. He knew that much.

"Are you missing a daughter, Mrs. Nellis?"

"What's wrong? Why do you ask?" She turned pale. "No, Annabelle's not missing, Sheriff La force. She's right upstairs. Just got back from visiting that Jamison woman. Hardly ever comes down otherwise."

"I saw her out there, Mrs. Nellis. She returned today, but she's not here in her room, she's at *my* place!" He was dog tired and wanted the woman to get her daughter out of his quarters, so he could get some sleep. "I've just returned from a long trip, myself, Mrs. Nellis, and went home to find your daughter curled up in my bed." He felt his temper rising. "I want her *out* of there. My God! I haven't slept much in four days, and now I find her in my bed tryin' to make trouble for me."

"It can't be! You're mistaken. She came home earlier today and she's up in her room." She opened the door for him to enter, headed for the wide carpeted stairs, and climbed them with unsteady knees. Jake was right behind her.

"My daughter hasn't been doing so well after that devastating attack," she informed Jake. "And anymore, I never know what the poor girl will take it into her head to do."

She reached Annabelle's room and knocked gently on the girl's door. Receiving no answer, she entered the room. Seeing the empty bed, Mrs. Nellis let out a scream. Perhaps, the immediate relief of knowing her daughter was alive and safe in the sheriff's quarters kept her from doing anything rash.

"She's gone, Sheriff. I never heard her leave, but she was here this afternoon after she returned from that woman's ranch." Her distraught face and the dark circles beneath her eyes, gave Jake a good idea what this mother suffered.

"Of course, she's safe, but I'd like her removed from my quarters. It's no place for a young woman. I never asked her there and I don't want her there." He waited impatiently for an answer.

"You didn't touch her, did you?"

In amazement, he realized the woman was ready to accuse him. *Can it be possible the whole damned family has laid a trap for me because of what Annabelle wants?*

"I just got back from Hettie's ranch myself, ma'am, worn out, and needin' sleep. I went to my quarters, and what the hell did I find? Your daughter in my bed. If you don't get her out of there right now, I'm arrestin' her for breaking and entering a private residence."

Mad as hell and ready to chew nails, Jake knew without a doubt, Annabelle was prepared to do anything she could to make trouble for him.

"You wouldn't dare!" Mrs. Nellis gasped out the words. "I'll get my husband. He can deal with this." She reached for a wrap and headed out for the hotel with Jake right behind her.

The chunky little woman walked so fast he had trouble keeping up as she pounded the gravel walkway toward Front Street.

At the hotel, she found her husband. Agitated and waving her arms, she told him where their daughter was. Together, they faced Jake. "So, you've got our daughter set up at your place," Mr. Nellis said. "Now you're done with her, and you're want to rid yourself of her!" His face was livid with rage.

"Mr. Nellis, I've been gone for four or five days. I just now went to my quarters, worn to a frazzle, and found your daughter hidin' herself in my bed. Now you'd better get her the hell out of there before I slap her little carcass in jail, and it ain't a nice place for a young girl to be!" His temper had hit a peak and he damned sure wasn't letting this family ruin his chances with Hettie.

"I'll go get her, but mark my word, La Force, you haven't heard the last of this. Her reputation has suffered enough!" Nellis, upset and trying to hide his embarrassment over his wayward daughter, would readily lay blame on another man, if he could. Jake led the man out and down the street toward his place, with Mrs. Nellis hurrying along behind.

When they reached his quarters, Jake took them in, immediately noticing how Mrs. Nellis sniffed in disdain at his humble, masculine digs. He felt pity for the woman because of her daughter, and her thoughts regarding his living quarters only made him smile. He led them to his bedroom where both parents found Annabelle shrinking under the covers.

Nellis rushed to her side. "Annabelle, honey, you all right?"

"No, Daddy! Jake attacked me as soon as he got here. He's always been after me, and now he's torn my clothes off me, and raped me," she cried bitterly, emitting enough broken sobs to convince any parent. "He's used me and now he wants to throw me out like a piece of trash! He's got to marry me,

Daddy, and make this right." She let out another deep sob and clutched the bedding tight under her chin.

"You don't want a brute like that for a husband!" her mother cried. She turned on Jake. "You filthy, rotten beast, how dare you do such a terrible thing to destroy my daughter's reputation, if not her entire life."

Her voice had risen to the edges of hysteria. Annabelle sat under the blankets watching her mother do her dirty work for her. Jake saw her look of triumph as she convinced herself she'd gotten what she wanted—him. She planned on having him and had set up this idea of a convincing trap.

"It'll be a cold day in hell before I'd have this miserable excuse of a female for my wife." Madder than a trapped cougar, Jake spat out the words. "She's plumb loco and you two have got yourselves one hell of a problem right here." He gestured at Annabelle. "Now get her out of here!"

His voice, deadly and filled with ice, told them he meant business. They went to their daughter and pulled her from the bed. Seeing her completely naked, Mrs. Nellis screamed. Jake quickly turned away, not wanting to see the girl unclothed, knowing her parents, seeing her that way, might reinforce her claim of rape.

Annabelle stood there, brazen as brass, not trying to cover her body or grab for her dress which lay neatly folded over a chair in the corner. Jake pointed to the dress. "Look at that. What rapist would bother to fold up his victim's clothes so neat?"

A look of comprehension crossed the father's face. The girl stood there with a smile on her face, making no effort to cover herself, while her mother grabbed at the dress and rushed to cover her child. Jake saw the look of shock on the father's face at the uncaring and shameless attitude of his daughter.

Jake watched the calculating glint cross Nellis's face. He knew damned well Jake was innocent, but if accusing Jake would save her reputation and sanity, he'd go along with his daughter.

Nellis faced him. "You sick bastard. You've ruined my daughter's life and her reputation. I'll see you hang!"

He waited while his wife dressed the girl and together they took her out into the night.

As they led the girl away, Annabelle screeched, "Remember what I told you. She's hiding plenty!" She gave him a last, long, triumphant look.

Jake looked at the rumpled bed. "Son of a damned bitch!" he exclaimed as he grabbed several blankets, rolled himself in them, took a stiff slug of whiskey, and went to sleep on the floor, but not before he wondered about those secrets Hettie had withheld from him.

CHAPTER 27

In the morning, Jake entered the jail. Lin met him at the door, his face white and wearing a questioning look. The man ran his hand through his hair and it stood on end. "Good God, Jake, what the hell have you done?"

"What do you mean by that?" Jake took a look at the papers on his desk and sat down. "What's got you all het up?"

"The whole town's goin' on about you an' that Annabelle, sayin' you attacked her and raped her." Lin swallowed and hurried on. "It cain't be so. I know that, Jake. You damned bet I know it!"

"Of course, it's not so. The girl's gone loco, Lin. When I finally got home last night after four, five days gone, I walked into my digs and found that little snip curled up in my bed without a stitch of clothes on." He snorted. "I couldn't get her to leave on her own, so I ran for her folks. When we got back, she starts in with this story about me attacking her, crying and actin' hysterical." Jake sighed then went on. "I wouldn't have any part of that girl if she was dressed in jewels and layin' herself out on a solid gold platter, and she damned well knows it!" He reached back to hang his hat on a rack of deer antlers behind him. "Then she says I have to marry her to make it right. Like hell I will. Hell'd have to freeze over before that'd ever happen, by God!"

"What a damned mess. Looks like that fool girl's got it in her head she wants you, Jake, and she'll do anything to get you." Lin paced the floor. "What'll you do? And what about the rape charge against Miguel? That's a real rape charge."

"I'm not doin' a damned thing, Lin. If this town is stupid enough to believe that fool girl, they can get themselves another sheriff."

He left his desk and headed past several cells to see Handy. He found the man polishing off a healthy breakfast, brought in from Ma James.

"Well, well, Sheriff, got your own self in a pickle, so I hear." Handy let out a chuckle, and Jake saw he was pleased as punch he wasn't the only one in trouble. "Now who's the big, bad hombre?" He stuck out his chin and Jake thought it matched his protruding gut. The good chuck from Ma's place seemed to be holding him.

"Get yourself a lawyer, yet, Handy?" Jake gave no hint of his feelings about Annabelle's nonsense. "Ought to have one, might help your case. Of course, we've got an eye witness against you." He didn't mind letting Handy know his case was hopeless.

Looking into Miguel's cell, he saw the man's liquid black eyes sparkling with enjoyment. Jake needed his testimony against Handy and he figured Miguel would use that to benefit himself if he could.

Miguel came to the bars, his eyes questioning on another matter. "*Señor, el caballo, Diablo? Muerte?*"

His face bore the traces of worry over the fate of the black stallion. For a man in his dire situation, he still had concern over a horse. To Jake, that earned a bit of respect for the man, rapist or not.

"*El caballo esta bien.* We brought him back, Miguel. He's in the big pasture with lots of grass. I'll go see how he is in a few days."

In spite of what Handy had told him, he wasn't sure how much the man understood, though his tone of concern told him enough.

"*Muchas gracias, señor. Muchas gracias.*" The glimmer of tears in those dark, sultry eyes told Jake the horse meant a lot to the man. It was all he had left of his brother and, killer or not, he'd been family.

"*De nada, Miguel,*" Jake said as he headed up to the front.

He had things to do around town. Ignoring the excitement over Annabelle's accusations, Jake thought of Hettie. He longed to see her again. *Hell, who'd be crazy enough to believe that little trouble maker, anyway.* He dismissed the idea from his mind. "Let her do her damnedest. I can't waste time worrying over nonsense."

He found it difficult to return to his living quarters after what had happened there, and after he'd taken care of business, he stayed at the office. Mel came in, edgy, fiddling with his hat. "That girl's stirrin' up plenty of trouble. There's some folks talkin' hangin', Jake. What the hell's goin' on?" His face wore a grim expression. "First it's the Mex, and now you." He rattled on, hands twisting his neck piece. "You've got to put a stop to this talk, man."

"Let them come and speak to me about it. I've got an earful for anybody out to hang me." Jake wasn't worried about anything coming from a girl gone plumb loco like Annabelle. He sat in his office chair trying to pay attention to things that'd piled up in his absence.

The door burst open and the mayor hauled his girth in, stopping in front of Jake's desk.

"Help you, Mayor Gibbons?" Jake took in the man's flushed features and awaited his blustering outburst.

"Jake, what the hell's going on around here? I'm hearing the most damnedable things against you."

He'd been a good friend and Jake knew him for a sensible man. "I'll tell you, Ben, if you want my side of it."

"I'd like to hear it, Jake. Nellis is raisin' hell all over town, about how you took advantage of his daughter."

"Have a seat, then." Jake rose to get the coffee pot and poured the mayor a cup of thick, strong brew. "Annabelle is just a kid. I've never given her a nod, but she'd been tryin' to cozy up to me for some time now, for a while even before her rape by Miguel." He shook his head. "I'd been out of town for four days, maybe more than that. I come home, dead on my feet, walk into my place, and find that girl in my bed, naked as a jay bird, just waitin' for me." He looked at the mayor and grinned. "I do have an interest in someone, but it's damned sure not that silly, spoiled, schoolgirl."

Jake went on to complete the details of the night in question. "That's all I know, Ben. If she's trying to force me to marry her…" He gave the mayor a look that said how he felt about the whole damned situation. "I'll take the hangman's noose before that ever happens."

"Thanks, Jake. I believe you and I'll try to quiet things down. Wouldn't want to lose the best sheriff we've ever had in Flagstaff."

"Well, not that way, anyway." Jake laughed and rose to see the mayor out. "Thanks, Gibbons, appreciate it."

The other two had overheard. "Sounds like that Nellis girl's been chewin' on some loco weed, don't it?" Lin said.

"Looks that way, Lin." Jake had decided something else, too. "Boys, I'll be out seein' Hettie at the Lazy J for a few days. Take care of the place, will you?"

"Don't forget, Miguel's trial. It's comin' up real soon," Mel reminded him.

"I'll be back soon enough, but this is pressin' business." He grinned and turned to leave after their nodded assents.

He went down to the stables for Bucky. The big horse was well rested and ready for a good run. He got a lunch from Ma Jones and heard her say in an undertone, "Everybody 'round here knows you never done what that fool girl's sayin', Sheriff." She handed him a thick package of sandwiches and gave him a big smile along with it.

He thanked the woman and rode out of Flagstaff into the clean smelling air of the high mountains and thick stands of orange-barked Ponderosas. As he rode away, he breathed a sigh and settled in his saddle for the long ride to Hettie's. He saw her face in the clouds and in his dreams at night. He loved her and planned to spend the rest of his life with her. They had a few complications to work out and this business with Anna-belle was another one.

Nearing dark, he arrived at the familiar ranch yard, saw no signs of activity, and felt his hackles rise. "What the hell's goin' on around here?" He dismounted, led his horse to water, then ground hitched him before heading for the ranch house. His knock on the door received no answer.

He opened it and saw no signs of Hettie inside. Her house was neat as usual and the bed made up. Feelings of alarm rose in him and made him say aloud, "Please, God, don't let any-thing happen to my woman."

Heading for the bunkhouse, he saw, to his relief, a group of horses ride into view, Hettie, among them on Patches. He waited in the ranch yard until she rode up to him.

"Jake!" she exclaimed, riding close. "What's going on?"

Was she glad to see him, or was that fear in her eyes? He worried she'd never really trust him again in spite of loving him. If he mentioned that million dollar blather Annabelle had gone on about, she'd never look at him again. He was damned sure of that. Would she ever tell him about these mysterious gold nuggets? He didn't know about that, but he knew for sure Hettie didn't take to questioning. He'd learned *that* to his sorrow.

At seeing her again, the feeling of coming home swept over him. He closed his eyes with contentment and smiled, feeling his mouth stretch wide. "Glad to see you, Hettie." He loved the way she looked at him and couldn't wait to get her alone. Nothing would keep him out of her bed tonight.

Jake's problems in Flagstaff came through in his voice though he tried to hide the mountain of anger and frustration he felt, re-living the ridiculous charges Annabelle had made against him as he felt Hettie's scrutiny.

"What's going on with you, Jake?" She dismounted and came to him. "Something's very wrong. And don't try hiding it from me like you hide everything else."

He planned to tell her, but right now he wanted her in his arms. He helped her put her horse in the corral, then his, and tossed hay in after them, without bothering to see if it got to the right spot.

They headed for the ranch house as the two cowboys, Windy and Larry, went to the bunkhouse. Once inside, Jake swept her into his arms and kissed her repeatedly. "I've waited so damned long for this!" He barely let her go long enough to remove her jacket. "Hettie, where were you? The place was so empty when I got here. I had an awful feelin'."

"What's *wrong* with you, Jake? What's happened?" She remembered his question. "We were out checking on newborn calves. Its' spring—lots of new ones." She gazed into his eyes, seeing the pain he tried to hide. "You'd best tell me everything, and don't try smoothing it over to spare my feelings." She hugged him in return. "I love you, Jake. You're not alone in this or anything else. Not anymore."

"Got some coffee?" He slumped into a handy chair and tossed his hat in the corner like always. He had to tell her about the charges Annabelle had made against him. The fact that they were ridiculous didn't seem to enter the minds of some of the citizenry of Flagstaff.

"Sure thing." Hettie bustled about, fixing a quick meal, and brewing coffee. Jake sat there bathed in the happy glow of a man seeing his woman busily doing things for him and making everything right. He relaxed and felt his heart expand with joy, watching her slim body moving about the kitchen, busily making supper. Her movements, practiced and sure, filled him with pride. Knowing what lay ahead for them both as the night fell into darkness sent him into a soft, heated glow of contentment.

Finally, she set down a plate for him and one for herself. She put meat and gravy out with a few left over biscuits, added a few early peas from her garden, and poured his cup brimming full of dark, rich coffee.

"I feel like I died and went to heaven, Hettie." He raised his troubled eyes to her, nodded, then dug in like a starving man.

They ate in silence. She waited for him to tell her not only what was bothering him right now, but those things from his past he'd kept hidden from her and anyone else who'd ever known him.

Once the meal was finished, they moved to the large front room. She sat across from him. The lamps were lit and made for shadows and softness.

"I have more than one thing to tell you, darlin'," Jake began. "I'll start with Annabelle's latest." He went into what had happened in his rooms and the vile charges against him she'd spread about Flagstaff. "My reputation could be ruined and there are some who want to hang me as a rapist, Hettie."

She pressed close against him. "Jake, only an idiot would believe what that girl is saying." She looked into his troubled eyes. "If it'll help, I'll tell them what I've seen out here. The boys will back me up on that, too."

"Thanks, Hettie, I may need all the help you and everyone else can give me. Her father's influential around town and there're some who'll go along with anything he's got to say." He looked at her, and sighed. "You need to know the rest of my story, too."

It was time and he was ready. He leaned forward, his elbows on his knees. "Goin' way back—I was married once, you probably figured that." He took a deep breath. "We were just kids, grew up together, maybe like it happened with you and Del. Martha and me, we started a little ranch near Prescott. It wasn't much, but we were happy together and worked hard to make a go of the place. In time, she gave me a son, and later we had a baby girl. We called her Jenny Lee. Our boy was Justin Carl, for my father. The time came when I had to go away—buying new livestock. I was gone a week, maybe ten days."

He took a deep breath before continuing. "When I come back, Martha lay sick with diphtheria, so weak she couldn't get up to tend the children, and they were both real sick, too. I rode for the doctor. They said he was out tendin' to another family, and would come as soon as he could. It seemed about everybody had it right then. It kind of swept through the area, and the doc went near crazy tryin' to take care of everybody. People all over the area were dying. Nothin' seemed to help."

Jake stopped for a moment and pulled Hettie close. "The doc did his best, but no matter what we tried, I lost my wife and two children within the week. I thought my life was over after we laid them to rest. I kept on with things, but ranchin' alone wasn't in the cards for me, and that house was like a haunted place after all that."

He wiped a tear away. "I sold off the stock and went to Texas, worked in the Rangers for a time. Finally, after hearin' this area up here was real good cattle country, and that they needed a lawman right then, I came to Flagstaff. I took the job and tried to go on livin' the best I could."

He sighed. "That's about it, Hettie. I was a dead man inside until I looked into your eyes that mornin' at breakfast, and heard your voice." He laughed in joy. "Not one thing's been the same since I looked into those cougar eyes of yours, dearest girl. Nothin' at all."

Hettie took his big body into her arms and moved against him. "I don't know what to say, Jake, but I'm glad you've told me. I know from my own experience how it is. But keeping that hurt inside for a long time like that is hard on you. I'm glad you've trusted me with knowing it."

She held him close. "We can go on and make a life together. Things don't always go bad. You've got to know that. We've got a good chance to make a go of this place, and we'll be together to handle things as they come along."

He flushed a rosy shade of red beneath his tanned features. "Darlin', would you mind if I took down that guitar? I've got this song workin' in my head and I'd like to sing it for you."

"You never said you could sing." Hettie sat before him in amazement, her hands fluttering to her chest. "Is that why you're always looking at that old guitar?"

"I reckon so. And I'm not sayin' I can sing, but sometimes I get somethin' in my head and it needs to come out."

At her assent, he walked over and took down the instrument. After running his hands over the finely wrought wood, he put the strap over his shoulder and settled it against his right side. He spent a few moments tuning it to his satisfaction then sat down, smiled, and looked her in the eyes. As he began his song, his voice, low, soft and deep, struck right down to the bottom of her heart.

> "I met a woman, soft as a thistle,
> "and strong and steady as a tree.
> "She bends but never breaks
> "from the worst adversities.
> "Shy and sweet, yet sometimes bold,
> "I love her caring, gentle way.
> "To wake up in her arms each mornin'
> "Is all I'll ever need.
> "Oh, Hettie darlin', I'm here to stay."

Hettie couldn't stop her tears. "Jake, that was lovely!" She sobbed for his losses and her own. In her mind, he'd always been a firm, tough, hard-bitten kind of loner. He'd never appeared overly sensitive or tender except in his lovemaking. And then she'd certainly seen his softer nature—that and more. But now, seeing her man with new eyes, she felt an even greater depth of love for him.

He put down the guitar and clutched her body close against his. "You're a strong woman, maybe a lot like Martha was. Could be that's what drew me to you. That morning when I came to your table in the hotel, I believe I fell in love on the spot. Took a while for it to sink in, girl, but you had my heart hogtied right then." He squeezed her so hard she could scarcely draw a breath.

"It didn't stop you from thinking I could commit murder, did it, Mr. Music Man?" She couldn't help but toss that into the conversation.

"I guess I'll never live that down with you, but I can think of a few ways you can make me suffer for my mistakes, if you're not afraid to come into your bed with me." He held her close, watching her face to see what she might say. Her expression often said much more than her words.

"What are you thinking, Jake?" Her narrowed eyes warned him not to try anything she might consider wrong. "Just what are you thinking, Mr.?" She drew away, her eyebrows furrowing.

"Aw, honey, I'll show you. Wonderin' if maybe you'd like to be in the saddle for a while." He laughed and grabbed her tightly, his eyes shining with excitement.

Hettie, secretly glad night had come because the darkness helped with her innate shyness, felt her heart rate nearly explode with anticipation. Jake was a devil when he got going, and she loved him for the wild feelings he aroused in her, even though she had reservations to overcome.

They nearly ran to the bedroom, throwing off their clothes as they went. She met him full on, fearful and beyond excited by this tall, taciturn man who kept her in a state of wonder. She never knew what he had in store for her, and that look in his eyes set her heart on fire. He kissed her over and over, going deep inside her mouth until she burned with rising passion as he pulled her onto the bed.

CHAPTER 28

They struggled awake. After a good breakfast, which took Hettie forever to put together, Jake took her in his arms. "Well, darlin', that was a good way to start the day, but as much as I hate the idea, I've got to return to Flagstaff and see what that blonde-headed little devil's got lined up against me, now."

Hettie detested the nasty fix in which Annabelle's lies had placed Jake. He'd been a good sheriff. It hurt her that some in town believed the foolish twit.

She figured his lassitude stemmed from their adventures in her bedroom last night and smiled her delight as she made him a lunch for his noon meal.

Before he left, he kissed her near to death then mounted up and rode away. She'd follow him soon as she made arrangements with the boys. Thinking of the vicious machinations of that silly, spoiled Annabelle, her hands shook with anger. "If I had that little baggage in my grip right now, I'd teach her a lesson she'd never forget."

Hettie's dander was up. Fed up with Annabelle's nasty shenanigans, she was ready to put that stupid girl in her place.

Larry and Windy were overworked these days, and she hadn't had time to find new help, but Jake and the strain he was under came first. It was late afternoon when the two came in, and she went directly out to them. "Jake's in trouble, and I'll be leaving for Flagstaff early tomorrow. I'll be gone for a while. I can't let him go through this alone, so I'm leaving the care of this place to you two."

Larry wore a puzzled look across his sunburned features as he said, "What's goin' on, ma'am? Any way, we can help, you know we will." He shuffled about in the gravel with his boots. "What's this about, then?"

"Annabelle is claiming Jake attacked her. When he got back to Flagstaff after finding Diablo, he found her naked in his bed. Doesn't anyone question how she got there? We know full well Jake didn't put her there. Imagine that, if you can." She laughed to even have to say it. It made no sense.

☙❧☙

Arrangements made, the next morning the boys saddled Patches for her while she packed a bag and some food for the trip. It'd be a while before she got back. Jake needed her now, and she planned to be right there with him.

Diablo limped about the pasture. Hettie watched him over the fence for a while knowing it'd be many more weeks before she could use him again. She missed riding that wonderful horse. Knowing Miguel's interest in him, she decided to speak with him. In spite of what he did to Annabelle, she respected his love for the horse and wanted to ease his mind.

He'd go to Yuma Prison or, worse, to the hangman's noose but she'd been touched to know he cared deeply for his brother as well as the horse. She also wondered what Diablo's name had been before he came to her.

It was late afternoon when she reached town. She stopped at the hotel, took a room, then rode her horse to the stables and left him. Jake had no idea she was coming to stand in his defense, but she was here and would do what she could for the man she loved.

She cleaned up, changed clothes, and went to Jake's office. He sat behind his desk piled with papers and equipment, his head bent over his work. He looked up to see who'd entered his office and Hettie thrilled at the look of delight spreading across his face.

"Hettie, what brings you into town?" He rose from his chair and came to her. It was unusually quiet in the jail, and she took notice of it.

"Why is everything so quiet all of a sudden?" She looked at Jake. "What's going on here?"

"Nothing more than what I told you. Annabelle's spreadin' it around thick, how I attacked her. There's been a lot of talk and some folks want to believe it." He laughed, but the hollow sound of it was painful to her ears. Jake had been a model citizen and sheriff for many years in Flagstaff, but Hettie knew the public could be fickle and swayed emotionally, all too easily.

"What's going to happen?"

She saw Jake's world crashing in ruins and hers along with it if the citizenry truly believed that crafty girl's wild story. Some people were always ready for that particular kind of excitement, especially those who'd come face to face with the sheriff and lost. Worrying that Jake might face a lynch mob made her blood run cold.

"Don't trouble your head about this, Hettie, darlin'. It'll blow over in no time," Jake said, but the worry lines etched in his face said something else. He repeated his query. "What brings you to Flagstaff?"

"I came to stand with you, Jake."

"Why thanks, girl, that means a lot. What hurts the most, is havin' people turn on me when I've done my best for the lot of them."

She saw Lin nod in agreement as he sat in his chair. He seemed worried, too, but said nothing. His concern filled her with a silent fear that froze her to the quick.

"Had dinner?" Jake smiled at her, remembering the accusing words about the gold business that Annabelle had spit out at him. He hadn't brought it up and decided he never would. Things were too good between them. He'd walk a million miles to avoid jeopardizing that.

"Starving, are you?" She smiled at him. "Where'll we eat?" Her thoughts went to Annabelle's father owning the hotel dining room.

"Right across the street in the hotel, I hear they got real good eats." He laughed at that and nodded to Lin.

They left the office with Hettie on his arm. Both of them wondered how the public would receive them as a couple after the windstorm of lies Annabelle had circulating about Jake.

Crossing Front Street, a man on horseback yelled out a friendly, "Howdy there, Jake, real good to see ya."

They kept on to the hotel and Jake warned, "Nellis may not even let us have a table, Hettie."

They entered the hotel lobby and in minutes, Nellis stormed out of his office. "I've been waiting to see if you had the gall to try coming in here!" Red in the face, and blustering, he hurried them into his office and quickly closed the door. Too many onlookers had already taken an interest in their conversation.

"Now you're dragging another woman in here with you! You've got a lot of gall to show your face in my place, La

Force." He'd lowered his voice as he faced them, his belly protruding like the prow of a ship.

"This is Hettie Jamison, Mr. Nellis. We're planning to be married shortly. Your daughter's been out to visit at her ranch several times." He kept his tone cool in the face of the man's towering anger. He felt a corral full of pity for the man. Nellis knew full well his daughter was lying about the rape, and Jake still held out a small bit of hope Nellis would quell the ridiculous charges his daughter had made.

The portly man faced Hettie. "It was at your ranch, she ran across that devil Maldonado, wasn't it?"

"Yes, it was, sir. I warned her not to fool with him, but she wouldn't listen or pay me any mind. I'm sorry to tell you, she flirted with that man every chance she got."

"What do you mean, fool with him?" His flushed features and heated state had Hettie worried he'd have a spell of apoplexy right in front of her. "You've got the gall to come in here and accuse her of that?"

"I'm very certain you know exactly what I mean," Hettie replied. "I warned her more than once that Miguel was from another culture and might not understand her girlish flirtations." The poor father, upset and frustrated about the turn of events regarding his daughter, caused Hettie to soften her telling of the things Annabelle had done. She offered her condolences. "I'm very sorry the way it turned out. Miguel certainly had no right to harm her in any way."

"I'll see that bastard hang!" he roared then, looking at Jake, he quieted and narrowed his eyes. "And you'll be right alongside of him."

Calmer, he turned to Hettie. "You two will *not* be served in this hotel," he continued. "Mrs. Jamison, I won't kick a lady out on the street, but I'll thank you not to take rooms here again." He opened the door and ushered them out.

Jake said in parting, "If I'm so guilty, why am I not in jail over there?"

Nellis gave him an angry glare, but had no answer. He turned from them, entered his office, and slammed the door behind him.

"I guess we'd better eat a bite at Ma Jones, darlin'. She's a great cook, but the atmosphere could use some work." They went arm in arm down the street to the smaller café.

Nearing the small eatery, Hettie smiled at the crookedly lettered sign in the window. It proclaimed the name of the establishment and a spider web in one corner further embellished the looks of the place along with a few dead flies on the inside window sill. Jake squeezed her arm and grinned.

Before they could enter the establishment, A deep male voice rang out, "Hey, if it ain't thet there rapin' sheriff we got in this 'ere town!" The man edged closer. "Look's like he's got hisself another 'un in tow. Better look out for that dude, lady!"

"Hell, maybe she ain't no lady, Tom. Likes it rough, does she?"

Hettie felt Jake stiffen and slow his pace. She tightened her hand on his arm. "Don't pay them any mind. Jake, don't!" But she knew he'd not hold with insults to a woman on his arm.

Jake loosened her hold on his arm and turned to face the two roughnecks who'd made the insulting comments. "Come over here and say that."

He stood ready for them. The two men weaved closer in an uneven shambling gait, and he knew they'd been at the Roaring Duck Saloon, just down the boardwalk.

"Hell, yes, we ain't afeard of no low down rapin' bastard like you, La Force." The staggering man sniggered. "I'd never do a thing like 'at, an' neither would you, Tom, ol' boy, eh?"

As they came closer, Jake saw it was the town drunk, Shorty Dykes, and one of his inebriated pals.

Jake tried to placate the drunks. "Tom, you'd best go home and sleep it off before you get yourself in real trouble. I'm still the sheriff, and until they hang me or put me in jail, you might want to do as I say."

Jake smiled at Hettie. "Sorry, girl. Guess the little blonde wants me up there on that hangin' platform if not in her bed." He scoffed. "I'd take that high wood walk any day, before I'd have her."

Suddenly, the sharp staccato of a gunshot rang out. Hettie smelled the burning powder and the sharp report of it left her ears ringing. She grabbed Jake's arm as he slumped over and fell to the ground at her feet and she screamed in disbelief. "Oh no, Jake! You're hit!"

The drunk, Dykes, yelled, "Oh shit, I've shot ol' Jake. I tripped on somethin' and my gun went off!" He'd sobered in an instant and stood white-faced in shock as people came running from many directions.

"Get the doctor, quick!" Hettie cried. She knelt down to see Jake's pale face in the glowing light from the small eatery window. She shook him gently. "Jake, Can you hear me?"

He didn't respond to her cries of despair as she saw blood pouring from his chest. Her future with this man drained away before her eyes, along with his life's blood.

She wanted to die right along with him. But she tore off her jacket, removed her thin blouse. She stuffed it inside his shirt and pressed it tightly against his wound. It staunched the flow a good bit. Kneeling at his side, she looked frantically about for the doctor. Jake needed help.

With relief, she heard Doctor Gentry's stern voice and commanding tone. "Make way there!" He pushed through the crowd to kneel at Jake's side. "What happened here?" he asked as he reached inside the bloodied shirt and pulled away Hettie's blood-stained blouse to examine the wound. A worried look came over his face as she told him what happened.

"Get this man up to my office and be quick about it!" the doctor ordered.

Men appeared from everywhere and soon Jake lay on a wide board or a door, she wasn't sure which, and was on his way to the doctor's rooms. They struggled up the narrow stairs and Hettie feared it would make his situation worse. She put her jacket on and if anyone had looked at her barely clothed breasts, she didn't care.

In the doctor's office, Hettie stood back and watched as he cut away Jake's shirt. The ghastly sight of the bluish, round hole in his chest, made her feel lightheaded. She wanted to scream, but instead, she struggled to remove his boots, trying to be useful. It helped her to stay busy.

After the doctor had Jake well in hand, his wife brought out hot tea. She served Hettie and sat with her, soothing her until Dr. Gentry called for his wife's services.

"I've got to remove that bullet. It's close to the heart, but hasn't hit it. He's got a slim chance if we can get it out." He turned to Hettie. "Don't get your hopes up Mrs. Jamison. He's in a real bad way."

Hettie sat there, wordless. Tight with fear, she watched the doctor's wife set out equipment and get things ready. The woman knew her business and Hettie, eager to grasp at any sign of hope, found that small fact reassuring.

When he was ready, Dr. Gentry attempted to shoo Hettie out of the room. She refused. "We're to be married. I must be with him. Please. I can't lose him, Dr. Gentry."

The doctor allowed it, and she realized by his confused expression, he'd heard the nasty gossip. She wondered how she figured in with Annabelle's complaint of rape against Jake.

She imagined her announcement of their forthcoming marriage didn't fit with Annabelle's wild accusations, either.

Hettie was aware that this doctor carefully followed the newest procedures requiring sterility of everything involving the patient. She'd heard it was a newly introduced method which improved healing and survival in many patients. These facts gave her comfort as she settled to await the outcome.

Dr. Gentry and his wife worked closely as a team, bent over Jake's still form. After dreadfully long moments, Hettie hear him say, "It'll be right about there, Millicent. I'll probe for it. If he starts arousing, get the mask ready. We don't need him thrashing about."

The woman quickly brought the needed surgical items to the area, laid them out over a cloth-covered tray, and covered them with a cloth, stiff and folded from steaming. Hettie clenched her hands together and beseeched God's help for the man she loved.

They began. Hettie sat, watching the smoothness between man and wife. They worked to save a man they'd heard terrible charges against, but Doctor Gentry knew Jake. He'd worked with him for years. Hettie wondered what credence he paid to Annabelle's nasty claims. He certainly knew the girl well enough.

"That's it. Thank God!"

She heard the relief in his soft voice and struggled to keep herself from hovering over the table where they worked.

"Stop some of that, dear."

She guessed it must be fresh bleeding from probing the wound. Bleeding would help cleanse his wound, and Hettie prayed even that small thing would help in some way. She heard the clink as a metallic object was dropped in to a dish.

Another hour passed before he turned to her. "We've removed the bullet. He's lost a lot of blood, but we have that stopped. He's got a decent chance, Mrs. Jamison."

He looked at her, though disheveled as she was, she felt his appraising eyes on her and didn't care what he thought. She had the steadfastness of a ranch woman, and that sustained her as she sat waiting, blood splattered on her clothing, wanting to help the man she loved.

"You and Jake are planning marriage, then?" the doctor asked, his puzzled frown only faintly visible in the lamplight.

"Yes, we are." She waited for him to comment, perhaps to mention how he felt about the charges hanging over Jake, but he said nothing more.

"You'd best get some rest, yourself. We'll keep an eye on him."

"I'd like to stay with him for the rest of the night. I'll never rest until I know he'll be all right." She stood firm, letting this man know she made a difference in Jake's life—one who proved to be a fit partner for the man he was. If Annabelle's charges against Jake had made a difference to Dr. Gentry, she saw no evidence of it.

"It could be days, my dear."

She wasn't leaving. "I've got the time, sir."

Mrs. Gentry came out of another room with hot coffee, and some hastily made sandwiches. "Here you are, my dear. Help yourself." To her husband, she said, "I'm going to bed, dear." Sighing, she wiped her brow and left them.

"I'll turn in myself," the doctor said. "But call me if…" He gave her instructions before he left and Hettie saw the look of respect in his eyes.

When the doctor and his wife were together in the next room, Hettie heard him murmur, "If that man ever looked twice at Annabelle Nellis when he had Hettie Jamison on his side, he'd be a raving fool. And we both know Jake better than that."

His wife offered a slight chuckle in reply.

Hours later, after dozing off and waking, Hettie heard Jake's voice, whispering and weakened. "Hettie, darlin'?"

She came awake from the depths of an exhausted slumber to hear the sound of a voice so dear and familiar. A voice she'd prayed to hear again. She struggled to get herself together from her pitiable bed on a small settee.

"Jake? You're awake." She went to his side and, in the soft lamplight, saw the ruddy color of fever in his return gaze. She wanted to ask him so much, but only took his hand and squeezed it gently, petting and soothing him.

"What happened, Hettie?"

"Remember the drunks we met? They were saying things we didn't like, and you braced them. The one called Shorty Dykes, I guess it was, tripped and accidentally shot you. He nearly killed you, Jake. Strange, isn't it, after all the time you've been sheriff in this town, to get shot that way?" She shrugged at the oddness of it.

"Well, looks like he wasn't much good at that either." He smiled. "You sure look good to this old man, girl." He tried to hold her hand, and the weak, feeble, pressure of his grip terrified her. But she hid it from him.

His fevered eyes worried her and when the doctor came out in the early morning, he examined the wound, redressed it, and turned to Hettie. "He's got some infection in the wound. Bullet wounds are the worst of the lot but I'll do all I can for him."

Lin came in for a short visit to worry and fuss over Jake, and Hettie worried right along with him. "How's everything going over there?" she asked, wondering if the man could handle things without Jake.

"Miguel's trial is tomorrow. Sure wish Jake could make it, but we'll have to go with what we have." He looked worried. "Annabelle is supposed to come to court and testify, and we don't know if she will. She's pretty near the whole damn case."

"I'm amazed at her, Lin. I saw her that night, too, scared out of her wits, sick, and all torn up from what Miguel did to her. She ought to do all she can to put him away for his crime."

But would she? Wondering what tricks the girl had up her sleeve, Hettie was certain it was nothing good for Jake or for her either. It filled her with uncertainty, and now Jake was unable to help with the trial or fight off Annabelle's vicious gossip.

CHAPTER 29

When the trial started, Hettie took time away from Jake to go to the courtroom located in a big, new native-stone edifice. She found a seat, wondering if Annabelle would show up. She'd have to wait and see.

The first hours were spent selecting the jury of twelve men. Then Lin brought in the prisoner. Miguel sat in front wearing manacles and a look of defiance across his dark, handsome features.

Annabelle arrived and sat between her parents. Hettie caught a glimpse of her face, tense and pale, her lips pressed tight. The trial itself started after the judge walked in and took his seat behind the high desk in the center. She'd heard of this man, the Honorable Rufus B. Jant. He was a tough but square judge, respected throughout the territory.

Lin stood up and read the charges. The judge called several witnesses, people known to have heard Annabelle's words on the night of her rape, including the doctor. His testimony, along with the oft-times wordy testimony of the other witnesses, was damning for Miguel. Finally, the judge called Annabelle to the stand.

Hettie had worried the girl wouldn't show herself in public, but she appeared bold as brass and dressed in her finest. Hardly the frightened, devastated victim, she was certainly no longer pale and trembling. Her shining, blonde curls were freshly done and she made sure they shook and jiggled charmingly about her head as she moved.

She answered the questions as to why she was out alone readily until time to identify the man who raped her. "He is not in this court, Your Honor," she proclaimed.

Hettie sat in stunned disbelief. Why on earth would Annabelle deny Miguel's guilt?

"You called out his name and claimed he was the man." The Judge's voice rose in frustration. "Miss Nellis, we have heard too many witnesses stating you named this man sitting right here in this courtroom, Miguel Maldonado, as your attacker for you to deny it was this man." He gestured at the Mexican.

"I did meet him, Your Honor, but it was just twice out at Hettie Jamison's place." She met the judge's glance with a firmness Hettie hadn't imagined the girl capable of possessing. Her jaw was set firm and her gaze direct.

"You may step down for now, Miss. I'd like to hear what Mrs. Jamison has to say." He asked the bailiff to bring her up.

Hettie rose to come forward, still struggling to believe Annabelle's testimony. She took the seat they indicated, was sworn in, and the questioning began.

"She did come to my ranch, sir. She flirted with Miguel both times she came. I warned her not to, saying he was likely to misunderstand her actions but she refused to listen to any of my warnings."

Annabelle jumped up and pointed at Hettie, her voice loud and shrill. "Ask her what she's got hidden out there on her ranch, Judge. She's the one killed her hired man. I saw the evidence. She stole something from him and I was the one who found it!"

Hettie, eyebrows raised at the outburst, answered, "I'm not sure what she's referring to, Your Honor."

"She's got a box of gold nuggets. They were in that pile of that old Elmer's clothes and things. I saw them, a whole lot of them!" Annabelle's voice quickly reached the higher notes of hysteria while she pointed an accusing finger at Hettie.

The crowd, whipped into a froth of excitement at the magic words, *gold nuggets,* quickly turned noisy and unruly. The trial was forgotten in the uproar as the gold-hungry men crowded around Annabelle, wanting to know more.

Judge Jant banged the gavel several times. "I'll have order here or you'll all get out of this courtroom, the lot of you!" His voice gentled as he looked at Hettie. "Can you clear this up, ma'am?"

"Yes, I can, sir. Annabelle must have searched the house while I slept. I had found a box of what *might* be gold in Elmer Greenup's belongings. I have no idea where they came from, how many years he had them, or who to send them to. He had no relatives that we could find." She paused then added, "I don't really know if it *is* gold."

"Since this has nothing to do with the case at hand, we'll get on with the rape trial." Jant banged the gavel and spoke loudly. "Order in this court!" He indicated for Hettie to step down from the stand.

He called Miguel. The young Mexican sat in the chair, his head held high, with a calculating smile across his face. Hettie could see, with his main accuser denying he was the rapist, Miguel was sure he'd go free and head for his home country. And if he found a chance, he'd steal that horse and take him, too, if Jake didn't go back on his word and bring charges against him for horse stealing. She'd not heard any word about the horse having been stolen, but she felt her anxiety rising.

"I understand you speak English. Is that true?" Judge Jant asked. He had the kind of way about him that brooked no nonsense.

"Yes, I do." Miguel's voice was clear with little accent.

"Did you rape the young woman in this courtroom?" The judge gestured at Annabelle.

"I don't know what is this...rape?"

It was explained in short order to the prisoner. Miguel replied, shaking his head. "No, I did not do that." He looked intently at Annabelle with a blank expression across his handsome face, and she hung her head with blazing cheeks. Hettie could almost read the man's mind.

After several more questions, where Miguel easily evaded supplying any truthful answers, the judge called Windy to the stand.

He was questioned about Miguel's whereabouts. "He wasn't at the ranch all that night, Your Honor. Handy Bates told the sheriff he was, but he lied for Miguel. They had a deal between 'em about stealin' Ms. Hettie's cattle. Sheriff Jake heard from Miguel about that. He told both me and Larry what he said."

The crowd was in an uproar. "Quiet in this courtroom!" Judge Jant banged his gavel smartly several times and Hettie wondered why the wood didn't split into a million pieces. "Since our sheriff's laid up, we'll go to him and see what he's got to say. I'd like to hear from someone who isn't likely to lie his dad-blamed head off."

Judge Jant looked angry. Incensed from the nonsense going on in his courtroom, he banged the gavel and roared, "Court's adjourned until tomorrow at ten o'clock!" The court emptied quickly, and Lin took the handcuffed Miguel back to the jail.

The courtroom cleared, and Hettie followed the judge and jury members over to the doctor's office, where they asked to see Jake. "Why sure, I believe he's up to a visit," the doctor said. He led them to Jake's bed side.

The judge spoke to Jake. "Son, we need to hear what you saw and heard when you went to arrest this Miguel." He looked down at the fever-ridden man who'd been the best sheriff they'd ever had in Flagstaff, a man who held the respect of nearly all of the townspeople.

Jake looked at the men standing there. "This about Miguel?" His voice held the weakness of the recently ill, but Hettie saw that his mind was clear.

"Yes, it is. We need to know what's going on. The Nellis girl has denied Miguel was her attacker, but we've had several other accounts on that. We'd like to hear your say, if you're up to it," Judge Jant told him.

"She denied it?" Jake exclaimed in disbelief. "Well, I'll tell you what I can." Jake detailed for the jury the condition and accusations of Annabelle on the night in question, and the fact that Miguel had indeed been gone from the ranch. He explained seeing what appeared to be bloodstains down the front of Miguel's clothes the next morning. He added that Miguel had confessed to him that Handy Bates had killed Elmer Greenup to keep him quiet about the cattle rustling. Jake honored his promise to Miguel regarding the black stallion.

The twelve men standing around Jake's bed nodded they were satisfied with his testimony.

"What about them gold nuggets old Elmer had?" A juror, Will Nelson, asked Jake.

With a look of amazement on his face, Jake lied straight out, "I hadn't heard anything about that, Will."

He noticed Hettie standing back against the wall, her face white. He'd speak to her later on that subject. It was nothing new to him after Annabelle's outburst in his quarters.

"Well, it was brought out in court by Miss Nellis. She said she'd seen 'em, a whole danged box of 'em!" Will Nelson couldn't seem to let go of the idea of gold being found in the area. Gold fever spread rapidly in any community and it had already claimed this man.

Judge Jant waved them out. "We've bothered Jake long enough. You men have heard the evidence and you can take it up in court tomorrow. Worrying about gold nuggets is not on our docket." They emptied the room except for Hettie.

She stood back, waiting a while, before coming to his bedside. "I found those nuggets in a tin box among Elmer's clothes and a few old letters after they brought me his belongings," she admitted. "I don't know why I didn't tell you about it, but being on my own so long, I guess I've gotten pretty quiet about a lot of things."

"Hettie, I don't care a hoot in hell about that gold, if it is that. Annabelle threw it in my face when she was hidin' in my bed that night, tryin' to make trouble for you. I didn't know how to speak to you about it without you getting' all het up again and I couldn't take a chance your feelin's might turn against me like before." He smiled at her and, seeing her relax, added, his voice deeply husky with emotion, "I couldn't handle that again."

Hettie kissed him. "It looks like we both have things to work on."

She left Jake's bedside and went to the jail. Mel was on duty and rose to take her hand. "How do, Mrs. Jamison. Jake's better, is he?"

"Yes, thank God. He's going to make it. The doc hasn't given us final word, but he's better all along." She smiled. "I'd like to speak with Miguel, if I may."

Puzzled by her request, he led the way back toward the man's cell. "Go right ahead, ma'am."

Seeing Handy in the next cell, she nodded. Her eyes narrowed and her jaw tightened, but she spoke only to Miguel. "I came to tell you that Diablo will be fine. He'll have the best home possible, fine horse that he is. I'm sorry you lost your brother, though by all accounts, he was an evil man."

She firmed up her tone and went on. "As far as Miss Nellis is concerned, you ought to hang for that, whether she flirted with you or not."

The man merely smiled and nodded, but Hettie read his thoughts. *The stupid blonde bitch didn't speak against him and because of it he might go free. If he did, he'd make damned sure to take Diablo with him back to Mexico.*

Hettie, seeing defiance in his eyes and certainly no repentance, felt no pity for Miguel.

Handy edged his bulk up to the bars and tried to speak with her. "Hettie, ma'am…"

The scowl she aimed in his direction betrayed her feelings of disgust. "Thanks for trying to hang me, Handy, but you killed that kind, gentle man and deserve to hang for what you did," she snarled, flinging the words at him.

She left the jail, feeling she'd avenged Elmer in a small way. Everything had been taken care of except Annabelle's charges against Jake. Her anger at the unfairness of the accusations against him firmed up her decision to pay the girl a call.

After making inquiries, she walked up Beaver Street to the home and knocked on the door, tense with distaste for the girl and the scene to follow. Hettie wondered if she'd be welcome, not knowing what to expect from an impromptu visit.

The door opened and a well-dressed, older woman stood before her. "Yes?" she said. After looking her visitor up and down, she peered about the street to see if anyone watched.

"I came to pay a call on Annabelle if she's at home."

"She's not seeing anyone. Not after what's been done to the poor girl and what she went through in that courtroom. And who might you be?" Curiosity was plain on her stocky face.

"Hettie Jamison, Mrs. Nellis. She's been out to my ranch several times to visit and I'd like to see how she's doing."

Relief flooded the mother's face. "Come in. I'll find out if she'll see you." She gestured at a thickly upholstered chair. "Have a seat. You know, since all these terrible crimes were committed against her, she doesn't go anywhere and refuses to see anyone!"

Hettie thought, *Well, except for my ranch, Jake's bed, and an open courtroom.*

Mrs. Nellis walked slowly up the staircase, covered with the same thick carpeting while Hettie took in the fine furnishings of their home. The wooden balusters sported brass trim done in intricate, lacy patterns and the cushions of her chair seemed stuffed with down. After several moments, Mrs. Nellis returned. "She says to come up. I'm so glad she's found someone to befriend her, the poor child." She turned to walk up again, beckoning for Hettie to follow.

Poor child, indeed! *If she only knew*! Hettie kept her peaceful mien and followed the lady up the elaborate staircase. On a white door, she knocked softly, heard a murmur inside and told Hettie. "Go on in, I'll just go downstairs."

She entered to see Annabelle propped up in her bed with a glowing *cat-that-ate-the-cream* smile on her face. "Ah, Hettie, you've come to see me. I wonder why?" She dragged out her words, making them as sinuous as possible, with that silly, victorious smirk across her face. *Could this girl possibly believe she has Jake cornered, and he has to marry her.*

"Just thought I'd come by and check on you. You've been through so much, lately." How easy it was to pull mock sympathy out of thin air.

"I'm glad you realize how much I've had to suffer, after all the awful things that have happened to me!" Annabelle snuggled the covers up under her chin and nearly squealed with delight at the sight of this woman coming to beg her to free Jake. But he was going to be *her* husband and not Hettie's, of that she was positive. After all, she'd taken steps to make it happen and her daddy stood ready to help.

"I see you're in very good spirits just now. How is it that you never come out of your room, well, except for a visit to an open courtroom? Your mother says you refuse to see anyone," Hettie queried.

"Some of my so called friends did come by to see me and all they wanted to know was all the horrible details of what that Miguel did to me. Would you believe, they actually asked me to tell them everything? After the second attack by you know who, I haven't been out where those nosy so-called friends can get to me. I'll show them in the long run, you just bet I will."

"Just whom are you speaking of—you know who? Who do you mean? It couldn't be Miguel since you swore in court he'd never raped you and I'd like to know why you did that, too."

"That Jake is so self-righteous. I wanted him to face defeat in seeing his prisoner goes free." She tilted her chin upward and slanted her eyes at Hettie. "That'll take him down a peg or two."

"There were many others, including me, who heard you name Miguel so he'll most likely be convicted. If he does go free, he could come after you again. Is that what you want?"

"Oh, my goodness, he wouldn't dare!" Her face turned pale and she quickly changed the subject to one that held far more interest to her. "You're way out on that old ranch and mustn't have heard a word about what happened around here. That old sheriff, Jake, tried to do the same thing to me that Miguel did, but my daddy got to me in time. He'll be lucky they don't hang him."

"You must be joking!" Hettie exclaimed.

"You'll never know if I am or not and it's too late for you to do anything about it."

"Are you saying Jake raped you?" She made herself sound incredulous. "Tell me, how did that happen?"

"He attacked me right in his own bed." She clutched the bedding closer. "I was so frightened of him. He's a very strong man, you know and when he attacked me, I felt completely helpless."

"Oh, he *did*, did he? Tell me, Annabelle, if you can, how'd Jake manage to get you into his bed? How did you get there?" Hettie queried in a soft voice "Tell me." She repeated. "I'd like to know how he did that."

Annabelle stopped in confusion. "I—er—he did do it, he did!" She started to cry. "I don't know how he did it, but there I was, and naked, too, after he ripped all my clothes off."

Hettie laughed her disdain. "If you were in his bed, you got there on your own, Annabelle. Think about it, for heaven's sake." She watched the alarm rising in Annabelle's face. "I hear tell your clothes were neatly folded, not ripped off. Explain that!" Hettie saw a look of resignation dawn across her face.

The crushing defeat Annabelle faced at Hettie's words drove the girl into a screaming rage. "You want him for yourself, you damned bitch, is that it?" The girl's voice quickly reached a high pitch scream.

Mrs. Nellis burst through the door. "What's going on in here? What awful things have you said to my girl to make her scream and cry, this way?" She faced Hettie, her face flushed and filled with anger, prepared to do battle for her distraught daughter.

Annabelle sat in her bed, gnashing her teeth and spitting fire. "Mother! She's trying to get Jake out of that charge of raping me!"

"I merely pointed out a few flaws in her trumped-up story against Jake La Force. If she goes into court with a lie like that, she'll be laughed out of this town." She repeated what she'd said to Annabelle. "I merely asked her if Jake came into this house, grabbed her out of this bed, and carried her kicking and screaming, down these steps, out the door, and all the way through town to his quarters." She turned to Mrs. Nellis. "Did he do that?"

Unable to face the truth of Hettie's words, the mother turned pale. She sat down on one of Annabelle's softly upholstered little chairs and put her head in her lap, her solid body trembling. "This has been so hard on our poor child."

Hettie stood before the white-faced girl, whose fists nervously twisted her sheets into knots. "Jake and I are going to be married, Annabelle, as soon as he's well enough." She didn't want to be cruel, but it was time this girl knew she'd met her match. She turned to Mrs. Nellis. "Please escort me down, if you will."

The woman, hovering over her distraught daughter, tried to sooth her but the girl screamed in anger at her mother. "Get out of my sight, you stupid bitch! You've never been on my side!"

Mrs. Nellis, crying, led Hettie down the stairs. "I don't know what to do with her anymore. I can't talk to her and her father can't or won't. I'm afraid she may be losing her mind. And after that second rape, she's even worse."

"Mrs. Nellis, face facts. There was no second rape. Think about it. You know the sheriff and have for years. As I asked Annabelle, did that good man come into this home, pull her out of her bed, and carry her kicking and screaming all through town to his quarters, and no one in this town saw it or heard it? If she was in his bed, it could only be because she put herself there. For some reason, Mrs. Nellis, Annabelle has taken it into her head that she wants Jake La Force for a husband and is doing whatever she can to make that happen." Hettie, seeing the look of understanding on the mother's face, breathed a sigh of relief. She hoped Mrs. Nellis had finally faced the truth of what she was saying.

"What will happen to her, Mrs. Jamison?"

"She may need some help getting those ideas out of her head. You might ask Doctor Gentry about that. And you folks might want to withdraw those charges against Jake while you're at it. Your daughter will be the laughing stock of the entire Territory of Arizona if she keeps on with this."

Hettie left that house, feeling she'd helped Jake, and hurried back to him. They had plans to make and not all of them for the wedding.

CHAPTER 30

Later, the next day they heard the judge's verdict. Miguel was sentenced to ten years in Yuma Prison. He would not hang since Annabelle had withheld her testimony, but the word of those who'd heard her cry out his name that night was enough to convict him. His horse thievery was not mentioned.

Handy's trial hadn't come up yet, but murder carried a heavier penalty. He'd face the hangman's noose. Everyone in town knew that.

           ❧❧❧

It was several more days before the doctor told Hettie she'd keep the man she loved. She'd slept on the small settee at night to be at his side and had only left him for the courtroom visit, the jail, and the Nellis home.

As he convalesced, they spent many happy hours discussing where they'd live. Jake decided he'd like to try ranching again. Tired of town life, living at Hettie's ranch suited him all the way. He'd come to love the place.

When he was able, she helped him settle on the thick pile of straw in the wagon Windy had brought to town.

Half the town stood around to see them drive away with Hettie sitting close to him, Windy driving the team, and Bucky tied on behind. Larry had stayed at the ranch, taking care of things.

After a long drive, they reached the ranch house and Jake looked about with a glow in his eyes.

"I've come to love this place almost as much as the owner." He reached for her with his lips for a long kiss before changing to another subject. "Darlin', let's take a look at that box of rocks and see what's in it."

Hettie laughed joyously. "I wasn't sure what it was, but I invited Alexander Hodges to bring his family out. When they come, he'll be able to tell us what that box contains. If it's gold, what would that mean for this ranch and us?"

"I don't know, girl, a wild gold rush, maybe? I only know I want to be with you and when I get stronger, we'll need to get this wedding in the works." He laughed. "But I confess, that box has my curiosity goin' wild, no matter what's in it."

"You're as bad as those men in town with gold fever," she chided with love in her voice. "Living out here will be a big change in careers for you, won't it?"

"Not if I keep a set of cuffs," he replied with a sly look on his face. "We could give them a try when I get stronger." He ducked from a gentle punch thrown his way.

"You're more of a devil than I ever imagined behind that sober-sided look you wear on your face. You know that, don't you?

He laughed, his joy complete, sitting next to this exciting woman. "Hettie, what did you tell Mrs. Nellis to get them to drop those charges against me?"

"I'll tell you some day. Maybe," she teased. "But right now I'm way too busy planning our wedding." She laughed with a joy long delayed, and Jake joined her.

The End

About the Author

Ramona Forrest is a retired RN. She keeps busy writing novels—and traveling whenever possible. Forrest has resided in the back country of Arizona, assisted in round-ups, worked in Saudi Arabia, and has had the pleasure of traveling extensively. She now resides in Phoenix and spends much time in gardening, writing, entertaining friends, and family.